Wakef

Chinese Whispers

Nicholas Jose grew up in Adelaide. He was educated at the Australian National University and at Oxford. He has lived in England, Italy and China, where he taught Australian Studies and was cultural counsellor at the Australian embassy, Peking between 1987 and 1990. He is the author of two collections of short stories and four novels, including *Avenue of Eternal Peace*, which was adapted into a television mini-series, and *The Rose Crossing*. He now lives in Sydney.

By the same author

The Possession of Amber (short stories)
Rowena's Field
Feathers or Lead (short stories)
Paper Nautilus
Avenue of Eternal Peace
The Rose Crossing

CHINESE
whispers Cultural Essays

Nicholas Jose

Wakefield Press
Box 2266
Kent Town
South Australia 5071

First published 1995
Copyright © Nicholas Jose, 1995

All rights reserved. This book is copyright. Apart from any fair dealing for the purposes of private study, research, criticism or review, as permitted under the Copyright Act, no part may be reproduced without written permission. Enquiries should be addressed to the publisher.

Edited by Michael Bollen and Elisabeth Klein
Cover and book designed by Design BITE
Typeset by Clinton Ellicott, Adelaide
Printed and bound by Hyde Park Press, Adelaide

National Library of Australia
Cataloguing-in-publication entry

Jose, Nicholas, 1952– .
Chinese whispers: cultural essays.

ISBN 1 86254 336 4.

1. Jose, Nicholas, 1952 – Biography. 2. China – Civilization – 1976– .
3. China – Intellectual life – 1976– . 4. China – Social life and customs – 1976– .
5. Australia–Asia relations. I. Title.

951.058

Publication of this title was assisted by the Commonwealth Government through the Australia Council, its arts funding and advisory body.

for Claire

---

who occasioned a lot of this,

with love

Author's note

For a small book, there are many people to thank, including the editors of the publications where some of the essays first appeared. I'd like to thank Ah Xian and his family, Geremie Barmé, Kathy Bail, Suzy Baldwin, Bruce Bennett, Michael Bollen, Stephanie Johnston and Elisabeth Klein, Ian Britain, Alison Broinowski, Peter Browne, Margaret Burke, Johnson Chang, Rosemary Creswell, Maryanne Dever, Susan Dewar, Tamsin Donaldson, Dinah Dysart, Guan Wei and Liu Pin, Paul Hetherington, Ivor Indyk, Ken Inglis, Linda Jaivin, Kate and Murray McLean, Humphrey McQueen, George Papaellinas, Cassandra Pybus, Claire Roberts, Sang Ye and Sue Trevaskes, Adam Shoemaker, Christina Slade, Max Suich, Ian Templeman, Neil Thompson, Wang Ziyin, Michael Xu and Neil Whitfield. Acknowledgements are due to *The Age Monthly Review*, *Art & AsiaPacific*, *Asian Arts Society of Australia Review*, *Australian Quarterly*, *Australian Society*, *Independent Monthly*, *Island Magazine*, *Orientations*, *Republica*, *Southerly*, *24 Hours*, *Voices*, and *Webber's*; to Rosemary Dobson, Randolph Stow and Fay Zwicky for permission to quote from their work; to Jacaranda Wiley for permission to quote from 'China ... Woman' by Oodgeroo; and to University of Queensland Press for permission to reprint 'Sang Ye: curio merchant'.

Contents

Preface	ix
'In Chinese' - A story	1
Shots through the bars	14
The embarrassment of the kangaroo	20
Translating China	35
Australia's China	44
Bridging people - *The Yellow Lady*	58
Asian impersonations	66
History repeats - Ernest Morrison's China	74
Romancers of Old Peking	82
Sang Ye: curio merchant	92
'The web that has no weaver' - Notes on cultural exchange	101
Oodgeroo in China	109
In the mountains under a blue sky	122
My search for a shaman - Contemporary Chinese art	133
Eunuch culture	142
The beat goes on	152
Screen dreams	159
Green oil - Media images of Australia/Asia	166
Taiwan: treasure island	171
Cultural trading - What have we got to show?	176
Out of Hong Kong - Timothy Mo	182
Ice city - How to make friends in China	189
Selected Bibliography	195
Index	197

Preface

Life-changing events are often a matter of chance. I never planned to get involved with China. It is an unexpected extension of my Australian cultural background and my training in English literature. The first step happened at Oxford twenty years ago. One night, sitting on the scrubby ornamental hill at New College, my friend, Alex Kerr, who had grown up in Japan and was studying Chinese and Tibetan on a Rhodes Scholarship, chastised my Eurocentrism and goaded me with the necessity of studying Chinese. I had already come to feel, being away, that the presence of Asia was a feature of Australian life I missed in Europe, although at that stage, in the 1970s, the Asian dimensions of Australia were not as clear as they are now.

Back in Canberra in 1979, I found a concentration of Asianists working in the academies and government who provided an incentive for me to take the next step and enrol in a course. I did not know how lucky I was to be with my remarkable teachers at the Canberra College of Advanced Education – but all along the way people have been remarkable. It is the human interest that makes the journey. I began in a state of wonder, and I imagine that the wonder, complicated and deepened by many humbling questions and realisations, will be part of my relationship with China to the end. For that reason I hope I'll be forgiven the whimsy of starting this book with, not an essay, but a piece of fiction inspired by those first toddler's steps.

The facts and fictions of China, as Australians move to re-discover and nurture our Asian connections, provide a running theme through this book. Although largely rewritten for publication here, most of the essays arose in response to invitations to write or speak on particular occasions – for mixed audiences, with a common interest in issues of Australia's involvement with China or, more broadly, Asia, or in my own experience of China, as an Australian. Partly autobiographical then, partly critical and speculative, partly for the record, these pieces look at various aspects of contemporary Chinese culture, and Australia's relationships with China, with a special interest in the personalities involved. I keep returning to Tiananmen Square 1989 as an epicentre. Five years later, the events of that time, their causes, consequences and implications, among many contending interpretations, continue to form the nexus for discussion of China's beyond-2000 confusions, as was re-confirmed for me on a return visit to Peking earlier this year.

Readers might wonder why I say 'Peking'. Isn't it 'Beijing' now? 'Bei' means 'north', 'jing' means 'capital'. The city has been China's northern capital on and off for many centuries. Its Mandarin name, *Beijing*, was pronounced and heard differently by different people. It became naturalised as Peking in English, Pékin in French, Pechino in Italian and so on, as *München* became Munich and *Roma* Rome. When *pinyin*, a new system of transliterating the pronunciation of Chinese characters was adopted in China, Peking became Beijing. It is a change of spelling, not a change of name (unlike, say, the change from St Petersburg to Leningrad). For the Chinese it is still what it has always been, a city with an ancient name and long historical continuity. To catch this sense in English, I prefer the time-honoured name, Peking.

I went to China in 1986 for what I thought would be one year and ended up staying for five, teaching English Literature and Australian Studies at Peking Foreign Studies University in 1986 and at East China

Normal University, Shanghai in 1987, then working as cultural counsellor at the Australian Embassy, Peking, from 1987 to 1990. I found myself involved in turbulent times of sometimes exhilarating, sometimes traumatic change. In 1986–87 I was writing the novel eventually published as *Avenue of Eternal Peace*. My working title was 'Searching for the Shaman', which indicates how I thought of what I was doing. As cultural counsellor, I saw my job as not only to facilitate cultural exchanges between China and Australia, but also to help Australians understand what was happening in China – which meant trying to understand it myself.

What do we want with China? In a more Asia-oriented Australia, what do we want from Chinese culture? I ask these questions in genuine puzzlement. Returning to Australia from Peking in 1990, I discovered how pressing – not to say fashionable – the interest in Asia had become in government, business and the arts. It is too early to guess at the enduring consequences of this wave; but already the ground has shifted from the days, as late as the 1970s, when an interest in China was considered more or less eccentric.

Having had the unusual role of a policy adviser who is also a novelist, I have tended, perhaps, to create dialogue between different parts of myself in considering what is most compelling, or most problematic, in my – or 'our' – experience of China. Where the policy maker may not know how to accommodate the novelist's flights and insights, the novelist will have a disposition to read policy documents as fictional artefacts. The zigzag between public and private, open-ended imagination and consequential policy decisions, can be confusing; but I hope brings a useful kind of energy into the discussion.

I am often asked if I have hope for China. What would *my* hope, or otherwise, mean? I'm not asked the question about Australia. In the case of Australia, I am simply *told*, as often as not by Chinese, that it is a place of hope. Surely, for both societies, if they are to survive and prosper, hope is indispensable.

Nicholas Jose
Sydney, 1995

In Chinese

A story

Entering the classroom John chose a place not too far forward, not too far back, and tipping, shoving, scraping, adjusted his chair to accommodate his body in a position of maximally receptive inertia. The others, as they arrived, busied themselves with their chairs as John had, then fell to cursory chat about the ordeal of study. They flicked in their folders for a clean page and doodled, stilling their thoughts. John drew a spiral around the punchhole in his page. They were not to be condemned. He had a theory: no matter how active their life elsewhere, they wiped themselves blank when they entered the teaching environment. Automatic primal therapy. They were ready for knowledge, in a dry fashion, yawning, shuffling, awaiting the lecturer, who was late. John, on principle, was passive too, because he was dedicated to openness and, anyway, he didn't stop at passivity. Beneath that layer he seethed with inventiveness, energy and decision. Did the others realise? He wondered if it was the case with them too. They eyed each other indifferently, looking content and compact – except for the old Christian Italian lady, who gave watery smiles to the air. They were dried fruit hoping to be dunked and reconstituted in the syrupy sweetness of truth.

The lecturer was a solid chap whose commitment to the subject had led him to acquire a Chinese sense of humour. He joked as he unpacked his bag, and the class stirred familiarly to reassure him. *How to tell the time in Chinese.* Like everything else in the language, it was sagely and wonderfully at odds with the way things were done in English.

The lecturer was giving the first example when the woman walked in. He stopped in his tracks to usher her to a seat. John had never seen her before: she certainly hadn't been there in the first semester. She sat on her chair, book and paper in her lap, and leaned forward at the lecturer, smiling keenly. With her hand under her chin, smiling, she welcomed the foreign sounds and the information. Her eyes were bright blue coals.

Behind her back the others in the class turned and made querying faces. Some frowned and were affronted. She couldn't just walk in like that after half a year and upset the group dynamic. Others pulled themselves up, or slouched back coolly, to intrigue and allure her. She didn't notice the rest of the class. Indeed, John saw, her attentiveness kept giving way to a tired dazzle.

She didn't sit back until the end of the lecture, when she turned to her neighbour and said, 'Isn't it *fabulous*! I'd forgotten!' She laughed, bubbling. 'But it's insanely *difficult*. I'm never going to catch up.' She flicked her fine, dust-coloured hair out of her eyes. Turning to the people on her other side, she looked, for a moment, terribly worried. 'What am I going to *do*? You're all so *good*.' Then she gave her rising tickle of a laugh again.

Her neighbour was Kevin Spike, the hawk-eye of the class. He stood up, buttoning his maroon blazer, and waited by the woman's seat, encouraging her to rise and leave under his escort. 'How come you're just picking it up now?' he asked.

She gathered up her things, still smiling, and, with half a turn of goodbye to the others, walked quickly ahead of Kevin out of the class. 'Well, you see, it was *hopeless*. I first – '

She was gone round the corner of the door before John could catch her story. There was only the string of images trailing behind her down the corridor, flashing through John's head, twenty-four per second.

The evidence was considerable. On a normal day John spent his time working methodically in his room. Now he was drinking coffee in the Union, looking up from the cup whenever a fair-haired woman of medium height appeared, whenever a brisk lively movement occurred on the edges of his vision. Where had she come from? Perhaps she had a connection with the lecturer and was given special treatment. In his mind John saw her park her hair behind her ears – where it should have stayed, except it fell forward and made her look mysterious and late-night. John couldn't wait for the next lecture. He had theories for everything, and speculated that this might be love.

He took the seat next to the one she had occupied, peeled off his parka and laid it across *her* seat. If his behaviour was obsessive, well, then, the others in the class were his rivals and would be equally devious. From the stairwell a clicking of heels announced her, rushing ahead of herself. John retrieved his parka only a fraction before she appeared in the doorway. She beamed, took the hint and collapsed in the empty chair. 'Hi!'
　　John responded as softly, as significantly, as he dared.
　　'What's the *time*?' she said. 'I thought I was ages late. God I'm disorganised. It was bumper to bumper all along Belconnen Way and I just couldn't *move*. My watch must be wrong. Anyway thank goodness I got here. It's absolutely pouring outside.'
　　She shook her hair and one of the raindrops fell on John's hand. As she settled herself he drew the hand back. Ceremoniously, with the tip of his tongue, he licked up the drop. She unwrapped her scarf and took off her coat: her chequered vyella smock underneath looked so warm John wanted to touch it. She gave a determined heave to slow her breathing. When her breasts rose they sent out a soft wave, as if she were throwing something off, stripping herself back to a kid who was ready to learn. But nothing was happening in the classroom, and she bent over to John, whispering that she'd *love* a cigarette. As she came near, he could do nothing but point, silently, at the No Smoking sign.

After a pause Kevin Spike leaned forward, offering a gold packet. 'Cigarette, Ginny?'

'Oh no, I don't think I will now, thanks.'

So that was her name.

When the lecture started she turned to John again, mouthing, 'I've forgotten my book?' He looked at her humorously and pushed his own book so far in her direction that it tipped off the table attached to the armrest. It spread-eagled on the floor, and he had to crouch to pick it up. At the end of the lecture John said, so flatly it was neither question nor statement, so warily it showed total disinterest, 'Off home now.'

'Well – ' she grinned, shrugging, 'via the bar.'

Kevin Spike pushed forward and asked if she was still coming.

'Are we coming?' she asked generally. 'We,' with John at her side. But she was walking towards the door in front of Kevin.

'I wouldn't mind a drink,' declared John.

He *would* mind it; he would hate it; but he would hear more of her magical chitchat.

He discovered that she was doing Chinese as part of a DipEd and had deferred the whole thing after six months to go travelling in Asia with a *really wonderful friend*. Now she was back to finish off the second part of the *year*. The last syllable of her sentences rose with unanswered possibility. After the first drink a good-looking man in his middle twenties came and took her away. He was got up, in punk style, like a battered schoolboy. Was he the *friend*? As quickly as possible after she'd gone – there was nothing to be said or done to Kevin Spike – John took himself off. He saw them then, in the distance, Ginny and the man, gliding behind the sheet-glass wall of Life Sciences, short-cutting to the carpark.

They learned many essential things in Chinese. They learned that in the opinion of some linguists there is no passive voice in Chinese. There is only greater and lesser activeness. There is no chance of withdrawing irresponsibly into a state of being worked on. On the other hand there is the compensation that *our* habitual passive can be strangely transmuted through Chinese eyes into an active living force. For example the character 爱, pronounced '*ài*' or '*eye*', meaning 'to love'. Typically it combined with other basic words to make binary compounds: you could take 人, pronounced '*rén*', meaning 'person', and put it with '*ài*' to make 爱人: *àirén*. Literally it means 'love person'. In English it must be translated as either 'lover' or 'beloved'. There is nothing in between. In the People's Republic it must be translated as 'non-sexist spouse', in Singapore as 'mistress'. But 'love person', the actively loving or the passively loved, John reckoned that in Chinese there could be no distinction. Simply by loving you would necessarily be loved back.

John was sitting behind Ginny, the day they learned about love persons. He looked at the back of her head and willed love over her in waves. It was an experiment and, if the theory were correct, she would become aware of him, start to fidget and, finally, turn for a quick smiling glance at him. But she didn't, and on the way out he couldn't look her in the face.

The class dispersed in various directions. John went by himself down the several flights of ill-lit stairs leading to the back concourse. Outside, his eyes were dazzled by the low sunset, fiercely orange behind the black mountains that threw light to the ends of the sky in stupendous spears. Bewitched, he pressed on, lost in it, until suddenly, crossing the concourse, he all but collided with Ginny.

'Hi,' she said and stopped. She was wearing sunglasses.

'Is it the same colour to you,' asked John, 'through those things?'

She smiled but didn't take the glasses off. 'It's better.'

They looked across ten miles of suburban development at the orange fusion. Four students with squash racquets came out of one door, walked along the building, and entered another door. 'There aren't many people *round*,' said Ginny.

'There never are,' said John, 'not real people. It's illusion. That's my theory.' His legs were apart and he had the weight on both feet, confronting her.

'That's what they say about you,' was her reply.

'They?'

She laughed and made her eyes bulge. 'A thousand million Chinese! Can you believe they actually communicate in that language? Anyway, see you.' And she pursued her geometric path towards an exit from the concourse rectangle.

John lived in a room in a hall-of-residence. By his bed, in a pot, there was a comfrey plant, an ancient medicinal herb that died in winter and came alive again in spring. But John, although he watered it carefully, had little faith that anything would grow out of the remains of last year. He looked at the old leaves, shrunk and crinkled like grey potato chips, and wondered if the comfrey were technically alive or dead. A book called *The Secret Life of Plants* had talked of the incredible sensitivity of all organic forms – to emotions, events, hopes, stimuli of every kind. So John stood in front of the pot and repeated his experiment from Chinese, emitting waves of love at it. When nothing happened he was consoled. If a mere plant didn't respond, why should he ever have thought a human would? Such ideas were superstitious snow!

That night, in the remotest passage of his sleep, he felt something tug him up from the deep. He kept his eyes shut, wanting to stick with his dreams, whatever they were. But slowly, sluggishly, he rolled over and edged across to hug the body in the space beside him. He reached out his arms to encompass the warm loved shape, but the sheets were cold in that part of the bed. He woke properly then and opened his eyes on the claustrophobic pitch of his room. A sorrow filled him, strong as fear. He found his body balancing along the rim of his single bed, making a place for the one he had loved in the night. But no one was there.

After the next Chinese class John intercepted Ginny in the corridor. 'Do you feel like getting together to practise for the oral?'

'Yes,' she said immediately. 'Yes, *great*,' nodding, 'come round to my place?'

'When?'

'Tonight.'

He nodded cautiously. 'Okay.'

Ginny lived in a group house: two females and two males. Marilyn suffered from anorexia nervosa and worked a computer in the Department of Veterans' Affairs. Ted and Todd studied Natural Resources. It was a townhouse in the far new suburb of Holt. The group was eating vegetable casserole and rice around the television when John arrived; Marilyn and Ted in their running shorts, Todd in battle trousers and a T-shirt.

'Will you have a drink?' Todd challenged, 'A beer?'

'Ah, no – thanks.' John stood there.

Ginny began to talk rapidly. 'Did you get here all right? It's incredibly difficult the first time. You've probably been driving round in circles for *ages*. Have you?'

'I rode my bike.'

Ted looked up with interest. 'Great,' he judged.

Ginny heaped a forkful into her mouth and, chewing, rushed with the plate to the kitchen. 'That was delightful,' she said, swallowing. 'Now John – '

While she was in the kitchen she continued calling to him. He stayed awkwardly in the living room, looking at the others who were looking at the television. When she returned she was in command, smiling and carrying a teapot and two small Chinese cups on a tray. 'We can practise better in my room,' she said for the benefit of the others. 'It's quieter there.'

Though it was not yet spring, her window was wide open and the room was fresh. There was a line of books in the room, a line of plants, a line of non-commercial lotions and a mushroom ring of jars, vases and boxes on a little chest. On the wall was a green Asian cloth, otherwise the room was white.

Ginny closed the curtains and lit two candles. They sat on the floor with the teapot between them. Ginny talked in excited bursts, then fell soulfully silent for a stretch. John spoke in single, laconic, equally spaced sentences. Whenever they ventured into Chinese they giggled, and sipped some more Chinese tea. They were still on the floor at two in the morning. John was propped against the bed and Ginny had smoked endless cigarettes.

'I better be going,' he said at last.

'You don't have to,' she said.

He put his hand on hers and she welcomed it with her fingers.

He was silent, then shuffled near and kissed her.

When they were in bed, when he was lying against her skinny, beautiful, fragrant form, when with her hands she seemed to treasure him, when she whispered 'John', he couldn't stop wondering why he had been chosen.

On the ride home, seven kilometres, tingling, he sang his tremendous luck. His luck that he knew was his love.

But was it love? He could afford to step back now. He noticed that the comfrey plant by his bed had put out two tiny spiky shoots. He regarded them with approval, and paused a moment to emit his remaining energy in their direction.

In the morning, when he awoke, he was refreshed and the shoots had doubled in size. There were four of them now, and the sun was shining. From his high vantage point in the residence he could look out and see mountains. In the morning light they were violet and airy, as if they belonged somewhere else, and they made John feel different.

That day he began to feel differently about many things. He saw a maintenance man sitting on a stone under a willow by the artificial pond in the college courtyard. For a moment the man was an elder in a scroll painting. On the approach to the residence block there were black plum and cherry trees studded with pale buds. They became Zen foreground. They had their mode of being as John had his, yet something linked them to him. Even the other students shambling about in the Union could be seen as fellows on the path, on the Way. But was this love?

He came early to the Chinese lecture and sat on the chair beside the one where Ginny would sit. He opened his folder and scribbled like the others, but now the idleness and inconsequence had vanished and the occasion acquired fantastic meaningfulness. Just before time, Ginny dashed in and whispered that she wanted to speak to John outside.

'How are you?' she said, pressing her back against the wall of the corridor.

He looked at her blankly.

'Listen, I can't stay for this lecture. I've got to see a *friend*.'

His tongue was a tangle of inexpressibles. He might as well have tried to speak in Chinese.

She was saying, 'What happened – last night – it was just something I wanted to happen.'

He gave nothing away. 'I wanted it too.'

'I know. That's all.'

'That's okay,' he confirmed.

'Anyway, look, we must see each other *soon*,' she said, smiling at him, turning from him, spattering down the stairs.

John spent most of the twenty-four hours until the next Chinese class in the Union drinking coffee. His favourite theory of all was that the individual should exert no pressure on the world. The being should be as if non-being. The world should do all the determining, all the moulding, all the pushing and shoving. He sat at one of the plastic tables overlooking his cup, moving only when the lady came to wipe the table. He waited until he was actually late for the lecture so he could make an entrance. But Ginny wasn't there. During the hour Kevin Spike tapped his shoulder and passed him a message on a piece of Defence Department notepaper. Kevin had written: 'I saw Ginny on the way here. She wanted me to tell you she's feeling crook and will catch up with you later.'

John's room in the hall-of-residence was small, but that night it seemed so enormous and empty he couldn't stand it. And there was the whole weekend to go.

At midday on Saturday , after he had busied himself all morning, he rode his bike out to Holt. It was the first sunny day of the season. Marilyn and one of the Natural Resourcers were playing frisbee on the nature strip. 'Hi!' they yelled, bouncing, offering nothing more. John went up to the front door and knocked. Todd, the other Natural Resourcer, answered. He was in his dressing-gown. He allowed John to walk into the living room, where the curtains were still closed. In the gloom, above the music, John heard Todd say that they hadn't seen Ginny for a few days.

'She could be at her parents.'

John had not imagined she would have parents.

'Wait if you want to,' said Todd.

But John wanted to return to the hall-of-residence. On the ride back an insect got in his eye and he cried. Why wasn't it working?

That Monday he was walking up the steps to the top concourse of the College of Advanced Education. It was early dusk and the view towards the sun was a fairytale. John couldn't help being enchanted. It was so clear and gentle. The mountains were blue-violet wash. The sun was silver. On the horizon a single green cloud rose in a zigzag, like a cartoonist's squiggle. All the way down the valley the planned development looked like scattered futurist cubes and carefree twinkling lights. John ascended the stairs as if advancing towards an unveiled dream city. The concourse was a high concrete plateau. It might have been an open-air stage for the mountains, or a slab from which the suburbs could witness sacrifices. At that moment it was depopulated, save for one couple. They were alone among the select native shrubbery. John saw the man put his arm around the woman. The woman stood up on tiptoes to kiss him quickly on the cheek, leaning into him, then lowered herself, pulled her sunglasses down, and was gone. The man walked on as if he were going somewhere. The woman was Ginny. John looked at the revealed city. It was a death metropolis fuelled by human dreams.

John and Ginny sat next to each other in the lecture. She greeted him solemnly. He felt the sharpness. They had a further lesson on binary compounds and the lecturer, beaming at the mysteries he imparted, introduced the word 博爱 *bó ài* – and its derivation. 'You know the word *bó* meaning "broad" or "wide", as in broadcast, sowing the seed wide. You know *ài* meaning "love". Put them together and you have "wide-love". What is this concept?'

'Promiscuity,' snorted Kevin Spike in a stage whisper. Beside John Ginny giggled.

'For the Chinese,' the lecturer continued, oblivious, '*bó ài* means "universal brotherhood".' He paused so the class could contemplate the celestial simplicity.

Wide-love, thought John. He could almost accept the concept, quietly and soothingly, almost. He turned to Ginny, whose eyes met his with an expression of indecipherable wonder. He had a theory. All right, he understood. It was wide-love that she practised. It was her version of universal brotherhood and was only proper. He had no special claim.

Afterwards John and Ginny went to the Union together, to speak in Chinese over their coffee as training for the oral. Suddenly the sensation of being with her came back, trying to assert itself. She held the coffee cup daintily in her hand, not quite keeping it level. It was surely that hand he had touched. But the more her sharp eyes shone at him, the less he knew whether it had happened or not. It was imperative not to be deceived by the illusion of an action. Everything reduced to passivity in the end. Everything reduced to receptivity. Everything reduced to dream. His own love was only one drop in the universal sea.

Ginny suggested they should arrange a time for further oral practice.

'It can wait,' said John gallantly. He didn't want to push her into something that wasn't real. 'Are you free on the weekend?'

She at once gave a great long uncontrolled speech about *all* the *things* she had to *do*, her *assignments*, her *parents*, her *house*, her *hydroponics*, her *really wonderful friend*, concluding that Saturday was fine.

John nodded. She brushed back her hair and laughed wildly.

'Great,' she said. 'See you.'

His theory was that it had never really happened. That seemed the right approach. In the evening he put himself in front of his books. The comfrey plant had exerted itself, and four large green leaves now sprouted from the pot. They were ridiculous. He laughed, to distract himself. He would see her next Saturday and they would talk in Chinese. He had behaved well. He had done nothing possessive towards her. He had done nothing at all. He shifted restlessly and turned the first of many pages.

Hours later there was a knock. The midnight intrusion startled him. He had been deep in study. Anxiously he went to the door. It was Ginny, face rosy, puffing. She'd been in the bar.

'Sorry,' she said clumsily. 'I'm sorry. Are you asleep?' Something had changed her since the afternoon.

She walked in and sat down heavily on the bed, bowing her head guiltily. John was at a loss.

'At least I got the right room,' she said. 'Sorry to bother you. I couldn't wait – '

John stood away from her, wanting to go to her but not doing so. 'Is anything wrong?'

She kept her eyes to the floor, shaking and altering position in great uncomfortable heaves. He couldn't stop thinking, nervously, about what was happening, watching for signs, wondering. The comfrey leaves had pricked up: the charge in the air would do them good. He prayed that she would speak – explain what was going on and release him from uncertainty.

'What?' he said, thinking she'd made a sound.

The room was monstrously vacant. Sunken on the bedspread, crouching round her knees, Ginny looked like an unwrapped parcel. John was hot, and heard thumping in the cave of his chest.

He went to her and put his hand on her head. At the same instant she spoke. 'What are you *doing*? Why don't you say *anything ever*? Why don't you do anything? What's going *on*?' She had been talking to the ground but now faced him. 'I'm sorry. I can't help it. I haven't done anything wrong. I don't want to hassle you but – oh God! – ' She put her head down against his knee.

She had done it. He gasped, half-yelping, half-mumbling. 'But I love you!'

In a convulsive motion, strong as shock, he jerked towards her.

'John?'

He had tears in his eyes.

They were together. It was real. Squeezing each other they understood that they filled the curiously matter-of-fact hall-of-residence room.

In the morning they opened the window – the world. They faced the furthest mountain, which was tipped with snow, and the nearer ones, glowing purple. Nearer still the suburbs were busy, packed with green. It was spring and the cherries and plums made pink and white spray. All was in proportion: background, middle and fore. John gulped the air.

They touched each other, and, as each traced a separate path over the other's body, their hands at last met and compounded.

They called the scene outside On a Road to the Yunnan Mountains, or, Approaching the Capital of the Southern Province. Overnight, overstimulated, the comfrey plant had produced two bellflowers which now tinkled in the morning breeze. There was no theory to cover it. Love person, love person, blew John in Ginny's ear. Together they looked out at the sprawling houses, all similar, containing rooms containing people, as blank and deceptive as Chinese boxes. Wide love could know them all.

1980

Shots through the bars

Friends told me about a matriarchal community in the remote southwest, out of bounds to foreigners and inaccessible to all but the hardiest Chinese backpackers. On an island in the lake stands a shining Buddhist-style temple that provides the community's spiritual and, until recent times, political centre. The man fishes in a long wooden boat rowed with one oar and, when he comes on shore, the woman in her large red-painted house with windowless upper storeys decides whether she will open the door to him or another. If a foreign man comes, he may be invited to share board and bed. There is no marriage as such. There is no word for father.

Was it fact or fable? The journey to the West for Chinese isn't always to New York. The country has its own land of romance, a potent realm of wonders far from Peking. I set out to see if I could find it.

In the foyer of Chengdu's top hotel, where saffron-clad American Buddhists wait for their delayed plane to Lhasa, capital of Tibet, the home from which the Dalai Lama is exiled, I bump into an old mate, an actor who has become a national television star for his role in a martial arts soap opera. The actor insists on lunch, and leads me through the city's maze of

Elizabethan-style houses to an eating place. For once I know what it feels like not to be stared at in China. All eyes are on the star, a handsome, chubby-cheeked guy with waved hair, in the best tradition of Chinese romantic leads.

Chengdu, capital of Sichuan province, is the city of hot food and hot tempers. The proprietor bellows the praises of his famed Chungking hotpot as he places stools around the earthenware stove on which a wok, full of stock, oil and red chillies, bubbles in readiness. You pick up the raw ingredients with your chopsticks, plunge them into the blood-coloured brew for a precise number of seconds, dip them into a chilli and garlic sauce – and eat if you dare. Squid rings, pigs' brains, geese tripes, congealed ducks' blood, and cows' trachea (the part that moos), are balanced with mushrooms, shallots and bean sprouts. Bodies sweat therapeutically. The actor poses for a photograph with a live loach – a cross between a baby trout and an eel – between his chopsticks.

Afterwards, the actor stops at a street stall to buy oranges. Polished cotton underwear shows through a tear in the vendor's shabby clothes. He sticks a cigarette in his pipe and joins the actor in transferring oranges from a big basket to a smaller bag. The actor makes a fuss of picking out the best oranges. The vendor, meanwhile, picks out the worst and drops them into the bag too. The actor then rummages for the worst ones to place them back into the vendor's basket, whereupon the vendor picks them out again and drops them back in the actor's bag, calmly puffing on his pipe. The routine continues.

The train goes south-west into mountains. In the musty velvet-and-lace compartment an old cadre eyes me with suspicion. At last, given a chance to brag, he softens. He is an ex-revolutionary pilot, engineer, herbalist, poet and elder, whose knowledge is supposed to go unquestioned. He explains that in most important respects China is more developed than the West. His own command of Chinese medicine has brought people back from the dead. In order to decline his offer of a cigarette, I say that Smoking is a Health Hazard. He asks me if I have relatives in Australia who could organise a promotional tour for him and his medicines. In return he points on the map to a shortcut to Ru Gu Lake, the site of the matriarchal society. Out of politeness I take his advice. I get off the train somewhere near the border of Sichuan and Yunnan. The elder has given me a letter of introduction to the manager of the local army hostel.

The town of Xichang is to become world-famous for its satellite launching pad. It is off-limits to tourists, but no one seems to mind that I am there. On the steps of the cinema, where *Love Story* is showing, the local young people play sluggish courtship games. Their dress indicates that they are Yi people, down from the mountains, members of what the government in faraway Peking calls a 'national minority'. They number some four million. The town also has an entrepreneurial off-shoot of the local electricity company, where you can pay to queue for a hot shower. Otherwise, I find little to do but eat while waiting for the next day's bus. The town serves the best roast duck and spicy beancurd in China, with a side dish of tender pea leaves tossed in oil. *Huajiao*, the local pepper, a kind of aromatic mustard, imparts the genuine mouth-numbing Sichuanese taste.

There is one clapped-out, chock-a-block bus a day that crosses the mountains to the last town before Ru Gu Lake. Its name translates as Source-of-the-Salt. A few kilometres underway, the radiator springs a leak. Since there is no way of fixing it, the driver decides to push on anyway, stopping every few minutes to pour in water. The trip takes twelve hours, at first through yellow-flowering fields and clusters of neat mud houses with upturned eaves. Spindly gums said to be introduced from Australia after the goldrush are the most common trees: the area is heavily deforested. Higher, through scrubby conifer forest, the road winds to a mountain pass where the travellers are given a few minutes to stare down into the mint-coloured waters of the Golden River a thousand metres below. The road then descends, tortuous and dusty, to cross the river on a narrow suspension bridge that marks the entry into the Autonomous Region of the Yi people. The appearance of the land changes from greens and blues to a bare moonscape as painted by an Italian neo-expressionist: black, magenta, chrome-yellow and ash-grey. The vegetation is minimal. The turned earth shows the peculiar colours of the mineral-rich soil from which the people profit so marginally. They are herdspeople, not cultivators. The best way to make ends meet, apparently, is to crawl down the tiny tunnels of the coal or lead mines, where the digging is done by hand. The work is dangerous: eighteen months is the limit permitted per stretch.

Dug into the bare black mountain slopes are the low farming settlements of the Yi. The mud walls are black and the grey planks laid for roofing are weighed down with black stones. Their sheep and goats are black or chocolate-brown and the herdsmen wear black, bell-shaped capes with long black tassels around the bottom. Under the cape they wear bell-bottomed trousers that stop below the knee. On their heads they wear big black turbans that look top-heavy. The Yi women wear headdresses of woven ribbons, bright striped towels and gorgeous stiff embroidery, built, with the help of their glossy black plaits and studs of silver jewellery, into great winged, peaked constructions, as if they belonged to some lost order of Dutch nuns. They complete their outfits with embroidered jackets and tulip-shaped can-can skirts of ochre, russet and red. Once the Yi were the rulers of a great southern kingdom that stretched as far as Laos.

As soon as the bus arrives in Source-of-the-Salt, I am spotted. An official from the administration leads me to the town office to meet the mayor. Although he is Yi, the mayor has taken a Han name. His authority is subordinate to that of the Public Security Bureau chief, a Han from outside the town. I am welcomed as a friend come from afar. The only other foreigner mentioned is an American pilot who crashed there in the fifties. The Yi put that funny ginger-haired creature in a cage and fed him scrapings. He married one of their slave women in the end. I tell the mayor that I have seen the movie.

The mayor promises to provide the visitor with every assistance in getting to Ru Gu Lake. There is no bus, the road is almost impassable, the last car to drive it overturned – but he promises to do what he can to rustle up a vehicle and driver. Meanwhile, he will fix up a bed in the living quarters attached to the town office, and he invites me to join him for an evening of spirits and television.

Two young men call on me in my room. The first is the town's only university student, who is home for the holidays from the Minorities' Institute in Chengdu. He is a pleasant, but melancholy boy determined to talk about the culture of his people, which dates back at least a thousand years, to the Tang dynasty. The language is still spoken, but not taught in schools.

The other man is a young Party official who is marrying a girl from the local bank. He has procured the four essentials necessary for marriage – fridge, washing machine, tape recorder and colour television – and has even managed a video recorder. For a boy from the backblocks, it is no mean tribute to the Four Modernisations. He turns on the television in the traveller's room. Slowly he has to admit that there is seldom any television reception in the area. And he has never seen a video cassette.

The mayor's summons comes. Dinner is served. The Yi people are renowned for their drinking, and toasts are proposed till the bottle is empty. The mayor jokes about the matriarchal community down the road and its legendary hospitality.

The sun is up early, and I prepare for the road. The mayor is nowhere to be found, nor is there any transport. One excuse after another is offered. At last the student arrives, cast as the bird of ill-omen. Higher instructions have been received. Before I may journey to Ru Gu Lake I must first go back where I came from to get my passport stamped. I am advised to take the first possible bus, back twelve hours over the mountain road. In the meantime I should rest within the confines of the town office.

It is a brilliant sunny day. I sit on a stool in the courtyard, by the locked gate, cursing the system. In the afternoon, kids on their way home from school come and stare at me. They are shy and giggle. I point my camera at them and take shots through the bars. The quest for the matriarchy has once more been prohibited by some mother of a patriarch.

If the way to Ru Gu Lake is blocked from one side, a roundabout route through Yunnan, the southern-most province, leads to an approach from the other side, through Dali, a city on the old Burma road between India and China. After the Yi Autonomous Region, Dali presents the opposite face of minorities' China. Dali, a prosperous place of 'fish and rice', lies between a lake dotted with sail boats and a range of snow-capped mountains. The pagodas are newly restored. In the fields farmers bless their new, but traditional-style mansions with fireworks, flowers and lucky pigs' heads stuffed with camellias. I am directed to the No. 2 Guesthouse, and from there to the Coca-Cola Restaurant, where cold beers and a pizza made from mountain cheese enable me to relax. Life is different now I am back on the Lonely Planet road.

I hire a bicycle to go to the next village, Lijiang, one stage closer to Ru Gu Lake. But at a certain point along the road I am pulled over and told that I need written permission from Peking. Ru Gu Lake is still out of reach, even though the lands beyond Lijiang have long since been opened up. Well, the journey, not the arrival, matters. Long may the matriarchs queen it serenely, safe from sticky-beaks and pestering anthropology PhDs. Closing the mosquito net around my bed in the No. 2 Guesthouse, I have reached the end of my exploring for the time being.

At night I am woken by a blood-curdling scream. Looking down from my balcony I see a sow running through the cobbled lane below with her throat slit, a gang of men shouting in pursuit.

1987

The embarrassment of the kangaroo

Taipei, 1994. The Leap Over.
I chew my first betelnut. It is eaten fresh from a packet that is kept in the refrigerator. You take two at once, cream-coloured balls, like two hazelnuts harnessed together with a strip of leaf, a tiny bikini top. Pop the whole thing in your mouth and chew. The taste is musky and anaesthetic, and after gentle chewing you feel a rush of heat to the face. Your earlobes flush, your senses lift. The body is subdued: not unlike a controlled exercise in glue-sniffing, or a very mild popper that peaks quickly. In five minutes the betelnut is a mass of tasteless red fibre. You can remove it from your mouth and delicately swallow, or you can spit a scarlet dart if your aim is good. You follow with a mouthful of beer, which tastes wonderfully sweet as your body expels its damps.

I am sitting in the New Phase Art Space in Tainan, old southern capital of Taiwan. In 1661 the people of the district besieged the occupying Dutch with ramparts of bamboo straw and left-over rice, and drove them out. Tainan boasts the ruins of Fort Zeelandia to this day. New Phase Art Space occupies a made-over commercial building from the 1960s, the days when Taiwan's now dragon economy was Newly Industrialising –

almost as long ago, now, as the seventeenth century. Gallery space, book and craft stores, seminar rooms, cinematheque, dance hall and Tuscan restaurant are included in this stylish private centre for contemporary culture run by artists and their backers. The enterprise is fueled by a combination of boom-time money from the 1980s and the 'Taiwan consciousness' that has intensified since martial law was lifted in 1987.

The courtyard café abuts an old wall made of beautiful apricot-coloured bricks held together by meandering tree roots. 'It's at least ninety years old,' the manager tells me. I could kiss her for her local pride. This is real history in a country that dates its calendar years from 1911. It's a refreshing change from mainland China, where everything is a glorious 3000 years old and no one knows the actual age of anything.

The betelnut is another difference. It belongs to a different cultural tradition from that of the Chinese mainlanders who crossed to the island in 1949, a difference as profound as between beer and wine cultures in Europe. In the south of Taiwan *bingnya* is everywhere. The artists sitting in the courtyard under the stars, exhausted by compulsive talk about the future of their place, chew it appreciatively as they sink into their tea leaves.

The bearded artist has a stoned glow in his eyes as he gives me a parting souvenir of betelnut. He waits for me to examine it. The logo on the green-and-gold packet turns out to be a kangaroo and her joey. It is Kangaroo Brand Betelnut. Green is a curative and refreshing colour, and gold is for the riches of sunlight – the island of Formosa, once the greenest place in the world, is now the place with the most gold. Marvelling at the piracy of images, I vow to treasure the gift. It comes from the deepest roots of this shamanistic, hallucinatory, as well as materialistic, culture, the power of which is here carried by the kangaroo and her joey, wearing a mantle of Australian colours.

When I tell my Australian friends back in Taipei, they warn me never to eat betelnut again. It's treated with chemicals to make it more addictive. The chemicals give you gum cancer.

I'm in Taiwan for the opening of 'Identities: Art from Australia', the first survey exhibition of contemporary Australian art to be seen here. My involvement in the project had its whimsical beginning in the air over the Snowy Mountains when my fellow passenger and I, strangers, abandoned our studied silence to admire the sparkling snow cover. We got talking. She taught at the University of Wollongong and told me about her Taiwanese graduate student who was agitating to take some Australian Aboriginal art to Taiwan. From there, it had been two years to this opening at the Taipei Fine Arts Museum, as part of Australia Now month.

Like everything else in Taiwan, the private artistic impulse achieves its dynamism, for artists, dealers, critics and buyers alike, precisely because it exists in a zone of resistance, not always comfortably condoned by officialdom.

We are taken to a private *Salon de Muse*, for example, where a dealer shows us his 'Ten Future Master Pieces', among them a painting of Botticelli's Three Graces belatedly reaching this once-paradisal island, tired, sallow and sagging-fleshed as they sink to the ocean floor beneath the weight of industrial devastation and cultural garbage.

The question of how art can discover a society's identity is no less compulsive to the private Taiwanese arts community than it is in public discussions in Australia. How can artists achieve a local *Taiwan* identity, removed from Chinese tradition at the same time as it is removed from Western internationalism? How should Australian arts export reflect cultural identity? The Taiwan partners in our largely state-sponsored project, wishing to market the uniqueness they find in the Australian works, somewhat inevitably suggest that the exhibition should be promoted with the image of the kangaroo. More than 100,000 Taiwanese tourists visit Australia annually. The trip would not be complete without their seeing a kangaroo on native soil. What more natural way of attracting Taiwanese audiences to an Australian art show?

But, despite its major Aboriginal and environmental components, the exhibition features no kangaroos. The problem is that the kangaroo is no longer kosher when our official effort goes into the promotion of an image of Australia overseas as hi-tech, innovative and pluralist. The kangaroo has been kept off the cover of the catalogue. Its bouncy form appears only in the Australia Council's logo. Then we discover that the museum staff have taken matters into their own hands. They have laid a trail of kangaroos from the entrance, across the marble floor and up the stairs to the haunting images of Australia.

Maybe it's lucky to have a few playful symbolic marsupials around to jump across these gaps. If we're not prepared to be cute, others will do it for us. I hear that Skippy the Boxing Kangaroo in the visiting Russian International Circus is the hit of this year's Chinese New Year holiday in Taipei.

The surprise success of Australia Now is the visit of Miss Australia – no, *two* Miss Australias, 1992 and 1993, lofty brunette and lofty blonde, who have the taxi drivers of Taipei queueing round the block to be photographed with them. One on each arm, perhaps? The laminated photographs will by now adorn many a rear-vision mirror. These Miss Australias come with impeccable professional credentials. *Diana* magazine, Taiwan's *Vogue*, headlines its photostory on Miss Australia at Phillip Island: 'Which Would You Rather Have, the Beauty or the Penguin?' Work that one out.

With unemployment at a twelve-year low of 1.45 per cent, only the seriously unemployable become taxi drivers in Taipei, either betelnut-chewing young locals or drunken veterans who came across from the mainland with Chiang Kai-shek's army in 1949 and are ready for a rave in the crosstown traffic jam when they pick the Peking accent in my mongrel Chinese. This particular driver was only a teenage kid when he hopped on board ship at Shanghai with a platoon of Nationalist soldiers, he tells me, leaving behind his family and friends. After a week the ship reached Taiwan where he has lived ever since, for most of his life as a bootlicker to a Nationalist officer waiting to re-take the Motherland. He has just been able to make his first trip back to mainland China. His sister waited for him at the provincial airport for five hours, with her limousine and driver. She was deputy mayor of the provincial capital now. My taxi driver had backed the wrong horse. He begins an obsessive litany about the unstoppable expansionism of China. 'Tibet used to be independent. It's returned to China. Hong Kong used to be British. It's returning to China. Mongolia used to be Soviet. It will return to China. Central Asia's returning to China.

It used to be Soviet . . . Korea . . . Vietnam . . .' I guess his logic is that Taiwan will return one day too. The only place that will never 'return' in this way is Japan, he claims. When he finds out I am Australian, he asks if it can be true that we are letting the Japanese build independent cities on Australian soil over which we Australians have no sovereignty. He warns that it is only a matter of time before these Japanese cities demand their own representatives in the Australian parliament – the thin end of the wedge. He has seen the Japanese fight the Chinese in the area around Nanking where he grew up. It is hard to argue with him. It is hard to explain that Australians, unlike East Asians, are mostly not given to five-year plans or long-term paranoias.

We leave it that as long as Australia has 'good air' it will continue to be an object of desire. It's true. Southern Sky, the largest Buddhist temple in the southern hemisphere, is being built by the Taiwanese Pure Land sect on the freeway south of Wollongong, which translates as 'Five Dragon Harbour' in Mandarin. It's clean and green and the *fengshui*, the harmony of the elements, is good.

I run into friend Lisa in Taipei. She is there to source seductive packaging for the deer penises produced in Goulburn for sale as aphrodisiacs to the Australian duty-free trade. I hear Barry Humphries's character Daryl Dalkeith, the embrace-Asia entrepreneur, gushing: 'I am thinking of bath gel, scented with West Australian wildflowers. We can put the dozers through the wildflower crop. We can pulp them up, get the juice out of them and bung it into the bath gel. They've never had it. They don't know they need it. You *invent* a market.'

Australia's international image is something our government would like to massage into better shape. But our image will probably never be much better than the substance that lies behind the image. And that substance is nothing more nor less than the agglomeration of all the different contacts that already exist between our community and other communities, often in crazy ways – ways which my experience tells me we are in no position to dictate or police, and which we would be foolish to resist or deny. Maybe we can learn some useful tips, even truths, by looking into these unlikely crossover points between us and others, and asking why. The spark only jumps when there is a build-up of charge on both sides. *Why* did more than 100,000 Taiwanese visit Australia last year? Was it just the low dollar? *Why* the kangaroo?

Australia Asia Airlines is what Qantas planes are called so they can fly to Taiwan, with which our national carrier may not have direct air links lest it upset the mainland Chinese. The flying kangaroo on the tail is replaced with flying streamers. The mostly young Taiwanese travellers sit enthralled at Yothu Yindi and Midnight Oil MTVs on the inflight video, and the *Best of Hey Hey It's Saturday*. They eat Sichuan chicken and gemfish with ginger. They are impressed that the inflight announcements are not only in English and official Mandarin Chinese, but also in Taiwanese, the majority language that is now associated with Taiwan identity and the movement towards independence. And the planes are always full, except during the ghost festival, when few Taiwanese would risk going up in the air. Flexibility, specificity, cultural sensitivity, business nous. Call it opportunism if you like. Only connect.

Different countries do not map neatly on to each other. Countries cannot 'mesh' thoroughly. The profoundest connections are unpredictable ones, and are often quite trivial at the outset. The translators, the mediators, the bridging people are our society's eyes and ears in this process, out in front, their antennae picking up the crackle in the air that means there is a message that *wants* to get across. It is a highly random, hit-and-miss business, in which misperception and fantasy play as important a part as accurate mutual apprehension. And the points of connection are not always flattering. In searching for the 'fit', it's necessary to recognise the points of non-connection too. And, since opposites can attract, the points of resistance, even of repulsion, may also reveal relationships, as between the twin halves of a duality.

Are Taiwan and Australia two island extremes that are being drawn inexorably to their inverse reflection in each other? The one to breathe fresh air, the other for a spin in the scarlet karaoke palace of economic superpowerdom?

The dynamos of Asia elicit a knee-jerk horror from many Australians:

corruption, crowding, cheap labour, exploitation, lack of humanity – a fouled nest, the flipside of Asia the Beautiful. Sometimes the horror is put to rest by the notion that Asians do, however, live by different values. They have their convenient oriental spirituality that enables them to passively endure suffering and hardship, to put up with bad environments and low wages, and other restrictions on their human rights, in the name of some higher ideal. At other times the moralistic horror response barely conceals the Australian's fascinated envy of the oriental opportunity zone. In that lotus land, to be sleazy – to give or accept deal-sweeteners, to jelly the truth, to pander to your and your negotiating partner's personal interests and appetites – is, after all, only to be polite. That's the way things have to be done, where corruption is fabled and accountability evaporates in clouds of unknowing. How unlike our own highly regulated home!

Whether horror or envy, moralism or blinkeredness, this kind of perceptual connection reveals an area of clumsiness or naivety in how we relate to the various societies that make up Asia. It is a problem aggravated by the fact that, with our government's encouragement, so many disparate activities are grouped under the heading of 'Australia's turning to Asia' – a nice-sounding idea that needs some qualification before it can really make sense. For some people the issue seems to boil down to whether we can only get involved with Asian countries if we turn a blind eye to what we don't like about them. Others respond, using the word beloved of diplomats, that a 'nuanced' approach is the best. It is easy to ridicule this, or see it degenerate into a craven double-standard, but the reality is that there are cultural differences, as there are cultural similarities, and that we are working across complex sets of assumptions and expectations, and that unless we are in there on the ground, we won't even know what they are. But that includes knowing what *we* are, and where we come from, and then using what we've got.

Dr Stephen Fitzgerald – Australia's first ambassador to the People's Republic of China, now director of the Australia Asia Institute at the University of New South Wales – writing on the 'Ethical Dimensions of Australia's Engagement with Asian Countries', develops the idea of Asia as a moral mirror or conscience for Australia. He notes how the decline in

Australian business ethics in the 1980s coincided with Asia's emergence as a priority area for government and business, and observes that the unseemly haste of the 'institutional discovery of Asia' at that time made the proponents of the new relationship oblivious to pre-existing histories of connection or to any understanding that looked to longer-term, perhaps unpalatable outcomes. Now, in the 1990s, our national Academy of Social Sciences is looking for an 'ethical framework' for business with Asia. It is no doubt a worthy consciousness-raising project, but it begs the question of whether we need different ethics for dealing with Asia, and, if so, whether that's because their ethics are different or ours inadequate.

Ethics is a big word. At one end of the scale, it can refer merely to matters of custom and etiquette. When do you take your shoes off on entering a home? When do you allow the other person to pay for your drink? If the other person insists on paying for all the drinks, are you then under an obligation to return the favour in some other form? At the other end of the scale, ethics is also a matter of moral choices, of good and evil; and in between are all those areas of passionate social concern – environmental issues, the status of women, policy towards minority and indigenous peoples, the preservation of cultures and heritage, consumerism, and so on. I am no philosopher or sociologist, but I suspect that the ethical dimensions of the behaviour of any one of us may be complicated by unfamiliarity where Asia is involved, but are otherwise neither more nor less demanding than the morality of our lives generally.

Externally imposed ethical frameworks don't have a good record of straightening the crooked timber of humanity, even when people do try to live up to them. It is hard to believe that there will be many subscribers to the ethical guidebook to Asia. Fitzgerald, being a veteran of many committees that have looked at issues of this kind, knows how often sensible recommendations go unheeded. Being as interested in nurturing a process as in getting results, he opts for an open-ended ecumenical approach, rather than anything too evangelical. He suggests that Australians should be encouraged to work together with Asian societies to seek a new commonality of ethical consciousness that goes beyond the existing moral givens of any one society. But it is hard to see how this would work in practice. We might exchange pieces of legislation, or family structures, or religious beliefs, or social support mechanisms, yet values are surely different. They are not swap cards. They are not tradable, unlike other commodities. They express what you are, even if you're not aware of it. They do not belong to you exclusively. Someone else, in another place, can have the same values, whether supported by their society or in defiance of it. Australian or Asian, it is a matter of individual consciences first and last.

Australia must be its own country, independently forming an array of relationships with different Asian communities, in a whole host of ways, where it is possible to do so, from trade and defence to the arts and tourism, and these relationships will include mutual ethical questioning. If you are committed to a spirited, open and confident sifting of your public and private moralities, as a distinctive part of social life, there is no reason why you should not expose that process to others.

The formulation of values and the creation of a good society could be one of the most exciting things about life in Australia, something some people will prize and others respect in a take-it-or-leave-it way. You can't just let go of your own values, however much of a nuisance they may be at times, so you might as well do something with them. What you believe and what you know are inseparable from what you are, the expression of a particular history, even as you are continuing to change all the time. Your values are what others see, even when you can't see them yourself. They're what others breathe when they're with you. They're what others may imagine, like the kangaroo. Why be embarrassed? They may even be the best thing you've got. Only don't be surprised when they turn up and are put to unexpected uses in strange places.

Peking, 1989. The Gap.

I had my own experience of kangaroo embarrassment.

With a reputation for being one of the most corrosive critics of the Chinese government, Liu returned to Peking from New York to take part in the protest movement. Skinny, with spiky hair and bad skin, he delivered outrageous remarks in a husky stammer. I liked him. He wrote that

Chinese intellectuals must become citizens of the world before their minds could be free. To be able to see China in a larger context, away from the centre, as he could, was already a big step. He had developed a taste for XO cognac. In the days of Tiananmen Square we got through quite a few bottles together.

The reason he came to my place the first time was to use the guest bedroom. Like some other fiery iconoclasts, he was irresistible to women. He had a loyal wife at home, a lover in the Square, and a new girlfriend. When it was all over I found two pairs of female knickers and one pair of his in the abandoned flat. His were like a child's. He had very narrow hips. I also found his Florida T-shirt. Palm trees against an orange sky.

Since a foreigner's residence was relatively convenient, he used my place as a base. He made and received international phone calls there. He could come and go. Writers, journalists, photographers, students – not all Chinese – did the same, and it became a drifting party, with dark intelligence flying around in cool counterpoint to what was happening a few blocks away. In the nearby Square thousands of impassioned people were calling for the overthrow of the government. Parades of support passed my building. Ferocious rumours of every colour were flying about. And, as the days went by, the running-down of momentum challenged my friend to take on a new role as activist. He placed an envelope in my desk for safe-keeping that contained, I believe, his Chinese passport and American visa, and $2000 from supporters in New York. He would need those things to escape. He did not retrieve the envelope until the eve of the army crackdown. It was in the backpack he left behind in the Square – incinerated, crushed by the tanks, or taken as evidence against him.

A visiting Australian theatre director nicknamed my place the Last Salon in Peking. From the seventh floor balcony you could see columns of smoke across to the west. Helicopters buzzed overhead. When the tanks occupied the intersection below, a barrel was aimed at the living room window and an officer shouted through his megaphone that we would be shot if we took photos. So the party moved to the other end of the flat, until the fridge was bare.

Before all this, what used to happen below my window, was a form of vocal exercise that the old men from the old low houses on the other side of the ring-road practised at dawn. I would wake to their cries, and look down at them lifting their legs to the perpendicular on to a bit of low wall, old men in the smoky haze of a summer morning that dissolved my views of the Temple of Heaven in the distance.

But now I wasn't at home much of the time. I had my work and my own involvement in what was happening, which I had lived every day for nearly four years, in private as well as professionally; bonds formed, allegiances and decisions made. And now everything was accelerating. I was out and about, aware of the gravity of events outside, and the danger of the comings and goings at my flat. I'd come home only to sleep, and to read a few pages of my bedside books. One was a study of Shakespeare's *Troilus and Cressida*, on the mixed meanings in great historical moments. The other was the *Six Chapters of a Floating Life*, an exquisite, intimate Ching dynasty classic.

There were persistent rumours growing that one part of the army would turn on those divisions responsible for the 3–4 June attack. Diplomatic missions were preoccupied with deciding whether their people should stay or go. An unexplained shooting directed at the foreigners' residential compound tilted towards a 'go'. It became my job to find and inform the Australian students and teachers living in the vicinity of Peking. I was also worried about my Chinese friends, many of whom had reasons to fear a clampdown. It was a very confused situation, unfolding by the minute. As our convoy passed army trucks burning on the road, we saw sniper patrols carrying out raids. No one went out on the streets who didn't have to.

By 6 June there was no food left in my flat except for some Bega cheese in the deep freeze. One Chinese man on the government wanted list had gone direct to the embassy, where he sought asylum. Liu was more of a problem. We made a plan that during the afternoon someone would collect him, his girlfriend and another friend from my flat and get them where they needed to go.

I was busy organising things until well after the curfew. After being out all day I had to go home one last time, a thirty-minute round trip, to pack a suitcase. Leave everything else behind. Throw perishables down the chute. Bring notebooks. Address book. Anything that should not be found in case of a search. A few personal irreplaceables.

The usual lift attendants had been off for days. Now a spade-faced plain-clothes cop had replaced them. On reaching my flat I found the lights on and music playing. The three people who were supposed to have gone during the afternoon were still there, waiting for me to return.

The security man studied us as we came out of the lift. I was lugging my suitcase. He noted the tell-tale plates of my car – the only car, only moving light, in all those vast dark boulevards. The petrified city of the future. I drove to where Liu's two friends had parked their bicycles and dropped them. Then I drove on with my friend, who had become, in official parlance, a Black Hand, a wanted man.

We stopped under the trees outside the embassy. The moment had come for him to choose whether to drive inside through the automatic gates with me to diplomatic immunity (a form of extraterritoriality such as had existed in China's concession ports in the old days), or whether to cross the road instead, to his friend's home, where his girlfriend would be waiting. There he could consider. He had said he wanted to call on the world's forces of justice to intervene in China's fate. Or he could run for it into the Chinese hinterland.

What happened is we reached out and shook hands. Firmly and for a long time. He opened the car door. Then he was gone, wearing my jeans, which were loose on him, and my jacket.

In the embassy everyone was smoking, although it was supposed to be a smoke-free zone. People waiting for the next day's evacuation flight were bedding down on the floor. There was much to be done, and the qualities of the players there showed up in the crisis, as if through glass. Some acted on a sure instinct of humanity, others, at a loss for any guidance of the heart, fell back on form, and still others were learning to embrace the decisions that the situation demanded. Around eleven o'clock, a phone call came through to my office from Liu's girlfriend. She and Liu had attempted to ride a bicycle to her house a few blocks away. At a certain intersection an unmarked van overtook them. Some men jumped out, dragged Liu into the van and drove off with him. The hysterical girl was ringing from a public phone. She didn't know what would happen to him after the arrest. He would be denounced. He would be tortured. He would be made to tell stories. She proposed to rush back to the embassy and jump over the compound wall.

Why had they done it? Why had Liu gone out with her on bicycle through those empty streets? Why hadn't they come with me? Was it to get fresh clothes? To make love? Was it the intellectual's intoxication with action? Did he want to proclaim his fearlessness? The jaws of a monster lying in wait in the darkness had snapped into place.

I lay on my back pressing the floorboards. The peculiar woolly grey of the Peking dawn came up before I slept, as it had done for centuries now according to the ancient calendar, over the low roofs of the walled city, the sacred groves of the emperors' outlying tombs, the craggy mountain fastness of the aspirant and the disgraced, and the yellow deserts beyond.

Should I have forced my friend inside the safety of the diplomatic compound for his own good?

He was a bright hope of China, one of few able to articulate what was needed to renovate this rotten place. Wasn't he? And now a person was gone, perhaps forever, down those jaws. I even wondered if I hadn't failed the China that had given me so much.

The most you can hope, perhaps, is to help a few people. But which people? Chosen on what basis? Those on your own side, or those you must cross the road for? I owed him nothing except that I admired him. And the reason for that was his rasping character. I liked him because of the way his taste for XO cognac enhanced the hoarse stammering delivery of his outrageous remarks.

In the end I had *allowed* him the choice of whether to come with me or go. Beyond a certain point I had not joined cause with him. I had not taken his life into my own hands. I had not presumed to know how he must act. His reckless caprice proved costly, and it continued to cause me pain and regret as well, whenever I thought of him.

He was an actor in a history that dictated its own merciless outcomes. I was only a bit player in that same history, at the point where it entered my life and where I was part of the connective tissue between China's epoch and our own subtler, wryer Australian history, in which different, democratic pulses can be heard. I was embarrassed, but reluctant to let go of the gap that held me from identifying with a Chinese friend who identified himself with his own people. That was always the basis of our relationship. He had his history, I had mine. The gap wasn't such a large one, it turned out – simply the moment in an idling car when an individual decides. I grieved for the existence of that gap, lying there on the floor. I understood in those anxious hours that I came from another place, that I should go home and wait another day.

In the small hours of the night on which martial law had been formally declared, through loudspeakers and under searchlights in the Square, I had walked back under the willows beside the palace moat and away into the maze of alleyways that was the city. I was walking with a wandering Australian scholar of China who knows more about all this than I shall ever know, when we met two girls making their way home.

'Our movement is defeated,' they cried out to us morosely. 'Our movement is defeated.' That's when I learned to read the dove-grey Peking dawn. It's no kangaroo fur. The light, so worn, is a blanket that can smother what might be, under the pretence of reinstating what is.

Amnesty, PEN International and other organisations made Liu's case a priority. He was vilified throughout China, because, they said, he had sold his motherland. But he was adulated too. Australian friends smuggled him a jumper of top-quality wool, Made in Australia. Sick in prison, he had been allowed Chinese classics to read. His face looked puffy, as if he had been beaten, when he appeared on television to tell a tailored version of his story. Then, after two years, he was released. He has even visited Australia to give lectures, which he is forbidden to do in China. But his views no longer inspire. So he must wait another day too.

And I, having recognised the gap, continue to explore it, probing the places where lightning can jump across and scorch.

Professor Yang Xianyi, a great literary translator, never approved of Liu. He said Liu was a mad dog. He wanted to move too fast. When asked what is going on in China, or what he thinks of Australia – are we part of Asia? – Professor Yang has a mouthful of Scottish tea and smiles. 'I like your koala. He is sleepy. He hates to move. I like your kangaroo. Although she cannot fly, she can leap. She can go faster than 100 miles per hour . . .'

In 1992 there was a Celebrate Australia week in Peking, featuring a preview of *Strictly Ballroom*, a grand barbecue, and support from Foreign Affairs (Austrade), Qantas, and Australian arts bodies. A feud broke out when it was suggested that the five-star China World Hotel, the host of the event, should get a giant kangaroo suit to enliven the festivities. Word came down the line – tacky tacky tacky. Chinese people were too refined to be amused by a bouncing humanoid kangaroo. Or if they were amused, it might mean they were laughing at us, not taking us as seriously as we deserve to be taken.

The costume is still available for hire.

1994

Translating China

A characteristic of traditional Chinese painting is the inscription of a text. Date, place and other circumstances of composition, and often a related poem, can be drawn on to the work. The word intervenes between viewer and the image the artist paints, becoming part of the image. The artist's depiction of the world is also a form of text. As Simon Leys, *nom de plume* of sinologist Pierre Ryckmans, has pointed out, Chinese literati talk of 'writing' a painting. Not only are the means largely the same – ink and fine brush – but the representation of landscapes, images and figures is less a process of depicting the external world than of reinterpreting a highly codified tradition, a process of reading and writing.

As painting can be a form of writing, so writing, in the form of calligraphy, is an equivalent to painting. When a work is finished, the author will usually stamp it with a personal seal, sometimes with an assumed, artistic name, to suggest that the work on paper was the creation of, or was creating, a different kind of personality. Friends might contribute additional inscriptions, and subsequent collectors add their seals, and the work takes its place in an historical continuum.

The written inscriptions that come to be an essential part of the painted scene offer an image of the way our contact with China is mediated, in many different ways, by the written word, and by the concepts and structures, stories and histories, that words delineate. Recognising the need for interpreters and translators, however, we don't always stop to think that the wall of words interposed between the two sides signifies a process of translation and inevitable distortion: a literary activity. Australia has inherited the Anglo monoglot vice of assuming that everyone in the world speaks English and that somehow translation is a transparent process in which all messages convert into a natural English form. Far too little weight is given to language expertise, the commitment involved in acquiring it and the relative depth of cross-cultural understanding it then enables. You have probably heard stories of how the interpreter stage-manages. When the Australian Foreign Minister, who was born in the year of the cock, made a joke to his Chinese host, also born in the year of the cock, about being 'born in the chookhouse together', the hapless interpreter thought it best to tell the audience that the visiting dignitary had made a hilarious, untranslatable joke and to ask them to laugh accordingly.

The special status of the written word in Chinese society perhaps helps explain why China has attracted foreign writers for centuries. From the earliest travellers' tales to reach Europe, to Voltaire and Coleridge, and on to the present day, China as strange, curious, awe-inspiring Cathay has drawn writers as a realm for tall tales, fantasy and the revelation of profound mysteries, a fabled zone of difference. Bamboozling the distinction between fact and fancy, China persistently presents the problem of how to take what is written about it. When Marco Polo offered his eyewitness accounts, scholars set to endless debating over the truth or otherwise of what he reported. Recounting his travels in China in *Escape With Me!* (1939), Osbert Sitwell put the paradox succinctly:

The stories of Marco Polo – which we know now, even when they are not accurate to an inch, to be so much truer than mere truth – were dismissed as falsehoods; constituted, almost, a standard by which to measure probability or its reverse.

What does it mean to be truer than mere truth? Writers about China have often been accused of fabricating, and, as in the antique business, so in literary works, fabrication can be a polite word for fake. One such discovery is George Psalmanazar, who 'arrived in England in 1703, claiming to be a native of Formosa', when he was actually born in the south of France. Translating the catechism into what he claimed was Formosan (a language he had in fact invented by himself), and presenting himself as an expert on the country, he deceived the dons of Oxford. After his eventual exposure, he discussed his techniques for deceiving people:

Whatever I had once affirmed in conversation, though to ever so few people, and though ever so improbable, or even absurd, should never be amended or contradicted in the narrative. Thus having once, inadvertently in conversation, made the yearly number of sacrificed infants to amount to 18,000, I could never be persuaded to lessen it, though I had been often made sensible to the impossibility of so small an island losing so many males every year, without becoming at length depopulated.

Psalmanazar is in a distinguished line that later includes Edmund Backhouse – subject of Hugh Trevor-Roper's study, *Hermit of Peking* (1977) – whose collection of rare books and manuscripts, now in the Bodleian Library, Oxford, still has experts arguing. How much did he forge himself? Was he really the Empress Dowager's lover, as he claimed? In his personality the distinctions between eccentricity, duplicity and sheer fantasy are well and truly blurred. Trevor-Roper makes the point that, whether Confucian or Maoist, the utopian nature of China to the Western mind lends itself to such artful deception. Later interpreters of China have been accused, if not of deception, then at least of special pleading: George Ernest Morrison, Wilfred Burchett, Han Suyin, Ross Terrill, Stephen Mosher and others. In the case of some of these writers, their interpretation of China was necessarily polemical, in order to combat entrenched and preconceived ideas. China expertise can become a liability when it fails to offer the counsel desired back home. Wilfred Burchett, who was in a position to know more about post-war Asian conflicts than almost any other Australian writer, was dismissed as a traitor.

Alternatively, when the China expert's interpretation is music to the ears back home, then the facts don't matter – a process Simon Leys has exposed in his essays. But who is Simon Leys? Tilting at demons with his polemical rapier, he is also his creator's invention.

The standard genre for writing about China is the eyewitness account, the report from the front that purports to tear aside the veil and reveal the real China. Such books continue to roll off the press. Peter Fleming's *News from Tartary*, Ross Terrill's *The Real China*, Tiziano Terzani's *Through the Forbidden Door*, Colin Thubron's *Behind the Wall*, and *Black Horse Odyssey: Search for the lost city of Rome in China* by David Harris, to name a few. Yearbooks, factbooks and handbooks churn out, from foreign and Chinese publishers alike, as if to suggest that fact is solid ground, that the real China can be found in statistics, if nowhere else. Such bald facts encourage another sort of façadism, and have squeezed out more imaginative kinds of literature. The difference between India and China in the area of English-language fiction, for instance, is striking. India has been embodied in the most sophisticated forms of imaginative narrative, rooted in but not confined to realism: *A Passage to India*, *The Raj Quartet*, *Midnight's Children*, Narayan, Naipaul, Ruth Prawer Jhabvala. The best known novels about China are André Malraux's *La Condition Humaine* (not an English novel), and *The Good Earth* by Pearl Buck, a widely denigrated Nobel-prize winner. Most of the novels in English with pretensions to art are little known, excessively artful and exotic, thinly autobiographical, or loose and sketchy. Among writers of the calibre of Joseph Conrad, George Bernard Shaw, Somerset Maugham, Harold Acton, Christopher Isherwood, Dorothy Hewett, Dymphna Cusack, and Alan Marshall, to name a few of those who visited China, none was inspired to produce major imaginative work from the experience – although Noel Coward wrote *Private Lives* in what is now the Peace Hotel in Shanghai. China has attracted writers, and turned people into writers, but has not helped to produce masterpieces. The contrast with India can partly be explained in terms of the history of colonisation and English-language education in India. But there are other reasons. The Chinese world-view creates a chasm between Chinese and others. The concepts of insider and outsider are fundamental at so many levels of life. The language, script and culture are expressions of this separateness, the manifestations of a society that is self-enclosed, hermetic and centred on itself. The visitor is always an outsider. The more expertly the non-ethnically Chinese China expert performs inside the culture, the more uneasy Chinese feel. Too often the expert ends up accused of being a spy or double agent. The contemporary novelist Wang Shuo confessed that he couldn't handle his Australian friend Geremie Barmé, who speaks Chinese like a total Peking insider. It was 'uncanny', in the Freudian sense; a freak of nature.

The traditional English-language novel depends on assumptions about human nature, about the individual in society, about cause and effect in the structure of a narrative. China challenges these assumptions, or prevents them from applying. The visiting novelist is largely denied access to Chinese human nature; he or she is restricted to external observation and imaginative projection, and both processes may say more about the writer than about the fictional characters. The Chinese may even challenge the assumption that there is one human nature. Maybe there is Chinese human nature and foreign human nature, as it is argued that there are Chinese human rights and foreign human rights. The Chinese may challenge the notion of individual autonomy, finding selfhood constituted by the groups to which they belong: family, locality, workplace, class, race. The kind of stories they live out may have a different teleology. Chinese narrative is characteristically episodic, rambling, picaresque and fragmentary. Essay, memoir, reportage, fable are more characteristic modes of Chinese prose writing than the novel as we know it. In all these ways China resists prose narrative. What remains is the foreign writer's reflection in a mirror.

Recent critical theory makes it easier to grasp the literary implications of these questions. The privileging of the written sign, with its peculiar relationship to the external world, has long made the Chinese master deconstructionists. Most spectacularly under communist rule, the period ominously known as Constructing the Nation, the manipulation of language, signs, history and culture, both on a grand public scale and into the deepest recesses of private brains, and the concurrent resistant countermanipulation, have produced cultural and social actualities that deconstructionist theory can rejoice in. (Among Western linguistic theorists, I.A. Richards and William Empson spent periods in China, followed later by Julia Kristeva.)

One of the best novels about China is George Johnston's *The Far Road*, published in 1962, nearly twenty years after the experiences that inspired it. It is the story of two men, an American and an Australian, travelling together through a region of southern China ravaged by war and the evils of war – people in thousands uprooted, starving and thirsting to death, victims of corruption and misinformation as much as of war itself – and the lengths to which people go, selling body and soul, in order to survive. The horrors witnessed by the two foreign journalists are felt personally as their relationship with each other struggles to withstand the assault on their individual value systems, their egotisms, and their desire for survival, until a point is reached where all values and meanings are questioned, including the point of existence itself.

The novel is not artfully written, nor consistently controlled. But it is palpably based on real experience, not a fable – unlike Albert Camus's *The Plague* with which it is in some ways comparable. The real experience is significant for what it does to the protagonist, David Meredith, breaking down his belief in power and empire, history, fact as the reporter knows it, fairness, and, most bitterly for an Australian novel – in mateship. What remains is a kind of freed vision, profoundly doubting, and the strength to look into nothingness. It is this quality and courage of vision that China gave George Johnston. He went straight on to write his best work, *My Brother Jack*, and the other two novels in his trilogy.

George Johnston's work has its seeds in his relationship with the poet Wen Yiduo in Yunnan after the second world war. For writers, a communication through art can be as substantial a way of experiencing another reality as direct experience. Wen Yiduo much admired the early Chinese poet-counsellor Qu Yuan, who committed suicide to protest being exiled in punishment for his loyal opposition to the emperor's policies. Wen Yiduo likewise stood firm in his convictions, maintaining literary and political activity even as the grim circumstances of the time drove him into marginality and near-madness. He was eventually murdered by the Nationalists in 1946. He resurfaces in Johnston's last novel, *A Cartload of Clay* (1971), when the narrator remembers 'Wen Yi-tuo asking questions of a blind universe'.

Principled artistic witness seems to be a quality of Chinese culture that has attracted Australian writers. Simon Leys has found inspiration and affinity in the savage indignation of Lu Hsun, China's major early twentieth-century prose writer. Rosemary Dobson, in 'The Continuance of Poetry: Twelve Poems for David Campbell', places herself and Campbell, and the inspirational language they share, in conjunction with Chinese poets of the Tang dynasty:

> *Two poets walking together*
> *May pause suddenly and say,*
> *Will this be your poem, or mine?*

A process of translation, a channel of communication, from Tang China to contemporary Australia, however subterranean, is acknowledged in Dobson's poem. Poet John Tranter has spoken of the inspiration he found as a young man in *The White Pony*, an anthology of Chinese poetry edited by litterateur and activist Robert Payne. After the Tiananmen Square massacre, Fay Zwicky, recalling a visit to Peking, remembers surprising a group of Chinese students by singing the Chinese national anthem as taught to her phonetically at a high Anglican Melbourne school by a communist teacher back in 1944.

In my own case, seeing Yuan dynasty painter Fan Kuan's painting *Travellers Among Mountains and Streams* in the Taipei Palace Museum in 1981 set me on the circling path that eventually led to my novel *Avenue of Eternal Peace*. The painting's title occurs as a chapter heading, as does the name of Qu Yuan's famous poem, 'Encountering Sorrow'. The wild lifestyle and passionate conviction of some contemporary Chinese poets were an inspiration for the novel, where the poets' dreams are set against the state's claims.

I was in Wuhan, in a hotel beside the Yangtze River near the spot where Chairman Mao took his famous swim in 1966. The river is immensely wide and flows fast, spanned by a huge flat bridge built with Soviet help, across which long trains, packed buses, people, cars, bicycles flow ceaselessly. I had been in Peking looking at post-modern artworks with people who at the time lived in unplumbed, pre-modern rooms, artists outlawed by a system that is at once high-tech sophisticated totalitarian and medievally feudal in what it demands of and does to people. In Wuhan I talked to a relation of the bodyguard who had accompanied Mao on his epic swim. The bodyguard was a peasant who had become a Communist Party member and security officer. He died in 1991, having lost all faith and hope in the system he had served with utmost loyalty all his life. At the time the man's relative had been among the hundreds of enthusiastic youngsters who had emulated Mao by swimming the Yangtze. But the young relative couldn't actually swim. By holding his hand up as he went down for the third time, to be seen and rescued, he managed, barely, to survive. The bodyguard told me that the present government was like boats floating on the surface of the river. They were on top, but they could do nothing to control the river's flow.

As I looked out at the river from my hotel room, and the surrounding tri-city complex of Wuhan, site of so many key events in twentieth-century Chinese history, I was struck once again with the impossibility of encompassing in words such fluid, endless immensity, such length and breadth, such dimensions of folly, tragedy and energy as is China.

In the 'Author's Note' to *Avenue of Eternal Peace* I struggled to find a way of explaining the relationship that existed between myself, the raw material of China, and the novel. I was tempted to quote Joseph Conrad's injunction, 'In the destructive element immerse.' It refers not so much to the sea, as to a zone of experience, another element altogether, which transforms the writer's consciousness. But the comparison was too grand, and 'destructive' was not quite right for what China had done to me. I adapted and paraphrased the remark, determined *not* to say that the book is about China. No creative work can be 'about' China in any meaningful sense. The best that one Australian writer's story can show is perhaps the encounter, the journey, the changes that China brings. I was amused, therefore, to see my author's note quoted as evidence that the novel was not eligible for the Miles Franklin Award. Professor Colin Roderick paid me the compliment of saying he would have voted for the book if he thought it was eligible. But to be eligible it must 'present Australian life in any of its phases'. As far as I am concerned one of the phases of Australian life is the attempt to translate. The process of translation, the journey of mind to make intelligible what we perceive at first to be only dimly part of our world, but which eventually becomes familiar and known, is what we are all about, one way or another, and is surely about all of us.

1992

Australia's China

Australia has a relationship with China that goes back before white invasion and has gone on ever since, with different elements of the relationship made visible, or invisible, at different times. China, in that sense, is part of what Australia is, as Australia is part of a Chinese world that includes mainland China, Taiwan, Hong Kong, Singapore and the Chinese diaspora, especially in South East Asia, as well as the Chinese in Australia. The story of China in Australia differs from the story of China in Britain or the United States, or in Malaysia or Indonesia, although all those stories are sometimes strands in the Australian story. And to talk of the Chinese in Australia requires fine differentiation according to where people have come from, how long they have been here, what languages they speak, and what cultures they identify with. There are many Australians of partial Chinese ancestry, which only at a certain point becomes meaningless or irrelevant to them – and then seldom finally. And there are all those non-Chinese Australians whose lives or whose ancestors' lives have been affected by China.

In *The Finish Line: A Long March by Bicycle through China and*

Australia (1994), Sang Ye writes of the people he meets on his bicycle rides across China and Australia. Travelling these routes, back and forward in time and space, he affectionately investigates the lives and attitudes of the people he meets along the way, especially those whose personal histories of hope, disappointment and renewed hope can be shared by the traveller-writer as reflections of the larger journeys undertaken by the two different societies over the last one or two hundred years.

Many of those he meets in Australia are of Chinese descent, and Sang Ye draws out the unusual or ironical connections between Australia and China that they provide. Nor does he forget those Chinese who have sojourned in Australia, sometimes for generations, before moving on. The Chinese concept of sojourner, as discussed by the historian of Chinese migration Wang Gungwu and taken up by Eric Rolls as the title for his pioneering history of the Chinese in Australia, *Sojourners* (1992), is useful here for encompassing 'expatriate' Chinese Australians too. Richard Hall, researching the background of heart surgeon Victor Chang for his book *Tiger General: The Killing of Victor Chang* (1995), has discovered that Chang's ancestors, for example, having come from China to Australia, were in the New England district of New South Wales earlier this century, but moved on – or back – to China and South East Asia, before their offspring returned again to Australia.

Sang Ye worked on the English version of his book with his wife Sue Trevaskes and myself. A sixth-generation Australian, Sue has one part Chinese ancestry six generations back. Queensland's Yappar River was named after her forebears. My great-grandfather went from Melbourne to China, where my paternal grandfather was born. It is threads of connection of this kind that show Australia's China to be a complex, various, historically evolved and specific entity.

A characteristic of Chinese culture has been its adaptability and transferability. Historically and geographically, Chinese culture has exerted a strong gravitational pull in Asia. Even where a major influence has been imported into China, such as Buddhism from India, it has been re-exported from China as a centre. Nowadays you hear talk of an Asian model or a Confucian model, which usually means something with Chinese culture as a source. Japan, the Koreas and Thailand can be seen in this way, along with Singapore, Hong Kong and Taiwan. Elsewhere, in Indonesia, Malaysia, Vietnam, Burma, Mongolia, Tibet and so on, a process of differentiation from, or symbiosis with, a Chinese model acknowledges China as a centripetal force. Although far from our nearest neighbour, China has been especially significant in the Australian experience of Asia. China and the Chinese have weighed heavily in policy decisions about White Australia, the Vietnam war and other 'Asian' issues. It is only in exceptional circumstances, such as the second world war, that we distinguish sharply between Chinese and other Asians. Likewise Japan's economic pre-eminence in recent times, in contradistinction to China, has forced a refinement of our understanding of Asia as a whole.

Inasmuch as Australia's identity has been formed through a dialectic (often silent) with what is perceived and feared as non-Australian, the relationship with the Chinese world reflects some of the not always articulated tendencies of Australian society and culture.

To illustrate how Chinese shared in the genesis experience of settlement Australia and its subsequent hierarchies, I can do no better than quote a sentence from Marcus Clarke's novel *His Natural Life* (1874), describing the inhabitants of Norfolk Island gaol in 1846:

These are creatures who openly defy authority, whose language and conduct is such as was never before seen or heard out of Bedlam. There are men who are known to have murdered their companions, and who boast of it. With these the English farm labourer, the riotous and ignorant mechanic, the victim of perjury or mistake, are indiscriminately herded. With them are mixed Chinamen from Hong Kong, the aborigines of New Holland, West Indian blacks, Greeks, Caffres, and Malays, soldiers for desertion, idiots, madmen, pigstealers and pickpockets. The dreadful place seems set apart for all that is hideous and vile in our common nature. In its recklessness, its insubordination, its filth, and its despair, it realises to my mind the popular notion of hell.

So multiculturalism begins – as does cultural exchange. The Norfolk Island prison, a version of English philosopher Jeremy Bentham's reforming Penitentiary Panopticon, found its way to China, in theory and practice, as a model adopted by the Chinese Communist Party for the prisons that underpin its ideology of reform through totalitarian control: the gulag/utopia.

Not many Chinese in Australia put pen – or brush – to paper, and fewer in English. Gradually, in piecemeal fashion, material to document the Chinese in Australia is coming to light. There are photographs, drawings, objects, a wealth of oral history, and, perhaps the most common form of record, the memoir produced for posterity by successful Chinese families. This can be a fairly literary form, subject to the usual embellishments, distortions and eloquence. One of my favourites is the testimonial of Taam Sz Pui, dated Innisfail 1925, as recorded by scholar Chan Wen Lung:

My grandfather passed away while I was seventeen. Four years later, there occurred in the village a terrible flood, which swept away all our fish and mulberry trees. This calamity left us in further reduced circumstances.

There was a rumour then that gold had been discovered in a place called Cooktown, and the source of which was inexhaustible and free to all. Without verifying the truth, my father planned to go with his two sons. We started from our village on January the 18th, 1877. On January 22nd we sailed from Hongkong and reached our destination on February 10th of the same year.

Oh, what a disappointment when we learnt that the rumour was unfounded and we were misled! Not only was gold difficult to find, the climate was not suitable and was the cause of frequent attacks of illness. As we went about, there met our gaze the impoverished condition and the starved looks of our fellow countrymen who were either penniless or ill, and there reached our ears endless sighs of sorrow. Those who arrived first not only expressed no regret for being late, on the contrary, they were thinking of departing. Could we, who had just arrived, remain untouched at these sad tales?

Thus begins a Chinese fortunate life.

48 | Chinese Whispers

Five years had passed, I now realised that to search for gold was like trying to catch the moon at the bottom of the sea. Forsaking it for something else, I worked in a restaurant at the wages of two pounds a month. At the end of the year I had already saved twenty-five pounds, sixteen shillings and six pence, after deducting expenses.

By the end, Taam Sz Puy can say of his life:

One would liken it to eating a piece of sugar cane from top down, the sweetest part would be last. I felt more than gratified.

As I am now growing old my eyes are becoming dim; my wife also is ill through continuous over exertion . . . Though I am still healthy and strong, I have passed seventy and come to the evening of my life. The sunset is certainly beautiful but I fear that the glow will not last long. My children have now grown up and I can entrust to them the business and relieve myself of this burden . . . Oh! Hing, my son, guide your younger brothers, Wing and Wah, and obey my commands . . . The experience of the past serves as the guide for the future . . .

The narrative has the magical quality of a fable, combining a strong sense of cultural continuity with an exercise in self-making that seems distinctively Australian. In some cases the process of self-presentation seems to involve a kind of impersonation of Chinese or Australian characteristics. Is it perhaps only in recent times, as we experience in William Yang's moving theatre piece *Sadness*, for example, that it has been possible for a person to be comfortably Australian and Chinese in one?

Such Chinese memoirs offer a transformation of experience that has been made available in Australian writing through other, cruder kinds of impersonation.

The Chinaman jog-trotted towards them, his baskets a-sway, his mouth stretched to a friendly grin. 'You no want cabbagee to-day? Me got velly good cabbagee,' he said persuasively and lowered his pole.

'No thank you, John, not to-day. Me wait for white man.'

'Me bling pleasant for lilly missee,' said the Chow; and unknotting a

dirty nosecloth, he drew from it an ancient lump of candied ginger. 'Lilly missee eatee him . . . oh, yum, yum! Velly good. My word!'

But Chinamen to Trotty were fearsome bogies, corresponding to the swart-faced, white-eyed chimney-sweeps of the English nursery. She hid behind her aunt, holding fast to the latter's skirts, and only stealing an occasional peep from one saucer-like blue eye.

'Thank you, John. Me takee chowchow for lilly missee,' said Polly, who had experience in disposing of such savoury morsels.

'You no buy cabbagee to-day?' repeated Ah Sing, with the catlike persistence of his race.

This passage from Henry Handel Richardson's novel *Australia Felix* (1917) is caricature, but sharply observed, not unaffectionate, in which Ah Sing plays up to a role that Polly can mimic. It makes us uncomfortable today. The example confirms that Chinese were experienced directly, at close quarters, at least in nineteenth-century Victoria. Perhaps this stripped Chinese culture of the more elevated dimensions of oriental mystique that were reserved for Japan. Accompanying visiting Australians to their meetings in the People's Republic of China in more recent times, I have noticed how often people want to make a connection between Chinese they have personally encountered in Australia years ago – childhood vegetable hawkers, families down the road, kids in the schoolyard – seeking a sense of identity that the Chinese officials they are meeting with seldom share.

Again the tendency of many Australians to seek a direct personal connection with China reinforces the point that Australia has a specific historical relationship with China. For this reason – and I suppose now is the time to say it – the discourse of Orientalism that this topic attracts is not always appropriate or easily applicable. Yet it is in the global ether. While in Australia there are political and social motives for putting Asia on the agenda, in academic and cultural institutions there is the added pressure of current theoretical interests and constructs, in which the critique of Orientalism is part of postcolonialism or Subaltern Studies. Orientalism has taken on a particular meaning since Edward Said's hugely influential book of the same name. Said's Orientalism describes a phenomenon, originating in the West's transactions with the Near East, in which perceptions of difference produced distorted exotic representations of other cultures that served the interests of the overtly or covertly colonising power. It is itself a powerful idea that has helped to bring previously marginal perspectives to the centre of intellectual attention, as Said's questioning of the motives or consequences of inquiry into cultural difference projects forward from past to present:

> ... *the metamorphosis of a relatively innocuous philological subspecialty into a capacity for managing political movements, administering colonies, making nearly apocalyptic statements representing the White Man's difficult civilising mission – all this is something at work within a purportedly liberal culture, one full of concern for its vaunted norms of catholicity, plurality, and open-mindedness. In fact, what took place was the very opposite of liberal: the hardening of doctrine and meaning, imparted by 'science', into 'truth'.*
> (Orientalism *(1979), p. 254)*

Said's Orientalism is also a monolithic idea. As Australian cultural theorists Michael Dutton and Peter Williams put it: 'the conceptual looseness of Said's founding work *Orientalism* is that it enables generalising and loose analysis of historically, socially and culturally specific and differentiated alterity practices on the basis of invocations of and appeals to Orientalism.' It has certainly been one factor prompting the gaze of intellectuals towards Australia's relationships with Asia. But it would be a pity if a needed redirection of attention were blinded to its subject by the very intellectual impulses that are nudging people in this new direction in the first place, by a failure to allow for the situation in Australia, in its relationship with China, at least, to be different.

A similar point can be made in relation to the other pressures that are encouraging our present interest in Asia: the national interest, the 'Asian thrust'. I worry when the process threatens to deny its own history. I suspect that our future, including our economic future, can be more soundly managed if we have a grip of the past. 'Don't Mention the War': an attempt to hold Prime Minister Paul Keating to this line during his visit to Vietnam in 1994 produced press brouhaha. It's just one example of what can go wrong if you massage history too much.

Although some public utterances seem to suggest that only now are Australians apprehending China, in fact many Australians who have spent time in or with China have left valuable written accounts. There is a body of diaries, memoirs, essays and analyses, some of which have become books. Examples include Mary Gaunt's *A Woman in China* (1914), C.P. Fitzgerald's autobiography *Why China?* (1985) and Cynthia Nolan's *A Sight of China* (1969). There are also the more literary works produced by visitors to China: poems, stories and novels that bear witness to the writer's experience, often retaining something of the journal entry. A blurring of imagination and record, fantasy and fact, is a characteristic of writing about China, even or especially by the so-called China experts. Australia, indeed, has a fine tradition of maverick sinology, in which the China buffs write well, get themselves into trouble, and play out peculiar roles between the two countries. They all belong to Australia's China.

And then there are those rare cases where an affinity with Chinese culture, however apprehended (and it need not be on the ground), informs work of independent literary value. Among poets I would mention Harold Stewart, Randolph Stow, Rosemary Dobson, and lately Fay Zwicky; among novelists, Beth Yahp, Brian Castro and Alex Miller. In works by these writers, the values of Chinese culture, philosophy or history actually connect with and enter Australian writing.

For the novelists mentioned, China is a source, and a resource, which their work variously relocates in relation to Australian experience. The hero of Brian Castro's first novel, *Birds of Passage* (1983), Australian-born, part-Chinese Seamus O'Young, has an alter ego, Shan of Young, descendant of Shan, a prospector, and Mary Young, a goldfields prostitute, from Young in New South Wales, near Lambing Flat where an infamous anti-Chinese outbreak occurred in 1861. Interspersed with Seamus O'Young's own contemporary story is an account of the original Shan's life. He left Ching dynasty China to sail for the goldfields, barely survived Ballarat and Bendigo after the failure of Eureka, and joined up with his Australian woman for a time. As Shan moves from a purely Chinese perspective towards a meeting of East and West, so Seamus delves into Shan's story as a means of rediscovering his Chineseness: 'I wanted to understand my whole history.' *Birds of Passage* is a stylish and ambitious performance that essays many of the strategies of postmodernist fiction well before they became habituated in Australia. 'There was no country from which I came, and there is none to which I can return,' says Seamus. Castro speculates on what might constitute a 'country' – a home, a history, an identity – for a person who seems heir to everything and nothing. He plays with asynchronous fragments in order to search for a whole; the result is a raw evocation of a doppelgänger's sense of dislocation and invisibility. In the end Seamus and his other self, Shan, merge across time and space in a symbolic union. Fiction here works against history, with all the traditional power of the Chinese word. 'Funny how writing is not a record for posterity or anything as fanciful, but is really a statement that one is not dreaming. It establishes oneself, puts oneself in control again,' records Shan back in China.

Birds of Passage is a meditation on identity and the conflict between Christian and Taoist/Confucian morality, especially sexual morality. Castro returns to these themes in his later novel, *After China* (1992). It is a work that also seeks its ends in journeys backwards, where, this time, the sought-after release comes in stepping away from the tidal pull of origins. 'There was no longer a future, no longer a possibility whose unknown had to be understood. So he had quite comfortably turned his back and settled for this self to which he had finally come, from which he would constantly remake himself.' *After China* reflects a more existential psychoanalytic position than the earlier novel, with China as almost a mode of consciousness, characterised by obscure intimations of profound wisdom and intricate, indirect, yet insistent links between one experience and the next – a form of life that today's individual will want to walk away from. Some of these qualities Castro's novel shares with Alex Miller's *The Ancestor Game* (1992). As the title brilliantly suggests, *The Ancestor Game* takes up the idea of realigning yourself through uncovering a hidden or alternative lineage. The novel traces a series of elaborately interwoven personal quests, expressed in relaxed poetic philosophising. It links a contemporary Australian writer and an elderly Melbourne Chinese in a search for heritage – their own, and by extension, a more layered heritage for contemporary Australia than is usually acknowledged. Or is it sleight of hand? China falls like an exotic backdrop, encouraging enigmatic ambiguity and opaque understanding.

It is to the other layers and other worlds that alternative ethnicity can conjure up that Beth Yahp also turns in *The Crocodile Fury* (1992), a meticulous recreation of a Malaysian-Chinese grandmother's world, a zone of stories and ghosts, superstition and unexpected liberation, hidden within, or just out of sight of, the ordinary. The writing is a conscious process of cultural transfer, from secrecy to communication, and Yahp's elegant, supple prose is well-attuned to its task.

Impulses of biography and personal positioning are at work in many of the Australian novels that refer to Chinese culture, keeping the connection between Australia and China in a social and historical ambit. The poets are looking for something else. Randolph Stow is a good example. He concluded his selected poems, *A Counterfeit Silence* (1969), with the sequence 'From *The Testament of Tourmaline* "Variations on Themes of the Tao Teh Ching"', the final poem of which can stand not only as an *envoi* to the book, but also as an epigraph on Stow's creative work as a whole: 'In the silence between my words, hear the praise of Tao.'

The line formulates a Chinese conception of the interrelationship of substance and void as mutually informing entities – as in Chinese painting the empty space becomes an essential partner in the dialectic of the composition. Tao (often translated as 'the Way') is the principle adumbrated in the riddlingly mysterious philosophical text *Tao teh ching* attributed to the Chinese sage Lao-tzu, who lived around the fifth century BC. Stow's sequence responds to several sections of Lao-tzu. Stow's poems also appear as fragments of intensely personal manifesto or apologia. Yet, as the elaborate title suggests, the personal impulse is veiled or counterfeited by a shuffling of masks, a dramatic impersonation, as if the author is finding a way to defend his decision to retreat from communicable meaning to meanings that exist only privately. The passionate clarity of these poems conceals puzzling paradox and seductive obscurity. Their clarion injunctions point to a spiritual renunciation that has its own subterranean eroticism, a sublimation of world and self into what is neither world nor self. Stow's Eastern conception seeks to go beyond traditional spiritual destinations to accommodate the oneness of land and people inherent in Aboriginal spirituality: 'Before God is, was Tao . . . the land and Tao are one.' In translating Lao-tzu into fragments of personal (and Australian) experience, Stow achieves an extraordinary purity of lyric utterance, transforming obscure private suffering into a posture of radiant absoluteness:

> *Deep. Go deep,*
> *as the long roots of myall*
> *mine the red country*
> *for water, for silence.*
> *. . .*
> *Silence is empire.*
> *Tao is eternal,*
> *flowering, returning,*
> *with water, with silence.*

In reconfiguring a Chinese world-view, the poet can sing the sources of his own creative energies, 'whose sound in time is nothingness'. In its complex strength and intensity, Stow's poem sequence is an expression of spiritual extremity rare in the literature of our country.

It is as if the writer turns to an Eastern position to expand the breathing space for values and attitudes that cannot grow, or only in a state of deprivation, in Australian soil. The poets who look to China are traditionalists in a special sense, concerned to reach modern renderings of ancient apprehensions, less interested in cultural melange than in refining or extending traditions. They wish to harmonise qualities in their Australian experience with deep, time-honoured (not exclusively European) springs of creativity. Fay Zwicky explores the idea of the enabling capacity of Chinese poetry for some Australian poets, including herself, in her essay entitled 'Vast Spaces, Quiet Voices: Chinese Connections in Australian Poetry'. She speaks of 'writers from a tradition of romantic individualism discovering something lacking in such a tradition . . . [and] trying to strike a more modest balance between action and contemplation . . .' In the process, some writers may turn to Chinese philosophy and poetry, attracted by qualities their own culture lacks. Zwicky observes that 'it takes a culture a long time to discover human limits in the illusory perspectives of limitless space'. China perhaps offers Australian writers a way of dealing with the apparent limitlessness of their own circumstances. In this sense, as Zwicky goes on to say, 'in the meeting of East and West, the West is learning to face the West, as it were, from the East'. The Chinese perspective feeds an understanding of Australia.

In Fay Zwicky's poetry this has meant, in her own words, a move 'from lyrical abstraction towards a more austere concreteness'. Her collection *Ask Me* (1990) begins with a suite, 'China Poems 1988', a series of tough self-interrogations prompted by the experience of China that is also the experience of moving through an enormous, alien geographical and historical backdrop, as in a contemporary version of a classical Chinese painting:

> *No language and I'm booked*
> *on China Airlines.*

And later:

> *I can't read a word. Who am I here?*

People seem to exist in a different dimension, not only physically, but spiritually 'out of this world', and, in responding, the poet herself achieves a state of sharpened, sceptical lucidity, a contemporary version of mystical exaltation:

> *. . . 'You like it here?'*
> *How can I tell her that*
> *I'm neither happy nor unhappy?*
> *. . .*
> *She might think I was seeing things.*

In other poems too, such as 'Push or Knock', China has an almost incidental capacity to freshen and clarify – a reminder that translation from one culture to another is surprisingly possible, and that, in the translation, an inexhaustible pool of wisdom almost comes in reach of the here and now. *Almost*. The poet's appreciation of the complexities and subtleties of a great and different culture also contains an abrasive reminder that its awe-inspiring value lies partly in its secrets, in what exists beyond our grasp. In a later poem, 'On the Acquisition of Four Famous Chinese Novels for the Senior Library and Related Matters', she writes:

> *There's more to culture than a useful acquisition*
> *as any dancer in the margin tells you,*
> *gentle hands mysteriously raised*
> *against the tides of vanished dynasties,*
> *no margin left for error.*

Zwicky's China is a place where personal encounters bring unexpected moments of enlightenment. Rosemary Dobson's 'The Continuance of Poetry: Twelve Poems for David Campbell' formalises a set of encounters with a friend, a poet, which are also occasions of encounter with particular settings and landscapes, and particular moments of literary discovery. Enacting the continuity from Tang China to an Australian present, the poems imitate gestures and inflections from Wang Wei, Li Po and Du Fu. The poetic affinities are a way of creating a habitat, planting the landscape, populating the scene. Transactions of poetry and friendship transform the landscape. Once that has happened, the landscape, and the friends, live in the poems:

> *Rereading the poems*
> *We are all late-stayers;*
> *Guests in your country.*

China has allowed an expansion of sympathy, a larger gathering-in of experience, so that emptiness is replenished, in a natural decorum:

Poems blow away like pollen,
Find distant destinations,
Can seed new songs
In another language.

Real and symbolic, transient in its manifestations yet imaging eternity, landscape is central in Chinese art. Chinese landscape painting – and poetry – embodies not only relationships between human beings and the natural world, but also between artists, as cultivated spirits in the endless line of descent that is tradition. This way of conceiving landscape can answer to an Australian need. To reconfigure the land, and our human relationships with it, in a quest for balance or harmony, is a task of perceptual cultivation that some writers have taken on, finding in Chinese culture their inspiration for imagining their own world in a richer way. How this particular form of cultural exchange serves the national interest may not be easily quantifiable, yet it does so, by allowing new conceptions of the nation's potentialities to take shape.

1994

Bridging people

The Yellow Lady

In an article headlined 'Government Blocks Migrant Spouse Scam' (*Sydney Morning Herald*, 4 August 1992), a senior official of the Department of Immigration refers to 'suggestions that some people were rorting the system' through 'a lucrative "sham marriage" racket involving Chinese students that is allowing a stream of Chinese to bypass the immigration queue to settle in Australia'. Marriages are brokered in Hong Kong, indicates the official, adding that 'it is not difficult for mainland Chinese to get to Hong Kong via Shanghai'. Then Minister for Immigration, Gerry Hand, is cited as saying: 'If chain migration was allowed to continue, the original 17,000 Chinese might increase to 300,000 by the turn of the century.' It is the Government's intention, the minister adds, to allow the sponsorship of dependents only 'on the basis of a genuine and continuing relationship between the husband and wife'.

Let's try to look at what's going on here from a Chinese point of view. From 1986 the Australian government, as part of its policy to 'export' education services, made it possible for Chinese students to pay their tuition fees and be granted a visa to study in Australia for a few months. Participants in the scheme were actively sought, and Australian administrators were caught off guard by the numbers in a position to take advantage of the offer. For many Chinese it looked like a golden opportunity. Once they got to Australia their period of 'study-sojourn' (*liuxue* – the open-ended Chinese term for the process) might extend to some years of profitable personal and professional development, leading perhaps to permanent residency. Come 4 June 1989 and the Tiananmen Square massacre, China seemed more than ever a place to stay away from, and the Australian government, responding to extraordinary circumstances, made possible a four-year visa extension. Student fees no longer needed to be paid, but it was unclear what would happen at the end of the period of grace. Flailing around trying to reconcile the prime minister's compassionate gesture with the government's determination to keep immigration policy, like a sacred virgin, 'intact', the Immigration Department indicated one avenue: students could apply for refugee status. Some Chinese have strong cases for refugee status. Others took it as the chief administrative means offered to extend their stay. Cynical perhaps, but hardly a surprising product of a society where cynical manipulation of bureaucratic edicts is a way of life. (China, I mean.) The only real alternative is to establish a marriage-type relationship of convenience with an Australian. Naturally a lot of marriages took place – again hardly surprising in a society where the *mores* of the film *Raise the Red Lantern* are not far away, where people routinely marry for pragmatic motives, such as to get a permit to move to the city, or a house to live in.

Patterns of behaviour that may seem strange can be quite rational when explained in context. The report in the *Herald* subtly demonises these Chinese students, using misinformation, innuendo and racist cliché, to make their behaviour seem threatening and un-Australian. The 'stream' risks become a 'flood' or a 'tide', as they show contempt for that very British institution of the queue – an image of a long line of virtuous sheep waiting for their chance to go through the straight gate into heaven. It is not true that Chinese can get to Hong Kong more easily from Shanghai than from anywhere else, but the mention of Shanghai, teeming and sinful, adds an extra nuance. The hint that these 'spouses' are selling themselves is set off by the passing glance at the 'genuine and continuing relationship between husband and wife' – the norm in our society? And having sold themselves, there is no end of it, if the astonishing feat of turning 17,000 people into 300,000 in eight years is to be achieved. Only a Chinese-proof fence will stop them!

The *SMH* article is mild by today's standards. The Immigration Department's position is motivated less by racism than the determination to win an interdepartmental dog fight. It was the Department of Education, after all, seduced by dollar signs, that invited these Chinese here in the first place. Nevertheless, writer-diplomat Alison Broinowski must have enjoyed this press report, since it so nicely supports her claim that our old attitudinal problems with Asia are as ineradicable as feral fauna. Part of *The Yellow Lady* (1992), Broinowski's book surveying Asian influences in and through the arts in Australia, touches on stereotypes perpetuated in the mass media, popular culture and everyday life. Cartoons are among her most fertile sources of racist caricature, playing on Australian fears of Asian takeover that go back well into the nineteenth century. She reproduces an astonishing example from the *Weekend Australian* in 1989, showing a cheerful, beer-drinking Australian worker mutating into a bent, bow-legged, laptop-toting coolie. The accompanying feature is entitled: 'The Age of Asia . . . and how to survive it.'

Literally hundreds of Australian artists, thinkers and public figures zip past in the pages of *The Yellow Lady* as the author throws the widest possible net, covering all the art forms, all of Asia and the Pacific, all of Australian white history and some before, from stock images in the press to esoteric allusions in specialised practice, from *The Mikado* to Richard Meale's Javanese gamelan-inspired compositions. Compressed from an evidently much longer manuscript, it provides an invaluable compilation of references, exhausting if not quite exhaustive. Subtitled *Australian impressions of Asia*, Broinowski's survey is tilted towards how Australians have approached and construed Asia (as opposed to assessing actual Asian contributions to Australia, if a distinction can be made). Artists' representations are taken to mirror the attitudes, fantasies and prejudices of the society as a whole. Broinowski investigates images, projections and caricatures, in an attempt to chart and account for what the author sees as Australia's inadequately developed relationships with Asia. Stopping just short of an indictment of racism, Broinowski finds evidence of a blinkered Eurocentrism that has not only blinded Australians to Asia, but also to where our own advantage lies. Delving deeper into this self-defeating national defensiveness, Broinowski finds archetypes in the (white male) psyche that may explain the peculiar handling and mishandling of (yellow female) Asia.

The work of cultural materialists on postcolonialism and Orientalism help the reader get a handle on these slippery topics, but I suspect Broinowski is too much of an historian to want to fly off into realms of cultural theory. Her book is organised chronologically, charting the major phases and events that have shaped and reflected Australia's involvement with the peoples and places to our north: the gold rush, turn-of-the-century *japanisme*, White Australia, the war with Japan, Chinese communism, the Vietnam war, the hippie trail, Zen, sex travel, refugees, real estate. The conclusion she draws is only partly of progress, maturation and sophistication. The dominant impression remains one of recurrent motifs, prejudices perpetuated, fantasies and bogeys reconstituted, wheels endlessly re-invented.

Broinowski reinforces the effect by overlaying on her mass of material a secondary pattern of organisation, where artists are grouped by attitude. So we have the Expatriate Shift, where an artist goes native and adopts the superior foreign viewpoint from which to judge the society back home. Or the Butterfly Phenomenon, where the Yellow Lady is exploited for erotic freedom-without-responsibility in a never-never zone of Illicit Space. Such generalisations tend to have a levelling effect on the more finely tuned engagements with one or other dimension of Asia in the work of pioneering individuals, such as artists Margaret Preston and Ian Fairweather.

Yet the mass of Broinowski's examples shows that, if Australia has not managed its relationships with Asia as well as it might, nor understood the creative and other benefits Asia can offer in developing a distinctive Australian culture, it is certainly not for want of trying. There has been a succession of what the author calls 'bridging people'. If there is to be a space for Asian cultural presence, it means working around the cultural and other barriers, and that depends on those who make the connections. In the case of China, they can be Chinese or non-Chinese, or a combination of both, and often they work in couplings, or even chains of several links. It may be less a matter of connecting with China, than of adapting what is available to meet the need for a sense of China. The cultural product that eventuates is inseparable from the contingencies of human links, networks of opportunity and mutual help, giving us a do-it-yourself China, constructed by, with and for people here, with a home-made actuality. It may not have much to do with China with a capital C.

The most stunning example of this process in recent times is *Wild Swans*, a miracle of composite composition, of bridging. It is not an Australian book, but it has been more successful here than anywhere else. Jung Chang took hours of her mother's recollections, translated them into English, added the impetus of her own personal story, worked with her husband, historian Jon Halliday, to create an historical, moral and psychological framework that would give Western readers their bearings, and with the editor to produce an unputdownable read, a book that for millions of people has brought a new expression to the Chinese mask. China, once again, as woman.

The Yellow Lady ends with a recommendation: 'It is clear that until Asia occupies a place equal to that of the West in Australian minds, the nation's pursuit of its interests will remain distorted. If Australia's identity and self-image are to change, they must therefore do so in a way that locates Australia in the Asia-Pacific hemisphere.' Once again Asia is being constructed to serve domestic political ends. As past experience shows, this is dangerous territory. If it works, the result could be an epoch-making realignment of the society that exists on this land mass, making for survival, vigour and a new synthesis of cultures and environment. If it goes wrong, there will be a backlash, as Asia is consigned to the too-hard basket, leading to I-told-you-so indifference, or worse, resentment, hostility, and the re-inscription of non-negotiable cultural exclusiveness as a factor defining our nationalism. As Foreign Minister Gareth Evans noted in a recent address in Bangkok, 'The product of generations of history . . . cannot be rapidly changed'. He added, nonetheless, that 'a very rapid evolution in recent years' seems to be occurring in attitudes towards Asian societies.

It is difficult to talk about racial and ethnic attitudes in Australia objectively. The violence and degradation inflicted on the Aboriginal peoples cast a shadow over subsequent attempts at demographic diversity, including migration programs that have, through good luck or good management, worked out well by most accounts. 'All Australians are boat people', as Broinowski puts it. But the history of Australian settlement reminds us at every turn how racism and good intentions can go hand in hand. The new public construction of Asia is a positive one, but what is it based on?

'Let's avoid using the words "Asia" and "Asians" wherever possible,' suggests Professor Jamie Mackie of the Research School of Pacific Studies at the Australian National University, as a first step towards clearing our heads about the countries in the region. He is right, of course. No person recognises themselves primarily as Asian. The first time they have come across the concept, usually, is in encountering the world as divided up by bureaucrats. In Chinese, for instance, a seldom-used character is taken over, in a non-natural way, to translate the Western geographical label. It has the same sort of relevance as 'Oceania' does when applied to Australia. Only the Chinese would edit official anthologies of Oceanian Literature, mixing Peter Goldsworthy with Francis Tekonnang from Kiribati. It is a convenient categorisation, like Asia, based on lines drawn across a map, and that's about all. In the same way, it is hard to imagine any policy or approach this side of fantasy that could apply with equal sense to any two Asian countries. South Korea and Bangladesh don't have much in common, save that both are east of Suez. A favour done to Cambodia becomes laughable if offered to Japan.

It was a notion of aiding overseas development that helped sell 'export' of education to Chinese students. The assumption was that, like the Colombo plan students a quarter of a century ago, the takers would go patriotically home at the end of their courses. It was also a spirit of fairness that originally did not exclude China from the markets for Australia's export education industry. Such fairness, designed to maintain a globally non-discriminatory immigration policy, rested on the tacit assumption that very few people from China would be able to lay their hands on sufficient funds to cover study abroad, and that Chinese students therefore would not present a serious 'visa overstay' problem. The emergence of so many Chinese applicants able to comply with Australia's financial and other requirements came as a surprise. More accurate information about the economic circumstances, attitudes and aspirations of the relevant strata of Chinese society at the time might have been sought to balance the prejudice that, for economic and political reasons, China simply did not count as a market for export of Australian educational services – which proved to be a product Chinese bought for their own reasons. Another kind of humanitarian impulse took over in the offer of sanctuary post-Tiananmen. Extending entry permits to family members showed a further impulse to do the decent thing. The problem is that such selective humanitarianism breeds resentment in others who are not accorded the same treatment – for example, asylum seekers from Cambodia, Sri Lanka and Lebanon. Clear-eyed pragmatism is a better way, where we know what we're doing. The Immigration Department has hired hundreds of extra staff for the elaborate process of trying to separate the sheep from the goats among Chinese applications. The Chinese students should be permitted to stay in Australia because they are here as a consequence of an exceptional series of Australian policy bungles and it is too expensive to do anything else with them.

I emphasise the issue of the Chinese students because the advent of a significant cadre of mostly educated, enterprising young mainland Chinese established in Australia is a real social change that has come about inadvertently, through good intentions and good will run amok. It will be interesting to watch how, as individuals, they contribute to Australia's involvement with Asia.

Australia's preoccupation with the monolithic diplomatic entity known as the People's Republic of China has for too long hindered appreciation of the complexities concealed within the term China. Peking, Shanghai, Canton, Tibet, Inner Mongolia, Hong Kong, Taiwan, Singapore, the Indo-Chinese, Cabramatta – all, in different ways, are and are not

China. It no longer makes sense to speak, for example, of artistic exchanges with China without specifying who you are talking about. Once every Chinese was expected to be a Mao-suited comrade working for the motherland. Now no one is. They're each on their individual long marches and with luck they'll get where they want to go in their own way. Part of the 'Asian thrust' involves making Asia more accessible. At best this is a matter of finding points of affinity and contact that make interaction work. At worst, accessibility, like misconstrued relevance, encourages simplification and superficiality.

Alison Broinowski has introduced us to the Yellow Lady. We know now that she prefers to drink green tea, with neither milk nor sugar. Next time we should be ready to meet some more particular human beings . . . Acehnese, native-born Taiwanese, Hong Kong Indian, Dayak, Khmer Rouge and Karen. But they won't all fit in one book.

1993

Asian impersonations

My grandmother, a traveller, always brought back dolls for my sisters. Some were quite finely made, others funny little souvenirs, but each, wearing her or his national costume, stood for the culture they came from.

Soon there was a cupboard full, and I was interested in trying to make them move. I had a puppet theatre at the time, and was an enthusiastic deviser of miniature extravaganzas into which I could co-opt some of these dolls. Put on a finger, they could be wagged beside the leading glove puppets. Then, when life-size clothing became available, it was tempting to act out pieces for ourselves. The pink silk bathrobe my grandmother brought back from Singapore or Hong Kong gave rise to a play called 'The Goddess' in which my sister – or was it me? – appeared from the wings at the end to put right the romantic miseries of those lost – 'amazed' – in some exotic clime. I don't know what our sense of the East, or the tropics, was based on; our primary references would have included *The Mikado*, *Madam Butterfly* and *South Pacific*, and my grandmother's photographs of herself in oriental dance spectaculars of the 1920s. I don't recall being much aware of an Asian presence in Adelaide in the 1950s and '60s, except for a visit to a Chinese restaurant on a special occasion, until my father started bringing home Japanese and Chinese businessmen for weekend barbecues – but that was later.

Yet in those childhood theatricals the elements were already present: tourism, costume, performance, ritual, and gender ambivalence. The Goddess who came down from her heavenly mountain in pink silk to put all to rights in the last scene was androgynous and all-bountiful, omnipotent yet all-merciful, pure, yet all-experiencing – and her embroidered vestments originated in a tourist hotel shop. In her bewildering array of attributes, she was – I would discover later – Asia, as first conceived in our scripting and enactment of her.

It is a site, or a trope, that merits subjection to cultural analysis. What interests me here is the identification of other cultures with their dress, the intimacy of our association of costume change with difference, and with the *possibility* of difference – different experience, different power, different wisdom. To put on someone else's clothes is easy, of course; to naturalise the look is much more difficult, and may not even be desirable, since that would miss the point – of slipping round the house in a sarong or *chinois* dressing gown, of the batik shirt, the Mao suit, the sari or the kaftan. Or, those looks that, epitomising the *un*desirable Asianisation, can never be worn: bound feet, elaborate Japanese kimono, elongated earlobes, coolie hat, or, for that matter, the salaryman's dark suit, tie, white shirt and Rolex watch. The idea that being Asian is a matter of dressing up runs into a conception of Asia as a zone of theatre, peopled by masks. Contrast this with Asian practice, where the identification of modernisation with wearing Western clothes (beyond the salaryman suit now to Levi 501s, Armani and Gautier) has been carried out so resolutely as to internationalise Western clothing, in both where it is made and how it is marketed, with the result that the West has no 'national costume' left, and is rendered into a transparent state of undress, tariff barriers notwithstanding.

In the People's Republic of China nowadays, for instance, the only place you see people wearing what is thought of as traditional dress will be in contexts of ritual and display, such as political parades, religious festivals and major sporting events, in luxury hotels and restaurants, for weddings and in the theatre. Equally, the anti-traditional costumes of the Maoist era are now confined to the military and enforcement organs, and menials. It is curious, then, that the China constructed for and by foreigners – I'm thinking particularly of cinema, but there are parallels in the visual arts and other areas of promotion – is so dependent on distinctively Chinese forms of dress. It means, in turn, that plots tend to revolve around theatrical performers (*M. Butterfly*, *Farewell My Concubine*), weddings (*Red Sorghum*, *The Wedding Banquet*) and concubines, the precursors of today's hotel and restaurant hostesses (*Raise the Red Lantern*, *The Joy Luck Club*). Heavy make-up is required. Can the outside world not see Chinese except as masks and butterflies (victim women), broken on a wheel?

This habit of imagining is partly a consequence of Chinese politics. China has masked itself to the world for so long. Chinese officials, especially those seen abroad, have had to be actors. Internally too, Chinese political life is a kind of theatre, with relationships between leaders and Party, and Party and people, stagemanaged by formidable propaganda arts, arts which reached their apogee (but not their end) in the Cultural Revolution theatrics attributed to Chairman Mao and his showbiz wife Jiang Ching. Unreality, if you like, *is* a Chinese reality. Blame it on the philosopher of Taoist paradox, Chuang-tzu.

Is it sensible for us, as Australians, to want to find a different Asia? Or is it mostly *fin de siecle* coincidence, come round again, that this postmodern (because pre-modern) quality of China – and other developing sectors of Asia – soothes anxieties that our world is destabilising and toppling, and suits our yearnings for an escape from the pressures of history, as new economic and political determinations affect us from outside?

The 1990s see us charmed by a new bamboo curtain of chinoiserie, and some comparable trends concerning other regional indigenous cultures. As so often before in Australian history, and in the broader evolution of Western civilisation, the East is looked to for inspiration, renewal, release, and even, in an ironic reversal of missionary roles, of salvation. To the Enlightenment, and under Mao, China offered models of Utopian government. To the late nineteenth century, China offered an escape from puritanism, and, to hippiedom, a new kind of spirituality. To the economic gurus of the 1980s and '90s China, via Confucianism and the Four Little Dragons, offers a regime of economic vigour. To Australia now, China, in this protean construction, is an essential ingredient in a new reflection of ourselves. It doesn't matter much what the diverse Chinese may actually make of us or what they may want. When we say to the Chinese, 'But we've remade ourselves in this image for *your* sake,' we may find them as bamboozled as we are when we observe Chinese diplomats following the rules of Western etiquette they've learned from their going-overseas manual: Don't Pat the Child and Kick the Dog – foreigners do it the other way round.

This is territory Chris Berry explores in a dizzying, brilliant essay, *A Bit on the Side: East–West Topographies of Desire* (1994). Discursing on Asian elements in cinema as seen and made in Australia, from an insider/outsider position (he comes from England via Peking and California), Berry tosses off some welcome insights into Australia's embrace of Asia. While he comments mostly on film, notably *The Good Woman of Bangkok*, a discussion text for which Cultural Studies must be grateful to director Dennis O'Rourke, Berry is at his best on the politico-psychology of the progression of 'identities' that is taken for Australia's cultural history: a commitment to British empire, displaced by nationalism, inflected to include multiculturalism as an extension of the 'fair go' ethos, barely accommodating Asians who arrived as refugees, only to be challenged by the claim that Australia, being part of Asia, needs further re-alignment. Berry points out the problematic binarism of all this: Britishness versus barbarism; free Australia versus enslaving Mother England; Australia *en face* with Asia. He imagines a new kind of relationship altogether, Australia-in-Asia, where identity ceases to be an either/or choice. 'The idea of a clear line between . . . male and female, oppressor and victim . . . Australia and Asia, begins to give and the space of "Australia in Asia" as a postcolonial space rather than a third self-conception based on the nation begins to emerge . . .' In this quest, Berry finds particular inspiration in the various constructions of Asian queerness seen in recent cinema, where the challenge to hierarchies of sexuality and gender in queerness implies a critique of the authoritarian structures by which Asian societies, or their governments, often see themselves constituted.

Moving from a discussion of homosexual rights (virtually non-existent) to broader human rights in Asia, Berry concludes his book with a timely warning against the Asian argument that human rights are 'relative' and by implication a Western invention and plot. This is a line put by Asian regimes disposed to trample over the human rights of their people, who may not concur that, because they are Asians, they don't have rights as humans. 'If . . . we allow the proposition to stand that homosexual rights (or women's rights, or worker's rights) are matters for only one part of the world, the game will be lost before it has even begun.'

But there are a couple of questions to ask here. The language and conceptualisation of these various rights have developed from the developed world (the coincidence of words identifies the package). What happens to these concepts as they cross cultures? The Chinese phrase *xitizhongyong*, 'a foreign concept given a Chinese application', by which early modern Chinese reformers rationalised their absorption of ideas from the West, remains helpful in understanding China's responses to the outside world. Jars of *Nescafé* are bought as cabinet display items; traffic control systems are imported for crowd control. So what does 'gay' or 'lesbian' become as an imported life? Can it be a form of dressing up? Whatever the answer, the discourse is on the move in translation.

If Edward Said has given his kind of Orientalism a bad name, there may be other places where something is to be said for the good old orientalist whose interest in China (for example) lies in its wonderful, weird, mystical, mind-boggling qualities, a China that has a place on no agenda. I know what I'm saying is heretical. But today's Orientalism might be a matter of finding ways to understand another culture that have nothing to do with trading ambitions or geopolitics. Orientalism is a way of finding something to love, to be ravished or amused or appalled by, in another culture, for finding inspiration there in things that are quite oblivious to the standards of the contemporary West – kitsch or sublime.

There persists a linkage of the Asian and the non-straight-male. It extends into such public areas as the desire, expressed by Asian leaders, for Australia to display cultural sensitivity in response to Asian values. It is as if the Australian ocker is being asked not to be too rough with the tender oriental flower. Asia is set up as already sensitive, exquisite and vulnerable. It is perhaps here a case of Asians self-orientalising to their own advantage. This is ironical given the virile warrior assertiveness, at least in performance, that energises the roles many Asian leaders play for domestic consumption. There Australians are asked to respond with a sensitive Asian impersonation of our own.

Oscar Wilde has been in my thoughts as I consider the question of our connection or disconnection with China. Wilde went west in his mission to Beautify America – an uphill battle – and approached the painter Whistler, another orientalist, about an expedition east, to Japan and Australia in 1883. Sadly the plan fell through. I have a feeling that many things would have turned out differently if Oscar *had* toured Australia and Japan. His poem 'Symphony in Yellow', an orientalist piece replete with silk, butterfly, jade and a temple (the Inns of Court, actually), inspired an Australian magazine to quote him: 'So they are desirous of my beauty at Botany Bay . . . whither criminals are transported to wear a horrible yellow livery. Even they are called "canaries". So I have written for them a Symphony in Yellow . . .' Wilde allegedly improvised a stanza:

> And far in the Antipodes
>   When swelling suns have sunk to rest
> A convict to his yellow breast
>   Shall hug my yellow melodies.

Australia was destined to remain for Wilde a parody place, a travesty Orient. He returned to England, eventually to dress himself in oriental costume as Salome, heroine of his own tragedy. Narrow England suffocated Wilde, or at least spurred him to conceive a defiant other world in which wisdom and wit were one and nothing human was alien – a vision he crystallised in epigrams of quasi-oriental inscrutability. As he wrote a hundred years ago, in *A Woman of No Importance*: '. . . the world has always laughed at its own tragedies, that being the only way in which it has been able to bear them. And that, consequently, whatever the world has treated seriously belongs to the comedy side of things.' It might be a Taoist master speaking.

The Australian poet Harold Stewart is a dedicated orientalist, having spent a great part of his life in Japan. He now lives in Kyoto. As his part in the Ern Malley episode shows, he was a genius pasticheur. Stewart's remarkable volume of poems, *Phoenix Wings: Poems 1940–6* (1948), written in Sydney during the war, contains stunning oriental pastiche or impersonation in sumptuous, hieratic language that summons to mind the poetry of Alexander Pope in *The Rape of the Lock*, if not the decadent exoticism of Beardsley, Wilde and Firbank a century and a half later. At that time Stewart was writing modernist mask poetry, in an agonisingly self-conscious way reaching for epic, for history, for a cultural or spiritual realm beyond the malaise of Europe (Australia). The poems belong, in their place and moment, more with, say, Australian artist James Gleeson's surrealism than with the expatriate fantasy to which they are usually relegated. Harold Stewart long ago discovered, in the way of a conscious and highly disciplined impersonation, an Australia-in-Asia space that enabled the transformation of the world he knew through the devising of another.

> *Eternal only is the Golden Flower,*
> *That fervent peace and liberation brings*
> *From bondage to the wheel of opposites*
> *In man, conflicting with the world's extremes:*
> *The separate hells of action and its choice,*
> *Tyrannic licence or disordering law,*
> *The painful pleasure in the loving hate,*
> *And evil reason against good desire;*
> *Which tear the unbelieving mind apart*
> *From the conservative and clinging heart.*
> *Eternal only is the Golden Flower,*
> *The solar petals of whose bowl comprise*
> *The rhythmic union of all plural things;*
> *Supreme and gnostic blossom of the power*

*And principle, which is not compromise,
But knows the chiaroscuro of the soul:
The conscious flame, the causal depths of coal,
And welcomes both, to live them as one whole.*

(from The Ascension of Feng)

Who else was writing like that in 1942? These poems are indeed, as Michael Heyward says, 'one of the secrets of the war'. The lines are quoted here from the original 1948 edition. Stewart has since substantially rewritten them, pending publication of a revised version of the work in his *Collected Poems*. During three decades of life in Japan, his work, which includes much translation and two epics, has moved far in the direction of simplicity and refinement. For Harold Stewart, the creative release he found may have led to exile and neglect, at least from the Australian literary scene. Or maybe his time has finally come around.

1994

History repeats

Ernest Morrison's China

Morrison of Peking by Cyril Pearl deserves its place among Australian classics. The historical ironies that have gathered since the book was first published in 1967 (coincidentally at the height of China's 'Great Proletarian Cultural Revolution') are evidence that it has more than one life.

George Ernest Morrison, originally of Geelong, was a characteristic late-Victorian schoolboy turned adventurer. As *The Times* correspondent in Peking during the Boxer rising in 1900 and the fall of the Manchu dynasty, Morrison became an authority on matters Chinese. He ended up as personal advisor to the first President of the Chinese republic – a post in which, like many a foreign expert since, he felt worse than useless.

The Manchu dynasty ended not long after the death of Ci Xi, Empress Dowager, in 1908. The Republic of China was established in 1911. The collapse of the late dynasty's feudal despotism gave way to a period of relative openness (or submission) to the outside world. Morrison's friend, army leader Yuan Shikai, seemed to be one of the modernisers. In the north there was talk of a constitution, democracy, and material progress in the form of foreign-developed industries, transport and communications.

More stringent demands for reform pushed up from the south, linked with the name of Sun Yat Sen. But Yuan Shikai was boss in Peking. He retaliated against reformist demands by turning the embryonic constitutional government into a mockery and securing himself as dictator.

Much later in China another despot, Chairman Mao Zedong, was to be denounced. Talk of modernisation, reform and democracy would follow, and progress would be made. But the godfather of the reform program, representing an entrenched elite, would subsequently respond to pressures for further democratic reforms by showing the other side of his Janus personality. Deng Xiaoping, 'an orthodox and narrow Stalinist bureaucrat' in the description of Simon Leys (*The Burning Forest*, 1985), said in 1986 that if a state has dictatorial powers it should, on occasion, use them. He was speaking in response to student demonstrations. Three years later, in Tiananmen Square in 1989, he showed he meant what he said.

Historical parallels are never exact. Yet passages from Morrison's copious diaries could be transcribed almost word for word by a foreign resident of China in later times.

Peking – a developing city pride – a healthier moral sense. Improvements: Roads – Police – Carriages and Building of public latrines and Rickshaws. Telephone Service, along the main roads. Prohibiting of indecent placards advertising: 'To-make-the-penis-as-if-it-were-iron-pills'. (1906)

Peking you simply would not be able to recognise except by its monuments. Macadamised roads, electric light, great open spaces, museums, modern buildings of all kinds, one or two of them on a scale that would not be out of place in Whitehall, motor cars (there are I think at least 200 in Peking), motor cycles – more numerous than we care for, and bicycles literally by the thousand. New roads are being driven through the city, in many directions and the Imperial City Wall is now pierced in a dozen places. (1916)

The change in Peking is most marked . . . Of the atmosphere it is difficult to speak, but here also I feel a distinct change. They are more corrupt than ever but there seems above and outside such common delinquencies a certain public articulate opinion (from a correspondent in 1919).

And yet:

What hope is there for China? None at all. Is there any improvement? None at all. No attempt at reform. The officials in power now are as stiff-necked and reactionary as those that brought about the convulsion. The most enlightened is the most obstructive of all. He plays only for his own hand. Let the country go hang provided he makes money! (1902)

And last, from a correspondent in 1919:

I suppose it is indiscreet to say so and still more to write it, but I haven't much faith in China.

If Morrison were alive today, his considerable vanity would be gratified by his prescience. Public toilets were renovated for the Olympics bid; billboards promoting 'bourgeois liberalisation' are sometimes banned; there is virtually nothing left of the Imperial City Wall, and many officials wheel and deal on the international finance market. His love of the Chinese people would be hurt by how little has changed. Despite repeated revolutionary turmoil, China has largely failed to realise the ideals of independence, prosperity and justice envisioned by her progressives a century ago.

Although a great 'friend of China', Morrison was not as effective in helping her as he might have wished. He felt strongly about preserving China's sovereignty and was adamant about the Japanese threat. Expecting a German victory in the first world war, Japan had been a lukewarm ally to Britain. Morrison discovered that Japan had made secret understandings with Germany in the hope of gaining territory on continental Asia. Calling the move 'China's first independent participation in world politics', and an action 'to vindicate human rights', Morrison pushed China into the war against Germany in order to strengthen her bargaining hand against Japan. In the event, the Versailles peace conference saw China carved up. On only one point did the 'Big Three', Britain, France and the United States, rebuff Japan's demands. The white powers refused to write a recognition of national and racial equality into the treaty. Here Australia, led by Billy Hughes with his eye on White Australia, took a firm stand. In compensation for the slight, Japan was given huge territorial concessions in China. 'Hughes, through vanity, demagogy, and stupidity, proved to be Japan's most valuable ally.' (Pearl) The seeds of Japanese expansionism in the second world war can be found here. Looking on, the young British diplomat Harold Nicolson, with his Bloomsbury liberalism, commented: 'Isn't it appalling that these ignorant and irresponsible men should be cutting Asia Minor to bits as if they were dividing a cake – Isn't it terrible, the happiness of millions being decided in this way?'

For Australians, the lesson is exemplary: a classic case of Australian grandstanding backfiring on itself. The English-speaking powers failed to analyse the Asian situation with anything like care or correctness. Morrison's perspicacity about the position of China, Japan and South-East Asia in the cross-current of geopolitical conflict went unheeded. Yet he was *The Times* correspondent. He had the voice of the Thunderer. What had gone wrong?

Like many foreign correspondents, Morrison complains of inadequate support and remuneration from his paper, but his stormy relations with *The Times* had a more serious basis. His dispatches from China were consistently altered or cut by foreign editors who were serving home interests. The case of Morrison and *The Times* illustrates how, without any overt manipulation, a nexus of personalities, markets and domestic interests can seriously damage understanding between states. By virtue of its prestige, *The Times* had something like monopoly status in regard to inaccessible China news. This trust, if you like, was abused in the name of erroneously conceived national interests. How much greater is the power enjoyed by the *The Times*'s present owner, Rupert Murdoch, who has developed a many-headed relationship with China through his print, film, television and publishing interests?

History repeats. Morrison's thumbnail sketch of the then Australian correspondent at the 1919 peace conference, in company with the 'woefully ill-equipped' chief cake-cutter and his white Australian stooge, makes intriguing reading today: '[Keith] Murdoch is a rather common ugly man, apparently on good terms with Lloyd George and Hughes, but despite his boastfulness, on terms less familiar than he had led [people] to believe –'

Morrison's judgment erred in his backing of military dictator Yuan Shikai as most likely ruler of a stable, modernising China. Perhaps he was dazzled by Yuan's urbane propaganda; perhaps, after so long in China, he was too embroiled in the shadow play of Peking politics to see that elsewhere in the country were other, better alternatives. For all his unremitting scorn of British administrations, Morrison never ceased to uphold the values of the Empire, which were part of his patriotism as an Australian: anti-colonialism was unfashionable then. Mass movements that threatened imperial or monarchical structures with any resemblance to Britain's he looked on with contempt and alarm. In China too, the Empress Dowager's abdication had been managed by Yuan Shikai with the utmost respect for majesty. That he should in time adopt a similar imperial standing was almost inevitable. Morrison preferred such authoritarianism to forms of constitutional republicanism that depended on a wider constituency – on the grounds that the Chinese were not yet ready for democracy, a view often recycled by Chinese today. The explanation may be that Morrison favoured the Chinese arrangement that most embodied his own imperialist values: a subtle kind of racism that prevented him from allowing the workability of systems other than his own.

The West has more than once backed the wrong horse in China. Has a similar kind of self-reflectiveness operated, in which the assessment of social realities gives way to support for whichever regime can be construed as espousing one's own values? The United States's backing of the anti-communist Nationalist Party even after the communist victory in 1949 is one case of such blinkeredness. Another occurred when the Western Left, the '68-ers, rallied round Chairman Mao's 'Cultural Revolution'. Then, in 1978, a more imperialist US, switching diplomatic recognition from Taiwan ('the Republic of China') to China ('the People's Republic') acceded to China's imperialist fiction that Taiwan was part of China. Deng Xiaoping's regime received added support for its recognition of the 'realities' of corporatism, entrepreneurship and market forces – from Westerners espousing such values themselves, pragmatic in the face of human rights abuses. Outsiders have been happy to forget that the reform policies rest on and serve an immovable foundation of Marxism-Leninism-Mao Zedong-Thought, as the Chinese will openly admit.

Cyril Pearl's biography skirts round Morrison's contradictory racial attitudes. The man who in youth was appalled by Australia's trade in Kanaka labour, whose deepest love was for the Chinese people, was at the same time both imperialist to his bootstraps and also overwhelmed by his pride in Australia. At the end of his life he noted that 'the White Australia policy – the most vital and most national policy in Australia – finds support from every section of the Australian people'.

Like cultural cringe, a protean racism comes with the insecurities of Australian national identity. Cultural inferiority and its arrogant obverse issue from doubts about the validity of latter-day Australian society, which began with a bloody and protracted war between whites and blacks. The vision of a multicultural society can also be built on historical distortion. As Vietnamese-Australian writer Uyen Loewald complains: 'Multiculturalism still means Christian or Western multiculturalism.' To be in a position to offer compassion, to dole out help, can be another confirmation of superiority. Australians frequently extend sympathy to refugees, to victims of violently repressive regimes, to those whose homes and livelihoods are destroyed, but we can be more grudging about sharing our birthright with apolitical middle class Hong Kongers, for example, who are trying to get their families out to Australia before 1997. Pressure for immigration into Australia comes pointedly and naturally from Hong Kong, whose five million inhabitants have had little say in their fate.

China plays to Australian prejudices too. It is economically and politically backward enough to allow compassionate superiority. Most tourists are surprised to find China 'much better' than they expected – whatever that means. It has a culture and history of unparalleled richness, which allows a new form of cultural cringe, a mixture of mystification, misconstruction, gullibility and cynicism, arising, at bottom, from unacknowledged racism.

If a dose of medicine is taken in re-reading *Morrison of Peking*, the pill is also sweet. An eye for bright detail, sharp insight into the personalities behind the scenes, and sardonic humour are qualities shared by subject and biographer. Morrison's relish for gossip is as unstinted as Pearl's interest in it all. The final years of ill-health, tedium and frustration are sobering as Morrison is increasingly caught between his two worlds in a state of non-belonging. At the time of his death Australia had forgotten him.

It is a relief to move from the mature Morrison's grappling with geopolitics to the young Morrison's travel journal. At thirty-two, when he walked the 3000 miles from Shanghai to Rangoon, he was still the boy adventurer who had once walked from Normanton, on the Gulf of Carpentaria, to Melbourne. His only published book, *An Australian in China*, published a century ago, records his first appreciative, amused, unillusioned encounter with the civilisation that came to enthral him.

For his walk, Morrison dressed himself up as a Chinese. The traveller who 'put his pride in his pocket and a pigtail down his back need pay only one-fourth of what it would cost him . . . in European dress'. He notes in his diary that 'there was a disposition rather to laugh at me than to open the eyes of wonder . . . But Chinese laughter seems to be moved by different springs from ours. The Chinaman makes merry in the presence of death'. A feature of the Chinese for nineteenth-century Western observers was their cruelty – a view that perhaps resurfaces in our concern with Chinese indifference to human rights abuses. Morrison was intrigued by comparative methods of correction too, yoking China to the Antipodes when he writes:

I question if the cruelties practised in the Chinese gaols . . . are less endurable than the condition of things existing in English prisons so recently . . . there are no cruelties practised in Chinese gaols greater, even if there are any equal, to the awful and degraded brutality with which the England of our fathers treated her convicts . . .

Morrison was not a very good bridging person, since he lost the wavelength of what the Western powers were prepared to hear. He was a realist rather than an orientalist. Or at least, as when dressing in Chinese clothes for cheaper travel, he put on orientalist garb for pragmatic reasons. It is shocking then to encounter the lack of sentimentality with which he writes about the immigration question in his 1894 diary:

We cannot compete with Chinese; we cannot intermix or marry with them; they are aliens in language, thought, and customs . . . Admitted freely into Australia, the Chinese would starve out the Englishman, in accordance with the law of currency – that of two currencies in a country the baser will always supplant the better . . . There is not room for both in Australia. Which is to be our colonist, the Asiatic or the Englishman?

Well, there is room now, we proclaim. Some room anyway. Morrison wrote those words in the 1880s, at the height of the orientalist movement in Australia, which was also the decade of Australian nationalism, the lead-up to federation, and embryo republicanism.

Australia's attention to Asia seems to coincide with our desire to find a new independence and identity in the world at large. As it occurred in the late 1880s and 1890s the phenomenon has too many parallels with the present for comfort if you consider how both nationalism and an open attitude to Asia were subsequently co-oped or aborted. But let's leave the warnings for later.

Morrison was an innocent Australian then, as we no longer claim to be. His gradual loss of innocence, traced through Pearl's biography, teaches some lessons about China, media ownership, and the handling of Asian political conflicts by Europe and the United States – and, at last, about Australia. As Morrison noted in his diary on a trip home in 1903: 'The commonest phrase in Australia was, "Well, I don't mind if I do."' Perhaps claiming a place has more to do with the claims you are prepared to make for yourself than with what the world is prepared to give you.

1987

Romancers of Old Peking

Old Peking – the phrase has a ring to it. More than referring simply to the Peking of yesteryear, it implies a way of life, a culture in all its minute details, a vanished world. When she styled herself *A Photographer in Old Peking* (1985), Hedda Morrison – German-born daughter-in-law of George Ernest Morrison – implies more than a literal interpretation of those words. She finds herself, like a time-traveller, or a space-traveller, in a zone that has its own characteristics, *in* it but perhaps not *of* it, in Peking in the 1930s and '40s to record, with the signally modern technique of photography, the riches of a world that has existed proudly and splendidly apart from modernity, technology and Western civilisation and which will now only survive, tragically, in the records of the outsider. For while Hedda Morrison is neither the first nor the only photographer of Old Peking (there are many valuable photographs taken by Chinese in the period), it is the case that the most coherent visual documentation of that vanished world comes from foreigners, informed by the ethnographic and 'heritage' consciousness that was a by-product of their modernity. For Hedda Morrison being a photographer in Old Peking was more than an idle hobby. It was her role, her vocation.

The phrase Old Peking, '*lao Beijing*', is still in use among the citizens of the city today, affectionately denoting a certain style or flavour, a look, an accent, an attitude, at the same time as it refers specifically to certain customs, sayings and foodstuffs. In some quarters it has degenerated into the equivalent of 'ye olde', the re-invention of a romanticised past for commercial purposes, as in the tea-house that provides 'Old Peking' snacks and entertainments. Its poet laureate is Lao She, whose writings, notably the novel *Rickshaw Boy* (*Luotuo Xiangzi*) and the ever popular play *Teahouse* (*Chaguar*), vividly evoke life in Peking in the first half of the century. Bittersweet movies regularly depict life in the old days in the lanes and courtyards of Old Peking, as people struggle to cope with upheaval. Recent examples include *Farewell My Concubine* (directed by Chen Kaige), *Blue Kite* (directed by Tian Zhuangzhuang, and banned in China). Despite the accelerating destruction of what physically remains of Old Peking, there are pockets of the city still redolent of this past world, if only through surviving placenames, and folk memories of what used to happen there. '*Caishikou*' ('Vegetable Marketplace'), for example, is known to be the old execution ground.

Old Peking implies a sense of the past, and with it a critique of the present. It refers to a human quality – salty, sarcastic, defiant – mostly in a passive sort of way. It refers most specifically to the chaotic period between the last years of the Ching dynasty and the founding of the People's Republic of China in 1949, with Peking as its capital, a time when the citizenry clung with dignity to traditional ways, or subtly adapted from within, while being inundated from without by waves of reform from the south and the Japanese from the north.

Peking came under Japanese occupation in 1936, followed by a period of Nationalist rule after Japan lost the war, until the city at last became the possession of the Chinese Communist Party. These successive regimes, and the influxes of outsiders they brought, went largely against the grain of the citizens of Peking, who proved adaptive yet resistant at the same time. In communist propaganda, the old society – and with it Old Peking – became an evil. The communists moved huge numbers of professionals and administrators into Peking, swamping the original inhabitants. But by 1989, when the communist leaders sent in the army to crush protest by students and Peking citizens alike, the troops had to come from far away, since soldiers from the Peking area would put their loyalty to their fellow citizens above their loyalty to the government of China. In other words, the Peking citizenry was once again defined by its opposition to external, military-backed intrusion, and people were quick to compare the army's invasion of the city in 1989 with earlier Japanese, warlord and Nationalist occupations, and, with greatest irony, to contrast it with the Red Army's own triumphant, peaceful march to Tiananmen in 1949. It was the spirit of Old Peking that re-asserted itself when millions of citizens flocked on to the street in 1989 to support the students, to oppose the government and the army, and, in true Old Peking style, to revel in the excitement, to take the stage of history, to invent satirical jokes, to beat up whomever they didn't like, to grumble and gossip about how it was all being handled, and to despair of the outcome. Not long after, the Australian ambassador asked an old Peking woman what she felt about the Chinese authorities' decision to use force to disperse the demonstrations in Tiananmen Square. She replied that in her ninety years she had lived under the rule of the Empress Dowager, the Republic, the Nationalists and the Communists and had learned one thing: governments always make the wrong decision. That old woman was a true *lao Beijing*.

The citizens of Peking, living at what was for such long stretches of Chinese history the heart of government, have politics, authority and hierarchy in their blood. That distinguishes them from foreign residents of Peking who, no matter how intensely they love the place, and even when they embrace Chinese political causes, can never be part of the body politic in the same way. In the sense of Old Peking found among the expatriates, the absence of politics is striking – even where politics is suspended like the sword of Damocles over the charmed life many of them enjoy. Many foreigners found in Peking a retreat from their own civilisation, or from the world at large. Peking seemed to offer something older, wiser and more refined – a 'cosmic consciousness' that the fortunate visitor might briefly share. But the seeming timelessness of the qualities

Peking offered also made visitors aware that they were destined to be transients, however long they stayed. They belonged elsewhere. So every delight is tinged with melancholy, and every moment of appreciation is doomed to evanescence. Those who felt alienated from modern Western civilisation, as was the fashion in the interwar period, became alienated in Peking in a new way, while of course enjoying themselves immensely.

The intimations of closure are felt, for instance, throughout American George N. Kates's classic memoir of Peking in the 1930s, *The Years that were Fat* (1952). No sooner has he established the house and household that is to be the centre of his existence in China for seven years than he writes: 'Like all the other foreigners, in time I became myself a visitor whose days were over, drawn again to join his fellows beyond the sea.'

Kates gives a loving account of Old Peking that goes beyond the physical aspects of place to all the human arrangements within it, large and small, in harmony with time-honoured customs and seasonal patterns, so that Old Peking becomes a spiritual discipline, a ceremonious work of art in itself, within which many lesser works of art have their place and meaning – among them the pieces of household furniture Kates discusses in another book, *Chinese Household Furniture* (1948), which has photographs by Hedda Morrison. Living in Peking, Kates's life itself becomes a work of art, which must be left behind when the end comes. Kates must at last decide 'to break the pattern. It was a conscious act of will. Another self now perforce took control; while the Chinese part, helpless, had mutely to watch itself step by step put out of existence'. Yet that Chinese self was always a flight from reality. Kates reminds himself at the end that he was after all 'of the West, of the one global civilisation of our time' and that wasn't going to change. Indeed it was the tough geopolitical fact of Western power and a battered and bruised China that allowed foreigners their special existence there. To turn away from politics, as Kates does, in order to achieve a sense of personal tranquillity, is perhaps the most subtle form of sympathy for China's plight, since China's historical predicament would be changed by costly and destructive forms of political activism. Kates's book has a special place for me since it was recommended as reading for my first trip to China by one of my first Chinese teachers in Canberra, Con Kiriloff, who was himself something of *lao Beijing* from the years he spent there renting a room just outside the walls of the Forbidden City. He had an ironic, historically-informed sense of the city and its changes over the years, and he loved the cheap liquor widely drunk in Peking, *erguotou*, bottles of which were always brought back to him in Canberra when colleagues or students visited Peking. I'm pleased to report that *erguotou* is now available in Australia.

Buddhist writer John Blofeld, in his book *City of Lingering Splendour* (1961), subtitled 'A Frank Account of Old Peking's Exotic Pleasures', presents a stark contrast between political exigencies and the life he enjoys in Old Peking in the years just before the Japanese takeover. One of his students, who has joined the communist underground, comes to warn him:

If you think that, when the change comes, you could get along with our people, please stay. We shall need teachers. English will still have to be learnt for all sorts of reasons, so do please stay. I shall be very much in a position to guarantee no harm will come to you. But, my dear friend, if you are still the same old John – lovable, but selfish, individualistic, romantic, a Buddhist and all that – then, for your own sake, don't be here when we come. Our people will not understand you or know how to appreciate you. English Buddhist? Ha, spy! Naturally they'll think that way. If you are still like that, and also wise, then leave Peking before – oh, before autumn of this year!

Actually I suspect this conversation, recollected in 1961, nearly thirty years later, contains more than a dash of romance. Blofeld's subsequent exile from Peking brings him to a sense of exile that generations of Chinese intellectuals have felt, in time, space and cultural value, when absent from Peking.

Today, like so many exiles from Peking, Chinese and foreign, I wander about the world grateful for whatever happiness I find and generally cheerful enough to pass for a contented man, but always with the conviction that nowhere else shall I find a life so satisfying to sense, heart, intellect and (for those who search diligently) spirit as Peking offered everyone who loved and understood her well.

High praise indeed! But then something that has gone forever readily shades into the stuff of legend.

Blofeld categorises the expatriates in Peking at the time – setting aside the stateless and disreputable White Russians and the Christian missionaries – into two categories. 'The larger consisted of those diplomatic officials, bank staffs and employees of mercantile firms who lived stuffy lives within the walls of the Legation Quarter . . .' while '. . . the more amusing Westerners were those who in varying degrees loved Peking and who lived scattered about the great city . . . For the most part they were Western counterparts of the Chinese literati – research scholars, university lecturers, writers and so on . . .'

Among them was C.P. Fitzgerald, scholar in embryo at the time, who, unusually, took a sharp interest in Chinese social and political developments. He later became professor of Far Eastern History at the Australian National University. In his superb memoir, *Why China? Recollections of China 1923–1950* (1985) he has left an unforgettable description, worth quoting at length, of the foreign community as he found it:

They floated, as it were, half way between the culture of the West and the civilisation of China. They had often virtually withdrawn from active participation in their own culture, largely because they found some aspects of it very little to their taste. There were many with homosexual proclivities, others who had no inclination to the world of business, or to any skilled profession. They were cultured, but unproductive, and mainly uncreative also. It is a significant fact that this community of intellectual people, and artists also, never produced a writer of fame, nor an artist of international reputation. They knew much about Chinese civilisation, they studied it with love and learning, but they did not succeed in interpreting it to the world at large. The few works of merit on the China of that age were written by visiting scholars and writers from the West, who lived in Peking for some months, absorbed and understood its atmosphere and character but, seeming to realise that it was a subtle but corroding force which would undermine their own creativity, left – to write perceptive books about their experience.

Bertrand Russell, Somerset Maugham and Osbert Sitwell all wrote such books, but none of them settled in Peking.

Peking had too strong a cultural force: it charmed the foreigner, but it sucked him out of his background without integrating him in its own. He was a foreigner, conspicuously so to any Chinese, however well he spoke their language. He had no family ties with Chinese, he was not subject to their often dangerous conditions of life; he might know and understand their social customs, but he did not practise them. To many younger Chinese he also remained an example of China's national decline and weakness, a by-product of foreign imperialism, perhaps a more agreeable one than the rest, but inevitably marked by the same stigma. Peking was a dream city for the foreigner; few realised that the dream must have a rude awakening before many years passed. One such erected in his courtyard a marble tablet in the Chinese style, inscribed 'Enjoy Yourselves; It is Later Than You Think'. A fitting epitaph for the foreign community of Old Peking.

I suspect the marble tablet may be a romancer's detail, echoing as it does the classic between-the-wars poem by W.H. Auden, 'Consider', written March 1930, with its 'immeasurable neurotic dread'. 'Seekers after happiness . . . It is later than you think . . .' But then Auden was discussed in Peking around that time, by poet and critic William Empson, who was teaching at Peking University, and I see that photographer Cecil Beaton, returning to Chungking in 1944, has a Dr Young quoting Auden and Empson. I suspect Dr Young is the gentleman known today as Professor Yang Xianyi, the eminent literary translator from the Foreign Languages Press in Peking. Auden was to heighten his dread in 1938, during his visit to Shanghai with English writer friend Christopher Isherwood, by looking at gangster boss Du Yuesheng's socks: 'Peculiarly and inexplicably terrifying were his feet, in their silk socks and smart pointed European boots, emerging from beneath the long silken gown'. It has become a classic image. The history of East–West relations is written in that sentence. Auden's 'dread' is a thirties development of the 'Decline of the West', a condition that quietly intensified – as a perceptive observer like Fitzgerald saw – for those who sought escape in Old Peking. For at their back was always the memory of the Boxer Rebellion (1898–1901), when the defiant Empress Dowager's xenophobic bravos were unleashed against the representatives of the Western and Japanese powers in an archetypal exposure of both Chinese hostility to foreigners and the foreigners' determination to show who was boss.

One of an earlier generation of foreigners who had been actively engaged in Chinese civil life, as influential as any foreigner could hope to be, was Sir Robert Hart (1835–1911), an Irishman who became Inspector-General of the Imperial Chinese Customs Service. Hart suffered in the Boxer rebellion and its aftermath – but it was he who had written in 1894, some six years earlier: 'Chinese blood has been well cooled by the training its brain has had the last twenty centuries, but I think it quite possible that one of these days despair may find expression in the wildest rage, and that we foreigners will one and all be wiped out in Peking'. Hart saw foreign ignorance of China as one of the fundamental problems that would eventually bring his prophetic scenario to realisation.

More than thirty years later C.P. Fitzgerald felt that things had not improved in that regard:

I had been for some years past impressed by the real absence of any profound knowledge of Chinese history among the foreign community of the various cities in which I had lived, and the total ignorance of the subject found in educated circles in England. If China was now regarded as a helpless, corrupt and inefficient state doomed before long to subjugation by the Japanese, as many believed, this judgement ignored the past: not the recent nineteenth-century past, which exhibited precisely these defects and had given rise to these opinions; but the earlier ages when China had been the most powerful as well as the most populous country in the Asian world, and had been in organisation and effective government far in advance of Europe . . . I could try to be a historian.

Fitzgerald at least shares with the romancers of Old Peking an estimation of the vanished glories of China's past, and I believe that he built, from a base of linguistic knowledge, idiosyncratic on-the-ground experience and subsequent historical scholarship, an understanding that proved influential in spheres well beyond the academies. He engaged with Australian and other governments as they strived to form policies towards China – not that Fitzgerald, like many a China expert after him, was necessarily heeded by the governments of his day.

I do not quite agree with C.P. Fitzgerald that none of the romancers of Old Peking produced works of merit. Although great fiction, drama and poetry is scarce, the writers did create their own superb Old Peking genre: autobiography or memoir that shades into fantasy, ethnographic or cultural study that turns into poetry, a form of writing that makes fact and fiction blur and interplay, perhaps because China is elusive to the observer. Classics in this vein include Kates's *The Years that were Fat* and Fitzgerald's own *Why China?*, and the book by Sir Robert Hart's niece Juliet Bredon, *Peking* (published in Shanghai in 1919), recommended by Con Kiriloff, which remains the most evocative guide book to the old city that haunts present-day 'Beijing' like a ghost. *The Moon Year, A Record of Chinese Customs and Festivals* (1927), co-authored by Juliet Bredon with Igor Mitrophanow, is even better.

These books have been reprinted in recent years and are sold at the Friendship Store to visitors and foreign residents. The categories of foreigner that John Blofeld and C.P. Fitzgerald identified are still pretty much recognisable today – or at least were in the Peking of 1986 where I set my novel *Avenue of Eternal Peace*, in one chapter of which I adopt the Chinese habit of dividing the foreigners into numbered types. There are still foreigners – including Australians – who want to call Peking home, by not living in the officially designated accommodation for foreigners but by finding their way into what's left of the *hutong* and courtyard houses, inspired by the dream of a China that is richer and stranger, more intimate and more dignified, than what the present seems to allow.

One young Australian who studied in Peking in the 1980s decided to stay on, eking out an existence as a business consultant. He rented a room in the back of a temple complex near the Drum Tower. The monks who supervised the site and the old woman who owned the room were willing to let it to a foreigner because it had bad *fengshui*. It was cold and someone had died there. The place wasn't far from the Bamboo Garden Hotel, a former princely mansion that became the house of Kang Sheng, head of the secret service. He built a nuclear shelter in the courtyard – or was it a dungeon? After his death the house was turned into a hotel and restaurant for foreigners.

After a time my friend found that people were calling on him, or going through the monks and the landlady, to demand fees and charges in relation to processing the permission for a foreigner to stay there. Then some damage was done to his motorbike and he suffered harassment on the street; smalltime standover tactics to ensure he paid up. It emerged that the whole quarter was run by an informal system of influence – a gang system that meshed with the local law enforcement agencies. The power behind the gang lay with relatives of Kang Sheng, who had died in 1975, Mao Zedong's Godfather. His descendants had managed to hold on to a slice of the action, and through them Kang Sheng's ghost still walked the streets. My friend paid up and eventually moved out. He would look elsewhere for a sweeter side of Old Peking.

1993

Sang Ye: curio merchant

As a writer, Sang Ye collects people, especially old people. He also collects old things, and I asked him why. He replied that old things have souls too. They carry the traces of the people who made them, handled them and owned them, even as they outlast the people who gave them their original purpose. The pathos of old things stimulates the imagination and warns against an excessively active approach to life. Sang Ye has a 1905 Deutsche Grammophon radio which he loves because it recalls for him the pride and joy its first owners must have felt on hearing its thin, crackly sound. Antiques are cold and theoretical, their value determined by a number of years and the marketplace. But old things are warm. They carry people's hearts. Displaced in time, their awkwardness makes them loveable. With a similar tragical whimsy, Sang Ye appreciates elephants and wombats, and beggars too, creatures which exist without inspiring any great confidence in life. His favourite cushion is called 'Elephant'.

Born Shen Dajun in Peking in 1955, he was at secondary school in 1966 when the Cultural Revolution broke out, a mass movement on an unprecedented scale, even in Chinese history. Those who were 'Red' were empowered to destroy those who were 'Black' in a restoking of revolution within the revolution. The young were urged to turn on the old. Children of the revolution were spurred to root out all remnants of the old society. Zeal, backed with force and political cunning, became the sole badge of merit. The movement was unleashed by Mao Zedong as his trump card in an internal power struggle designed to sideline his rivals, among them Deng Xiaoping, China's subsequent paramount leader. At the same time, it was driven from below, by young people using the Red rhetoric they had imbibed from birth to hasten the Maoist Utopia they had been told the revolution should bring.

This coupling of leadership and youthful masses was effected through the children of the elite, the senior officials and professionals in the major cities. A centre of this connection was Qinghua University High where Sang Ye went to school. When his parents were sent out west to 'learn from the peasants', Sang Ye was left in Peking with his grandparents and sister at a crucial stage of his adolescence. Schooling was erratic in those years, and once a year the school kids were packed off to be farmers. Sang Ye went as one of a group of five friends, all children of academics. There was not much contact with the real peasants, but they did learn the peasants' methods for seizing an advantage from a situation, no matter how small. As they worked the rows, harvesting wheat, they would grab a handful from the next person's row when no one was looking.

Of the five friends, Sang Ye ended up a writer. The violinist dropped out, and was later imprisoned for rape. The one who liked to dance *The Red Detachment of Women* died of brain cancer. The artist got a scholarship to study scenic design in the United States. The fifth one is studying librarianship in Japan. In a tiny way, the diverse fates of the group reflect the upheavals that have characterised life for many Chinese in recent decades. For Sang Ye's generation, the Cultural Revolution was the pivotal experience of change and release, disillusionment and victimisation.

In 1971 Sang Ye went to work as an apprentice at an electrical engineering plant in the region outside Peking, near the thirteen Ming tombs, where heavy industry is concentrated: a chemical weapons plant, a nuclear power plant, a steel mill. Designed in the Soviet Union with thick walls suitable for Siberia, the plant inspired his first story, 'The Fourteenth

Tomb'. He missed university entry in 1977, the first intake after the Cultural Revolution, but got into a short-term mathematics course at Peking Normal University in 1978. By 1980, his journalism had developed and he was doing regular features for the Hong Kong and overseas Chinese press. There was research work for the newly established Madame Sun Yat Sen Museum and on some Peking local history projects. Prepared to live by freelance writing, Sang Ye was able to cut himself free from many of the formal structures of Chinese society.

In 1983 the Anti-Spiritual Pollution Campaign was launched, attacking, among other things, liberal, westernising and humanistic tendencies in literature. The novelist Zhang Xinxin, whose fiction had been criticised, was looking for a way of writing that would engage with the realities of contemporary Chinese life and be publishable at the same time. Influenced by Studs Terkel's works of oral history, she and Sang Ye decided to collaborate on a series of a hundred or more interviews, which started appearing in December 1984 and was published in book form in Chinese, to great acclaim, in 1986. *Beijingren* (published in English as *Chinese Lives: An Oral History of Contemporary China*, 1987) sets out to explore who and what the Chinese are today. There was one question asked of all interviewees: Do you think your life in China is good or bad? It asks – obliquely – whether people buy the revolution, the myth of social transformation that has dominated Chinese history since the end of the Ching dynasty. For almost everyone interviewed, the Great Proletarian Cultural Revolution (officially dated 1966–1976) was a formative event. Not one person had a good word to say for it. At the same time, the interviews are set against the background of post-Maoist China, the 'open door' policy and Deng Xiaoping's seemingly pragmatic, market-oriented economic reforms. Indirectly, as early as 1984, *Chinese Lives* documents the moral, social and even economic bankruptcy of the reform program, which almost derailed in Tiananmen Square in June 1989.

To give an ordinary person the right to speak and be heard is itself subversive of a system where your place is determined by a hierarchy of power and your views by the Propaganda Department. Individual realities undermine the grand, empty rhetoric that structures the Chinese state.

Ironically, however, it was the orgy of collectivist and idealistic rhetoric fostered during the Cultural Revolution that rendered the Party's claims valueless for most of the people interviewed. An older and wiser Red Guard puts it with damning simplicity: 'You can only be yourself.' The remark is a stake through the heart of the Chinese system. It denies the collective and also the possibility of ameliorative change. You cannot change yourself, and you have only yourself.

From people to things. The work on *Chinese Lives* sharpened Sang Ye's sensitivity to what is denied or obliterated in official discourse. In 1986 he rode his bicycle for three months along the old course of the Yellow River, the birthplace of Chinese civilisation and, socially and ecologically, one of the most devastated areas of the country. He could find no way to shape his perceptions and experiences into written form. A conference took place in September 1986 on the relationship between revolutionary memoirs and the burgeoning genre of investigative journalism. The Chinese Communist Party, privileged to define the facts of history, has resisted the revisionist probes of historians, journalists and biographers. The conference split into two camps, the elders and loyalists who had a clear sense of the sort of revolutionary memoirs they wanted written, and the younger writers who wanted to achieve a history of their own. The latter group further divided into those of the 1950s generation who wanted the record put straight on the Anti-Rightist Campaign of 1957, which had been calamitous for the intelligentsia, and those of the 1960s who wanted to tackle the Cultural Revolution. In the comparative leniency of late 1986, it almost seemed possible that someone like Sang Ye might be able to work on a warts-and-all history of New China. But the student demonstrations that erupted in December 1986, to be answered by a renewed campaign 'Against Bourgeois Liberalisation', put an end to the plan.

Sang Ye set aside his program of Cultural Revolution interviews in order to visit Australia on an invitation from the Literature Board of the Australia Council and the Australia–China Council. He remembers arriving on May Day 1987, when there was an airport strike and the cost of public phone calls went up from twenty cents to thirty cents. He travelled all over Australia, by pushbike from Adelaide to Darwin, by coach from Brisbane to Cooktown, talking to many Australians – from Gough Whitlam, Chairman of the Australia–China Council, to an eighty-eight-year-old Australian-born Chinese who had gone to Shanghai to work for the British-run Customs and later returned to live in Queensland. In Canberra he met his wife Sue, a sixth-generation Australian, who has some Chinese in her ancestry too. The contrasts between travelling with no official escort through Australia and travel in China – especially the journey along the Yellow River – set Sang Ye thinking again about who and what the Chinese are.

By the time he got back to Peking in 1988, joined by Sue and living in his mother's flat, he had become obsessed with collecting Cultural Revolution materials. Nothing was being properly collected in China, and his investigations abroad showed that none of the major foreign oriental collections – Harvard, Tokyo and so on – had anything like complete Cultural Revolution archives. A market for Mao badges and memorabilia was developing meanwhile among tourists to China. As the Cultural Revolution receded into history, China's institutions began to clear out their files. Enormous amounts of material were either deteriorating or being sent to the tip. Sang Ye, who knew what he was after, managed to buy one institution's entire archives, which had been sold for paper recycling. He amassed 700 or more versions of *The Little Red Book*, numerous rare monographs, recordings, posters, several hundred Red Guard publications, runs of local and provincial newspapers, and other miscellaneous items, building a major collection of hitherto unobtainable documentation of the Cultural Revolution, much of which is now lodged in the National Library of Australia. The history of one of the strangest episodes in our strange century is only now being told – in books such as *Wild Swans* by Jung Chang. As Sang Ye says, every Mao badge – and he has many – is eloquent testimony to the bent life of its wearer and the folly and pity of the Cultural Revolution.

On 7 June 1989, following the Peking massacre, Sang Ye left for Australia with Sue and their daughter Shen Yi.

Sang Ye says that there are no human beings in the literature of modern China. The books he read and re-read as a young man are the classic tales and annals of the individuals who made up China's past, including bandits, outcasts and weirdos. He read Sima Qian's Han dynasty *Records of the Historian* (a Chinese cross between Suetonius and Aubrey's *Brief Lives*), savouring the gaps left to be filled by speculation. He read the classic Ming dynasty novel *Water Margin* (translated by Pearl S. Buck as *All Men Are Brothers*) and the sardonic sketches of Lu Hsun.

The collector, archivist and connoisseur of oddity is one type among the gallery of not-quite-reputable Chinese eccentrics. It was Ye Qun, wife of Mao's comrade-in-arms Lin Biao (whose death in a mysterious plane crash in 1971 is still unexplained), who assembled the largest collection of Mao badges. She had 10,000. They would be worth something, now that Mao has been revived, as a camp youth cult, as a sign of nostalgia for the never-never land of revolutionary heroics. Sang Ye's collector's nose has served him well. In 1992 he waltzed off with the prize, a round woollen carpet produced in 1967, handwoven in brilliant colours by 3000 weavers, showing a three-metre Mao face radiating over the scenes of his revolutionary triumphs.

When asked about China, Sang Ye replies, 'China is just a great big freak.' Since coming to Australia he has paid close attention to the effect China has on Australians, particularly those in the universities, government and the friendship societies who have a professional interest in dealing with this freak. Does like attract like? What reflection does the freak mirror show? How, people-to-people, do the two countries treat each other?

Sang Ye has inherited a tradition of recycling the past that can be traced back in his family. During the chaos of the 1930s in China, his paternal grandfather left Zhejiang province for rural Hebei province, where he worked the soil. Then, after the Japanese invasion – reversing the Chinese adage that in times of minor unrest there is advantage in moving to the city, while during major unrest it is better to go to the countryside – his grandfather moved to Peking and opened a second-hand store, which lasted in the family until 1954 and still exists as a junk shop in Flower Market Street. His grandfather used to remake people's jewellery, and Sang Ye came to see that each time a piece was refashioned, given a new lease of life, there would be a fraction less gold. Dealers in old wares can also be cheats.

Sang Ye's father joined the Communist Party as a schoolboy, and studied law. His mother came from Manchuria, where her father had worked for the occupying Japanese as a lawyer – a bad background for which the man suffered successively under the Nationalists and the Communists. He had stashed some gold rings in a jar for a rainy day, the last of which were cashed in to pay for his daughter's schooling. She went to St Joan's Girls College in Peking where she was educated as a Christian. In the New China of the 1950s, she became an instructor in physical education. She and Sang Ye's father didn't get on, and he eventually divorced her in 1971, putting his training in civil law to good use. Divorce was relatively uncommon in China then and Sang Ye felt stigmatised each time he had to enter his parents' marital status on a form. The divorce came during the stressful years of the Cultural Revolution when Sang Ye was separated from his parents. His father was a typical communist official, and he was responsible for the family break-up. Sang Ye experienced at a vulnerable age the gulf between noble words and shabby conduct, and the misery caused by double standards and hypocrisy in Chinese society.

His first published work was a poem in praise of Chairman Mao on the fifteenth anniversary of Mao's labours at the Ming Tombs Reservoir. Sang Ye's poem hailed the azure sky reflected in the rippling waters of a reservoir that had, in fact, never been finished. (Today it is the site of a Japanese-built fun park.) From then on his work has been concerned with carefully peeling back the skin of illusion to reveal the tender, pitiful human rawness beneath. For Sang Ye, one stubborn fact can topple skyscrapers.

He has inherited his parents' athletic frame, skinny and gangling as a result of malnourishment during the years of famine that followed the Great Leap Forward, with a toothy grin and a smokers' laugh. His name can be interpreted as 'bright mulberry'. He is one of the few writers I know who can turn his hand to any electrical work going. I first met Sang Ye in Peking in 1986, at the home of Yang Xianyi and Gladys Yang. Then I saw him in Canberra in 1987, and we argued about Australian immigration policies, Sang Ye taking a sterner view than I did. Sue and Sang Ye were back in Peking by 1988 and I remember meeting Sang Ye again by the railing outside the China Art Gallery at the opening of a retrospective exhibition of Chinese news photography. Sang Ye installed an answering machine in my flat in Peking so I could get some rest. He saw me as an Australian sheep being rounded up by the Chinese sheepdog. Or was it an Australian sheepdog being pestered by Chinese flies? Those were years when virtually everyone you met in China was involved in getting someone to Australia 'to study English'. After embassy staff were evacuated in 1989, following the massacre, and visa processing was suspended, the mail bags of applications made a pile large enough to fill the embassy's own Great Hall.

In *The Finish Line*, Sang Ye reflects on China's upheavals when he considers how he comes to be making a new life for himself in a leafy Brisbane suburb. Some travellers feel a need to keep discovering new places. Sang Ye is not one of those. He is a traveller who has found his path and returns to it again and again. In travelling round Australia, he notices individuals whose quaint, self-defined certainties stand in marked contrast to the huge and vague mysteries of the continent; whose sense of value and dignity in simple, often eccentric human acts appears in relief against the enormity of the land and the drifting country evolving in it. The enormity he registers in China is not emptiness but density: of population, of history, of disaster, of enmity. Against that background people work through their lives, struggling with bureaucracy here, seeking a little advantage there, and generally surviving in a spirit of inextinguishable self-belief that can seem almost absurd.

At the core of Sang Ye's travel diary is the split in that massive Chinese entity brought about by politics and civil war, Nationalist against Communist, brother against sister, leading to division across the water between Taiwan and the mainland, and the continuing exodus of Chinese on migrations to remote parts of the world such as Australia, where the dream of home is never quite abandoned. The brutality of severance among nearest kin, the violence and folly that pits one person against another, is the source of the pain that lies behind Sang Ye's rueful comments – the point where the writer can do no more than witness. As he puts it, recounting a battle in which more than half a million Chinese bloodily defeated another half a million Chinese: 'History cannot allow everything to be a poem . . . Penned in blood, it can only be blood.'

Sang Ye makes his own furniture and loves nothing more than to remake a piece he has picked up second-hand, often turning it into a Sino-Western hybrid. He continues to be a kind of Christian and a kind of pawnbroker, sifting through rubbish with an appraiser's eye and a compassionate heart, making it worth something.

1994

'The web that has no weaver'

Notes on cultural exchange

Sang Ye went on a journey to a village in the mountains beyond Kunming in south-west China, in an impoverished area populated predominantly by the non-Han Chinese Yi people. A foreigner had come to the village in 1904 and spent the rest of his life, until his death in 1944, working with the village people. He introduced Christianity to the village, bringing to an end the practice of human sacrifice that had been a characteristic of the traditional tree-worshipping folk religion. He established a health clinic. He built a college, run on modern educational principles, to teach theology as well as other subjects. There was no script for the Yi language and he devised a romanised script that is used to this day. When the Red Army came through in 1935, he negotiated with the then commissar Yang Shangkun (later President of China) to give the communists safe passage through the area on condition that not so much as a blade of grass would be taken from the people, a promise that was honoured. On his death, the people cut down the totem tree at the centre of their village to make a coffin for this man they believed had come to them from heaven. Ten thousand people attended the funeral and his grave became a shrine.

After the communist victory in 1949, the Party took on the trappings of local Christianity to win over the people: 'The Party Central Committee is the shepherd and the Yi people are the sheep of its pasture.' Later, all traces of Christianity were suppressed. In the village the Party won the two-line struggle against the foreigner's legacy, and human sacrifice was revived until, following the disasters of the Cultural Revolution, the people realised that the socialist heaven was unattainable and returned to a grass-roots form of Christianity. By 1992, a local variation of Christianity had become the predominant faith among the Yi people in the area. The foreigner's shrine has been rebuilt. Even when he was alive they did not know his real name. The stone reads:

The man who carried the new sun. Born 1876, arrived in China in 1904, returned to God in 1944. This gravestone does not hold his remains. The makers of this stone have lost his name but we have kept his religion.

This man has become a local spirit. His name, unknown to the people who worship his memory, is John Williams and he came from Ipswich in Queensland – possibly the first person from Ipswich to be deified. Tracking down this story, Sang Ye encountered difficulties from suspicious local officials. One old witness seemed to remember that the foreigner had come from a place called Australia, but one of the officials, hearing that Sang Ye was interested in the story because of his Australian links, said it was really Austria.

In this enduringly effective case of cultural exchange, the Australian connection has all but disappeared, suppressed or forgotten. The man who has become a god to the local people, and whose presence is physically remembered by the mature eucalypts that cover the landscape, is literally anonymous. He is as unknown in Australia as he is in China. Presumably his motives in going to China originally were not 'Australian' in any simple sense (although an historian of imperialist/sectarian attitudes in turn-of-the-century Ipswich might have relevant insights). 'God loves all' was apparently the attitude he applied to letting the Red Army of Han Chinese, traditional ethnic oppressors, pass through Yi territory. It is of little relevance to the Yi community that John Williams's legacy comes from Australia; and since the Han Chinese-dominated People's Republic of China actively deplores the assistance given by imperialist missionaries to primitive, superstitious minority tribes, there can be no record of John Williams's work as a contribution to Australia–China friendship. Yet the durability of his imprint must be the envy of the many and various official cultural exchange programs that have been carried out in the twenty years of Australia–China diplomatic relations.

True cultural exchanges are about the interactions of people, of their nature often invisible and unrecorded. They are not costed or carried out according to policy guidelines. Their effects are unpredictable, sometimes even regrettable according to the values of hindsight, and it is impossible to measure what they add to how China sees Australia or the other way round. Yet the developments that happen through what people actually do provide incontrovertible evidence of cultural interaction, and, in that sense, Australia has been engaged in cultural exchange with China for a long time. From before European settlement, Chinese traders sourced trepang (*haishen* – sea slug, or *beche de mer*) from Aboriginal societies along the coasts of northern Australia.

By virtue of its size, sparse population and, apparently, abundantly exportable natural resources and primary products (wool and iron ore are the best known in China), Australia is seen as a rich land given rather unfairly to a small group of whites rendered lazy, if not slow and stupid, by the ease of their circumstances. Australia is felt not only to need people, but poses a challenge to a Chinese sense of proletarian justice, or at least a sense of what the Chinese could put to good use.

The majority of enquiries about study in Australia in the 1980s came from Shanghai, Guangdong and Fujian, outward-looking areas with a strong migration history and long historical connections with Australia. There have been misperceptions and misjudgements, of course, and many dreams have been disappointed in the process that has brought tens of thousands of young Chinese to Australia in recent years, most of them to stay. But the information sent back home, however distorted, has filled in the picture of Australia with more detail than ever before. When Prime Minister Bob Hawke wept for the dead of Tiananmen Square in June 1989, everyone in China with an interest in Australia soon knew – through

Radio Australia, other foreign media reports, and Chinese word of mouth, which can operate with staggering effectiveness when it matters. The news only confirmed people in their view of Australia as a place wanting to give young Chinese the future denied them in China. In terms of creating an engaged awareness of Australia in China, and developing a host of durable ties between Australians and educated, urban mainland Chinese, the mismanaged export of education services from Australia to China has probably done as much for Australia–China relations in the long term as the millions of official aid, education, cultural and scientific dollars spent by Australian governments since 1972.

So what about official cultural exchange then? From the way its appearance followed closely on the establishment of diplomatic relations, I suspect that 'Australia–China cultural exchange' (*wenhua jiaoliu*) may be a Chinese-sponsored euphemism for what can prove to be something of a one-way traffic in terms of funding and benefits. In 1979 Foreign Affairs Minister Andrew Peacock announced the establishment of the Australia–China Council as what the Chinese might call a people's organisation, to raise mutual awareness in the two countries, to enlarge areas of contact, and to act as a feeder to inform policy-making. Until the late 1980s almost all Australian academic, cultural and sporting exchanges with China in some way involved the council, which endeavoured to cast its net as wide as possible. Reading the council's newsletter for the early 1980s, I am struck by the exuberant range of activities pursued and the optimistic confidence with which barriers were pushed back. Punctuated by political visits of increasing moment, from then Vice-Premier Li Xiannian (now deceased) in 1980 to the meeting between Prime Minister Bob Hawke and then Premier Zhao Ziyang (now disgraced) in 1984 and then General Secretary Hu Yaobang (now deceased) in 1985, the relationship's growth encompassed such diverse events as the China–Australia Ampol Soccer Cup; the Entombed Warriors exhibition; 'Mood and Moment: Australian Landscape, 1830–1930'; a joint quaternary studies project that showed Australia and China were closer together 300 million years ago; work experience in sheep handling at Haddon Rig for Chinese from Gansu; training assistance for *China Daily* in its infancy; the development of an enduring relationship with the National Library of China; Chinese heart specialists working with Victor Chang; Australian mountaineers climbing Everest from the Chinese side; and the first official visit by Chinese Christians (which in the positive language of the day helped expose 'misinformation'). One early member commented that the council had an 'unusually generous brief' that had been 'interpreted with imagination and some flair'.

Not all was rosy, however. Founding Chairman Geoffrey Blainey's introduction to the 1981 annual report, a succinct model of historical sooth-saying, notes that the heartening relationship between Australia and China rests on shaky foundations. 'A well-educated Chinese citizen knows little of Australia, except perhaps about kangaroos,' while Australians as tourists are 'easily exalted in and excited by lands where the liberties of the local citizens are sparse and where economic life is tightly controlled.' He warns that the test of a relationship is not the honeymoon but how 'setbacks and rifts' are handled, predicting that as Chinese goods increasingly compete with ours, and China imports less of our raw materials, we shall look on China's economic advancement differently, and that unemployment in Australia may sour the welcome to increased numbers of Chinese immigrants. His basic point is that friendship must be turned to understanding and that in Australia's case, in a democracy, 'that understanding . . . has to be widely dispersed'. It is at once a noble and a pragmatic point. In a society such as ours, policy and practice towards China are too important to be left to a small administrative elite. The general public must discuss and substantiate the issues, and on an informed basis. Hence the vision of the Australia–China Council as an organisation linking Mandarin policies to as wide a section of the community as possible.

A routine review of the council's activities from 1978–1985 acknowledged a high degree of success, but noted that 'its work had been relatively more successful in Australia than in China'. At the time the Council considered that academic institutions were not keeping up with the relationship. The Executive Director until 1985, Dr Jocelyn Chey, is quoted as saying, in 1984, that 'tertiary level research, training and teaching [on China] are dangerously insufficient'. The other worry that emerged was a lack of positive co-ordination and information exchange between institutions, especially government departments.

Lack of Australian expertise, lack of coherence in co-ordinating and implementing the response to China (I use the word 'response' for what in the language of the day was more of an 'approach'), and uncertainty about what difference the council was making to Australia's presence in China, could easily be attributed to the peculiar difficulties of dealing with a China finding its way in the post-Mao years. But in his parting words as chairman, in the report for 1985–86, Professor Wang Gungwu politely turns the tables, suggesting that the problem has less to do with China than with ourselves:

We are in fact unique, no less so than China itself. And if less strikingly so, the subtle differences in Australia are often harder to grasp. Certainly our perceptions of our neighbourhood and the world are peculiar to ourselves.

Even our background of economic, cultural and strategic dependence on others is an elusive subject requiring careful study. For the future, our distinctive characteristics will be increasingly important. If we want our relationship with China to endure, we must not hesitate to tell the Chinese more about who and what we are.

In other words, we are mad buggers, and we can't expect other people to know where we're coming from unless we learn to translate ourselves. And to translate yourself also means learning the other language, how you look from the other fellow's point of view.

The objectives of the Australia–China Council were reviewed again in November 1989, towards the end of what was perhaps the most difficult year for the political relationship since 1972. The new objectives signalled focus on particular priority areas, with a stronger economic emphasis than previously. The introduction to the report submitted by Chairman Gough Whitlam addresses itself to administrative matters, expressing some reservations about the grant application process. 'Council members . . . noted that the grant applications received did not apparently reflect the breadth of community interest in this relationship.' Too many applications are from academics, we are told, and too many fall outside the 'priority areas' defined by the council. Co-ordination with other government organisations has proceeded to the extent that a number of the council's areas of activity have been handed over to other bodies: development of language skills, educational exchanges and cultural exchanges are finding other sponsors.

As the narrowing of the council's areas of interest is described, the tone of enthusiasm heard in earlier reports is replaced by sobriety, even scepticism, with the council seeking projects that will make 'a *genuine* [my italics] contribution to Australia–China relations'. Further frustrations are voiced later in the report as additional restrictions are laid down. Funds are not available for conference travel. Matching funding must be provided by China for projects of mutual interest. The response by companies and government bodies to the council's training scheme has been 'quite disappointing' and so on. Ten years after its establishment the Australia–China Council has moved far from its original conception as a flexible and broad-based bridging organisation between government and people, and has been re-absorbed, with a diminished role to play, into the structure of government.

I wonder how much difference our cultural diplomacy has made to the way Australia is able to operate with China. Perhaps the most significant achievement is the development of a network of people – principally Australians, or people with a good understanding of the Australian context – who know China well, who are well-connected in China and who have sustained relationships with China over a long period. There is a web of personal relationships and experience that has been nurtured by public funds and by generous sharing (or at times anxious competition) among individuals caught up in a common interest, or passion, or fate. The network weaves in and out of government, but is independent, and sometimes critical, of government's ways of working. Neither in Australia nor in China does the network have fixed political affiliation. The generational baton has been passed, so that, for example, those who were hardy students in Peking in the 1970s when Jocelyn Chey was a youthful cultural counsellor are now key mediators in different areas of the relationship, and Jocelyn Chey herself has become Australian Consul General in Hong Kong.

The basis of the network is Australian, but it has been able to pull in exceptional Chinese expertise, in Australia and in China, to give flesh and blood to its work. Examples, among many, include Professor (and former ambassador) Ross Garnaut's research on the Chinese economy with senior economist Liu Guoguang from the Chinese Academy of the Social Sciences; the documentaries about interaction between Chinese and Australia by filmmaker Wang Ziyin, originally from Peking; the contribution of Peking critic Li Xianting to exhibitions of contemporary Chinese art in Australia; the work of Melbourne's Playbox Theatre, directed by Carrillo Gantner (another former cultural counsellor), in creating relationships with Chinese performing artists; and the sustained involvement with Australian literature, for more than ten years' translation, publishing and liaison, of Hu Wenzhong, Chairman of the Australian Studies Association of China. They are instances of individual commitment, often with complex personal stories behind them, including sometimes a less than smooth relationship with the governments of the peoples whose co-existence they make more meaningful.

What I am talking about here in terms of a network of personal links is what the Chinese call *guanxi*, connections. It is something to be proud of that Australia has its own invisible, unquantifiable share of the huge *guanxi* network that is China. Australian *guanxi* have developed, as they have been primed, haphazardly but indispensably, by our efforts at cultural diplomacy. It is a case of, to adopt the title of a well-known book on Chinese medicine, 'the web that has no weaver'.

Our administrative problem with how to institutionalise such links, so they exist beyond the individuals concerned, palely reflects what is almost at the core of China's prolonged crisis, the question of how to make the transition from power vested in persons to power vested impersonally in institutions, administrative procedures, and law. To the extent that Australia's effective presence in China is defined by a net of *guanxi*, we have already become a player in this transitional process too. Our cultural diplomacy has helped the web spread wider.

1992

Oodgeroo in China

The poet Kath Walker, as she then was, visited China from 12 September to 3 October 1984 in a delegation comprising Caroline Turner, as leader, Eric Tan, Rob Adams and Manning Clark. The delegation was organised by the Australia–China Council (ACC), under the auspices of the Department of Foreign Affairs, in response to an invitation from the Shanghai People's Association for Friendship with Foreign Countries, an arm of the Chinese Foreign Ministry. In the composition of the delegation, with its broadly cultural focus, you can perhaps see the hand of Geoffrey Blainey, the ACC's first Chairman, and Jocelyn Chey, then executive director, who must have enjoyed advising the Shanghai authorities that Oodgeroo's 'father was of Noonuccle Tribe, Carpet Snake totem'. Caroline Turner, Deputy Director of the Queensland Art Gallery, was an ACC member, as was Perth surgeon Eric Tan. Rob Adams represented the Australia Council. Manning Clark had the distinction of having his *Short History of Australia* published in China in 1973, for internal distribution in government circles only, with the warning 'the author is a bourgeois historian. Many of his opinions are not in line with Marxism'.

The visit came at a rosy time in Australia–China relations. China's 'economic reforms' and 'open-door policy' were well underway and the devastating extremities of the Cultural Revolution were being firmly repudiated. From the Australian point of view, China had been identified as a regional and trading partner to be cultivated. The ACC, along with other Australian organisations, was implementing a vigorous program of activities designed to extend people-to-people as well as official ties. The 1984 cultural delegation was a highwater mark in this process, a happy and well-managed visit that pushed back the boundaries of what was possible and resulted in enduring recommendations and initiatives. To look back after ten years is to discover, perhaps with some surprise, the long-term effectiveness of cultural relations in enabling insights and contacts that can be built on in the future. A whole range of training exchanges for young people developed from the delegation's recommendations, for example, with medical students from the University of Western Australia spending part of their course in Chinese hospitals, and Australian students of Chinese language being placed in organisations in China for work experience. A vigorous sister relationship was established between Shanghai and Queensland, which has facilitated the exhibition of treasures from the Shanghai Museum in Australia, and Shanghai's representation in the first Asia-Pacific Triennial of contemporary art at Queensland Art Gallery in 1993. There are many more such flow-on benefits.

Part of the agenda came from the Shanghai authorities, who in 1984 were keen to establish in the minds of Australian administrators that a whole range of activities was possible with Shanghai, more or less independently of Peking's control. Thus a lasting message was sent about devolution (and rivalry) in China, as the monolith of centralised power fissured. Australia identified the need to develop polyvalent relationships with China. The delegation's visit took place in the wake of the short-lived, but chilling, Anti-Spiritual Pollution Campaign of 1983, a conservative backlash against liberalisation, pluralism and Westernisation in the ideological sphere, which set the critical parameters of how the Chinese Communist Party (CCP) would handle the consequences of social change and modernisation. The policy of Australian governments, then and now, has been to support liberalising and reforming elements in Chinese society, and the distinguished cultural delegation's visit in September–October 1984 can be seen against this wider diplomatic background. The delegation's official host, Mr Li Shoubao, held the post of Vice-President of the Shanghai Friendship Association, among his other designations, and has proved over the years a highly effective servant of his government's interests. At the October First National Day banquet in Canton, the delegation met Mayor Ye Xuanping (son of revolutionary Field Marshall Ye Jianying) and Provincial Party Secretary Xie Fei, both of whose reformist stars continued rising during the 1980s. Meanwhile, back home, Geoffrey Blainey's cautionary analysis of Asian immigration to Australia was causing a local variant of an anti-spiritual pollution campaign as his academic colleagues widely denounced him, and the debate became 'something of a catalyst', Caroline Turner recalls, for the travellers' sense of themselves as Australians while in China.

Their itinerary was mostly a standard one, combining historic and scenic sites with cultural visits: Peking and the Great Wall, Xian and the Entombed Warriors, Shanghai, Hangzhou, Guilin and a cruise down the Li River, and finally Canton. A highlight of the meetings arranged for the group was a lively seminar with staff and students of the Australian Studies Centre at Peking Foreign Studies University.

Manning Clark, who had undergone major surgery a year earlier, was thrilled to stand atop the Great Wall. Dr Tan advised him to take it easy. Manning's fear that he might have cancer (he didn't) heightened his experiences during the visit. He wrote later: 'We were all very excited. We were all like human beings who had fallen in love at first sight'.

In Xian the group visited Huxian, where the famous peasant painting movement began in the 1950s. They were fascinated by the lively work, with its blend of folk exuberance and contemporary socialist realism, and by the management of a movement that, with a modicum of intervention, allowed working people to give seemingly spontaneous expression to their lives in a form that could also succeed in the marketplace. During a meeting with the artists, Kath Walker passed Rob Adams a Qantas postcard on which she had scrawled: 'If you love me, you'll pinch that painting off the wall for me'. There are parallels between the Chinese peasant painting movement, which by the 1970s was seen by some outsiders as a representative achievement of Maoist cultural policy, and the development of Aboriginal art in Australia from the 1970s. Perhaps, at Huxian, Oodgeroo saw in action some of the possibilities she was working towards in her own community cultural centre, Moongalba, on Stradbroke Island.

In Xian, Kath and Manning sang Waltzing Matilda to a group of Young Pioneers, the CCP's cubs and brownies. In Shanghai, preparations for the National Day celebrations were underway when the group visited the Shanghai Municipal Children's Palace, and this time Kath talked to the children about Aboriginal art, while Manning danced with them. The group was in Canton when October the First arrived, and they watched on television the military parade through Tiananmen Square that marked the thirty-fifth anniversary of the founding of the People's Republic of China. It was the first such parade since 1959, and, according to an official spokesperson, 'was not intended as a show of force, but as a display of defensive strength', boosting the morale of the People's Liberation Army, which was unhappy about aspects of the country's modernisation drive and now, under Communist Party leadership, was well on the way to becoming a sophisticated fighting force. There was another reason for celebrating, which would not have been lost on the citizens of Canton. The joint declaration between Britain and China confirming the return of Hong Kong to China in 1997 had been signed across the border in Hong Kong only a few days before, on 26 September 1984.

I can only speculate on how the members of the Australian cultural delegation responded to the momentous events going on around them, to their encounters with China, or to their sense of themselves as representatives of Australia, which they were invited to articulate at meeting after meeting. Accounts of the trip exude euphoria, perhaps not an unusual response for first-time China visitors (all except Tan), but enhanced here by the determined optimism of China in 1984 and by the personal chemistry of the group. Clark claimed it was the happiest such trip he'd ever been on. The delegation members developed friendships with each other that were to endure. In writing and conversation they convey a great sense of warmth towards each other and towards the China they experienced together.

The central element in the group dynamic was the relationship between Kath and Manning. While she had tremendous respect for her old friend, Kath was not overawed by him. When Manning gave a panoramic picture of Australian history, Kath was not afraid to present a different version, emphasising the white man's invasion of the country and blood in the streets. Oodgeroo saw herself as an ambassador for Aboriginal culture. It amused the Chinese that one black woman would dare to differ from the great historian. A photo taken, of all places, at Chiang Kai-shek's villa, shows Kath cheekily resting her head on Manning's knee, as he looks sternly at the camera, in an ironic tableau that might be captioned 'the Patriarch and the Piccaninny'. At first Kath may have been overwhelmed by the impact of Chinese culture, acknowledging the contrast between its achievements and the fate of her own comparably ancient culture. She was homesick, and the tug of home led her to relate China always back to her own cultural heritage, which she had a tremendous capacity to share with the people she met. In this way Oodgeroo connected herself with China too.

Within the group, and within Oodgeroo herself, a momentous event of another kind was taking place. She had written no poetry for six years before her trip to China. Her life was extraordinarily busy, activist and public. She had private problems to deal with too. She had an established literary reputation. But for any writer, not to write, however easily explained, is an uncomfortable condition. One morning Kath said to Manning, 'I'm pregnant again.' She meant she had started to write poetry. During her three weeks in China she produced a suite of sixteen poems. The first one, published as 'China . . . Woman' was inspired, if I have reconstructed the circumstances correctly, by a tour of the Forbidden City ('in a word overwhelming' according to Caroline Turner) in Peking on 17 September 1984 and written over the next few days. By 19 September the travellers had flown to Xian, which was where Rob Adams photographed Kath sitting on a step outside the Wild Goose Pagoda apparently writing the first poem of the series.

'China . . . Woman' is general and synoptic, giving voice to the affinities Oodgeroo found with China. As an Aboriginal she compares the

Great Wall to the Rainbow Serpent; as a woman she conceives China as dignified and fecund; as a revolutionary she registers the weight of the past, the struggle for change and also, in a sharp image of Beihai, the once-imperial park, some of the ironies of the present:

> *High peaked mountains*
> *Stand out against the sky-line.*
> *The great Wall*
> *Twines itself*
> *Around and over them,*
> *Like my Rainbow Serpent,*
> *Groaning her way,*
> *Through ancient rocks . . .*
> *China, the woman*
> *Stands tall,*
> *Breasts heavy*
> *With the milk of her labours,*
> *Pregnant with expectation.*
>
> *The people of China*
> *Are now the custodians of palaces.*
> *The wise old*
> *Lotus plants,*
> *Nod their heads*
> *In agreement.*

In their published form, in sequence, the poems offer a journal of the trip, and, as befits diary entries, they are informal, spontaneous, catching fleeting pictures and unresolved thoughts, tied to the specific evanescent occurrences of the visit. They are not without a sense of comedy at the situations in which the visitors find themselves:

> *Manning and I*
> *Offered to sing*
> *Waltzing Matilda for them.*

> *I think they liked it,*
> *Or, maybe, they were*
> *Showing us,*
> *How polite they can be.*
>
> *Then, they sang a song for us.*
> *A song of the young pioneers.*
> *We liked it too*
> *And before we left,*
> *We cupped our hands, and called for them*
> *Our*
> *Australian coo-ee.*

Elsewhere there is a sense of the irony of scale, as the travellers find their own personal connections with, or reactions to, what is laid before them.

> *We are shown the pavilion,*
> *Where they caught*
> *Chiang Kai-shek.*
> *It's halfway up the mountain*
> *Of the black horse.*
>
> *Later . . . I sketched a pearl shell*
> *and gave it to Caroline.*

Impromptu and seemingly effortless, the poems enact an open, fluid, wry and insightful response to China, in straightforward terms, aware too of sadness on the other side of hope:

> *We saw a giant panda*
> *At the zoo.*
> *He wasn't very happy,*
> *He was sick.*

China hands say that if you go to China for a month you write a book, for six months maybe an article, but if you go for a year or more you will never write anything, as the ever-increasing complexity of your knowledge reduces you to silence. Short-term visitors are faced with a barrage of bewildering, often incomprehensible impressions and, under the pressure of journeying through a hugely different world, they struggle with exhilaration and exhaustion to formulate reactions. Oodgeroo's response, in her effusion of poetic fragments, sidesteps the need to reach conclusions, while registering with sensitivity the wonder that she experienced. The underswell is the personal reference back to herself and what she knows. In the 'Reed Flute Cave at Guilin', for instance, she writes:

> *I shall return home,*
> *And I'm glad I came.*
> *Tell me, My Rainbow Spirit*
> *Was there just one of you?*
> *Perhaps, now I have time to think,*
> *Perhaps, you are but one of many guardians*
> *Of earth's people . . .*

The China poems are less public, less oratorical than her more familiar work. In their free, spare, elliptical immediacy, they have an imitation-Chinese quality, reminiscent at times of Maoist revolutionary verse.

Oodgeroo may have been relieved to escape for a while from her public role in Australia. She enjoyed herself in China. She took the toasts at banquets while others piked out, and Eric Tan and Rob Adams had the job of sourcing the liquor for after-hours. She let her creativity flow. Throughout the trip she made pastel drawings, and, after Eric Tan bought her Chinese brushes and inks, she experimented with Chinese painting. She copied out her freshly composed poems and decorated them with snakes and other personal emblems and presented them to people she met. She was less impressed by great historic sites and occasions than by the direct experience of place, people and lived history. She enjoyed walking round markets and countryside, for example, or meeting students with whom she engaged as the sparkiest sort of teacher. She was happy spending time with children – partly because they took her back to her own grandson and the children who visited her on Stradbroke Island. As Caroline Turner recalls, Oodgeroo 'grew in energy all the time throughout the visit . . . She had a marvellous intuitive sense of place which came in part from a poet's sensitivity and in part out of her Aboriginality but also from her acute intelligence and ability to respond to people'.

Oodgeroo was happy to go home, but she came to China gladly. She remembered Chinese sailors who had come to Stradbroke Island and mixed with her local people. Chinese, through Macassans, were trading sea slug in Australian tropical waters from the late seventeenth century, as Oodgeroo seems to know when she writes a caption to her drawing of a Stradbroke Island sea slug:

There are many different types of sea slug. The sea slug that the Chinese people like to eat, is very very different; it's very hard and it hasn't got any pipes. It's what people call a sea cucumber.

She was also aware of the international communist role in opposing racism and oppression of indigenous peoples. An important memory of Kath Walker's youth was of the public stance taken by the Communist Party of Australia in exposing a racist incident in Queensland. China under Mao had styled itself the leader and advocate of developing peoples and the Third World. In 1974, Gary Foley, the first Aboriginal person to visit the People's Republic of China, had brought back ideas about people's communes.

By the 1980s, however, China's credentials in this regard were wearing thin, as relationships with the developed world took priority over support for developing countries. China had more interest in trade than aid. China's treatment of her own minority peoples had come under scrutiny, and China's occupation of Tibet was an issue on the global agenda. China's sensitivity on these issues led to the propaganda use of a 'pot calling the kettle black' approach to other countries. In the case of Australia, the Chinese government focused on the plight of Australian Aboriginal peoples as part of a larger indictment of capitalism. There was some hypocrisy in this concern. Chinese xenophobia can take particularly repellent forms in relation to black people: even at its most benign it delights in the strangeness, the 'colour and movement', of black cultures.

Many Chinese have shown an excited curiosity about Aboriginal culture, with an appreciation of its antiquity and distinctiveness, sometimes even recognising similarities with ancient Chinese culture, at other times mainly savouring it for its perceived exotic and primitive qualities. Since 1984, different kinds of Aboriginal art have been exhibited and favourably received in China. There have been further Aboriginal delegation visits. One included Aboriginal photographers who were retracing the links between the Rainbow Serpent and the Great Wall.

Oodgeroo went into this complex environment in 1984 and no doubt she saw it all for what it was. I don't imagine it changed the view expressed in the first poem of *My People*, 'All One Race' (illustrated, incidentally, with a caricature of a pigtailed Chinaman):

> *Black tribe, yellow tribe, red, white or brown,*
> *From where the sun jumps up to where it goes down ...*
> *I'm for all humankind, not colour gibes;*
> *I'm international, and never mind tribes.*

But there were some awkward moments. The seminar at the Shanghai Foreign Languages Institute was less dynamic than the counterpart occasion in Peking. 'The students and audience in Shanghai seemed confused by many of the things we said,' comments the report. This may have been because the students were insufficiently informed about Australia. It may have been because of internal resistance at the institute to the development of an Australian Studies Centre (it subsequently transferred to East China Normal University, Shanghai). Or it may have been because the imposing official Shanghainese presence intimidated the Chinese participants, causing open inquiry to become entangled with diplomatic façadism. The audience seems to have been uncomfortable about the delegation's frank criticism of aspects of Australia. In the wake of the Anti-Spiritual Pollution Campaign's repression of intellectuals, the audience must have hoped that the visiting intellectuals would identify Australia with pluralist and humanist values. Students may have been puzzled to hear Manning Clark speak of China as a beacon to Western intellectuals. Sinologist Geremie Barmé was in the audience as an uninvited guest, and recalls it as a distasteful occasion. Regulations were in force at the time to prevent 'unattached foreigners' from mixing with the local populace. Barmé's independent presence in Shanghai – as against the carefully managed presence of the delegation – meant that he came under secret police surveillance. It seemed to him that his fellow Australians were irresponsible not to consider how their remarks might be taken or used in the local context. He remembers feeling a sense of 'national betrayal' that led him to question his sense of himself as an Australian who was nonetheless deeply committed to understanding China.

By the time the travellers reached Guilin, they were aware that there had been virtually no contact with China's so-called minority nationalities. In Guangxi Zhuang Autonomous Region, the area around Guilin, the 'minorities' make up seventy per cent of the population. The group was joined by Roger Brown, then Australian Consul General in Shanghai, who, with Eric Tan, sought to rectify the omission in the program. Oodgeroo was interested, although it was not something she pushed for. In the event the delegation met some official representatives of the Zhuang people, but there was recognition by this late stage of the trip that the program had been filtered. 'We were keen to meet with minority people, and thanks to the admirable Mr Fu [of Shanghai Friendship Association] this was done. However, we felt our local hosts in Guilin could have arranged a one-day trip to visit the minority people considering the time we had available in Guilin,' notes the report. The minorities in the field would not have presented as smartly as their official representatives.

Among the many results of the visit was a proposal to publish the poems that Oodgeroo had written during the trip in a bilingual edition, as a joint venture between Jacaranda Press in Brisbane and the International Culture Publishing Corporation of China. The proposal was brought to fruition by Jacaranda's John Collins, thanks to his well-established contacts with Chinese publishers, notably Mr Xu Liyu, then Vice-President of the Chinese Publishers Association. The suite of China poems was published in 1988 as *Kath Walker in China*. It included an enthusiastic foreword by Manning Clark and evocative photographs of the trip taken mainly by Rob Adams. The Chinese translations by Gu Zixin are accurate, although inevitably with minor differences. The lines about the sick panda, for example, become: 'He wasn't very happy *because* he was sick'. This slightly shifts the directness of Oodgeroo's sympathy for the (highly symbolic) giant panda's plight.

The book is unique in many ways. As far as I can establish, it contains the first Aboriginal writing published in China. It is the first single volume of an Australian poet's work published in China, male or female, and the first joint literary publication. 2000 copies were taken for distribution in China, the remaining 850–1000 sent to Australia. They arrived in Brisbane not long after the Tiananmen Square massacre of 3–4 June 1989. Witnessing Tiananmen Square at a happier time, Oodgeroo had written on 18 September 1984:

> *The big square*
> *Welcomes*
>
> *Her sons and daughters . . .*

The tragic, and potentially embarrassing, irony of these lines would not be lost on Australians. A new dustjacket was printed, incorporating on the back cover a new poem, 'Requiem', condemning the male politicians everywhere who 'Derive new ways, To uphold ignorance, To keep slavery alive'.

> *In Tiananmen Square*
> *History repeats itself.*

This final poem lacks the subtle freshness of the China poems of Oodgeroo's late fruition in September–October 1984. It brings her back to the harsh public world of political struggle.

Perhaps because of its peculiar publishing history, *Kath Walker in China* seems to have dropped from sight. The book is not widely known, and the poems have not been given much of a place in Oodgeroo's *oeuvre*. This is a pity. The poems document the kind of excited progress through China that so many thousands of Australians, from prime ministers to package tourists, made in the 1980s. They also give utterance to the continuation of a long faint thread of Aboriginal Australian–Chinese relationship. Furthermore, they show a face of Oodgeroo that would not otherwise be seen. Oodgeroo in China may have been 'pregnant', and a little hysterically so, but her condition proved more fertile than any 'hysterical pregnancy'.

Kath Walker in China shows Oodgeroo as a poet in her response to an extraordinary world. That is an especially valuable and lasting result of the 1984 cultural delegation. Judith Wright wrote to Oodgeroo in 1975, after Kath had sent her the poem 'Sister Poet', encouraging her to go on writing, whatever else she did. 'Keep writing,' urged Judith Wright, 'it reaches more people than you'd think and we've only got one Kathy Walker'.

1994

In the mountains under a blue sky

That grand old lady of Chinese letters, Ding Ling, visited Australia in 1985. She was in a motel room in Canberra when an episode of the documentary series *The Heart of the Dragon* came on television. It was about culture, and showed an interview with the elderly writer Shen Congwen and his artist nephew Huang Yongyu. The narrator said that, if any Chinese would win the Nobel Prize for Literature, it would be Shen Congwen. Ding Ling nearly choked. Through the window of a television screen in a foreign land, an apparition had risen up to torment her. She and Shen Congwen had been enemies for forty years.

The cause of their feud is unclear. Ding Ling and her lover, who was later assassinated, had been Shen Congwen's closest friends. Maybe Ding Ling didn't like his literary portrait of her after she took up with another man. Ding Ling, having joined the communists at Yanan, went on to become one of the most powerful cultural officials of the People's Republic. Whether her animus towards Shen Congwen was personal or political, it helped keep him under a cloud. He worked as an obscure researcher at the history museum and for forty years published almost no new literary works. The suspension of his output after 1949 disqualified him from the Nobel Prize, in fact, but Ding Ling was not to know that. She saw looming out of the foreign television set the threat that posterity would reverse the positions she and Shen Congwen had enjoyed in life under the Communist Party. Ding Ling died in 1986 and was given a fitting send-off. Shen Congwen followed in 1988, his death hardly noticed but for a few mean-spirited obituaries in the Chinese press. He is among the greatest writers of our century.

Ding Ling's visit was a window for me into Shen Congwen's writing, and Shen Congwen became a looking glass through which I tumbled into the other world that lies behind the surface of Confucian order, ideology and modernisation in China.

Shen Congwen – or Shen Tsung-wen as his name was spelled when his stories first appeared in English in the 1940s – was a native of West Hunan, an inaccessible mountain region of rebels and émigrés and non-Chinese people driven into the hills by Han and Manchu, and later Nationalist and Communist pacifications; a bloody, passionate and magical borderland haunted by the beauty and tragedy of a people kept literally beyond the pale. In the Communist 'liberation' in 1950 an estimated 30,000 people, mostly of Miao ethnicity, died.

Legend has it that the Miao lost their written culture in the Yellow River when they were driven southward by the Han. Today they have no written script. Supposed descendants of the lyrical shamanistic culture of the Kingdom of Chu, their cosmology and 'history' exist in their oral tales, songs, and in the story images that appear in embroideries and carvings. Shen Congwen was part Miao. His fame rests on a small group of stories and sketches written mostly in the 1930s, evoking the life of his homeland and in particular the beliefs and customs of the Miao. The style hovers between ancient and modern, marrying an ethnographer's insistence on detailed observation with a fabulist's imagination. They are written with archaic freshness and sensuousness, presenting a world beyond time as it steps into its poor, pitiful place in history, fantastic tales, grim fateful accounts, or indictments of superstition and violence.

The Miao of West Hunan divide into land people and river people, embodying a division between the stay-at-home farming culture of the hills and the trade culture of the boats. The boats brought contact with towns and cities downstream, and, with it, the breath of prosperity and the sediment of despair. Shen Congwen's most famous story, 'The Husband', is about a land husband whose wife goes down river to work as a prostitute on the boats, earning money from traders to support them both. The forced opening of a maiden world is caught with painful understatement. Like moments in Thomas Hardy, Chekhov or Marquez, Shen Congwen's stories and images make an imprint that seems to go deeper than literary effect.

I copied down the rules for life that, in old age, Shen Congwen passed on to his nephew:

1. *Give all your love to the people and the soil.*
2. *If you fall, get up and keep going. Don't waste time admiring the place where you fell; don't stop to lament.*
3. *Hold fast to your work and never, never let go.*

It is powerful advice that reflects the author's character and also an attractive quality to be found in many Chinese people, who can be practical, resilient, tenacious, in love with the world that nourishes them. I know better than to generalise about the Chinese, and Shen Congwen, a figure of minority background who nonetheless made a name for himself in the metropolis, is no ordinary Chinese, but in the great world that is China there is a quality of obdurate vitality that has enabled people to transform and survive, often against terrible odds, for centuries. Shen Congwen links the people with the earth, and that seems essential. *The Good Earth* was what Pearl S. Buck called China in her 1931 novel; a recent study of China's ecological catastrophes calls it *The Bad Earth* – soil which cannot feed its people; Yellow Earth, leached of nutrient, parched, deforested, yet of the same substance as the sons and daughters of the Yellow Emperor who populate it so pressingly, making the fate of the earth also the people's fate. The source of *ch'i*, the breathing power that animates them, is located low in the belly filled with grain produced from the Yellow Earth. It is near the centre of gravity when people squat to return their meagre human fertiliser to the soil. People and earth are matter endlessly transforming into spirit: tales, rites, signs, histories, dynasties, ideals, traces, ghosts. People and earth are creative energy as well as raw material. They are the created work, in all its fecundity and pathos, as well as the mass of mud and ashes and numberless unrecorded Wangs and Zhangs to which the creation returns. The earth is everywhere modified by human activity that pulses with a struggle for life, or is pushed down into dormancy, like the earth.

I wanted to see the earth of Shen Congwen's writing. How could written words carry me into the world of these people who had no writing? How could their world, as the writer conjured it up, be swollen with the humanity and earthiness that always seemed to be missing in the orthodoxies of contemporary China? How could it be real, when the ordinary, officially contoured Chinese life I dealt with every day so often seemed false?

Finally, in the autumn of 1989, when the Australian embassy's work was in suspension after the Peking massacre, I got the chance. The first part of the journey was to Changsha, the capital of Hunan province. The land-locked province borders to the south-east on thriving Guangdong province, which abuts Hong Kong, and along its other boundaries on the far less prosperous provinces of Jiangxi, Hubei, Sichuan, Guizhou and Guangxi. In Guangdong, arable land has been given over to industry, forcing the well-heeled entrepreneurs of Guangdong to come over the border in to Hunan to procure food and raw materials, bartering manufactured items such as clothing, shoes and electrical goods in payment. The free market price for grain has soared above the state price, leading to shortages in the local shops while large quantities of grain cross the southern border, often illegally. After fulfilling their quotas to the state, farmers are turning to cash crops to supply Guangdong factories, in haphazard cycles of scarcity and glut, flax one year, kiwi fruit the next. Unable to manipulate the situation to their advantage, Hunan officials cling to the centralised system they grew up with, making their capital, Changsha, a junction between old-style socialism and the hybrid capitalism that is working up from the Pearl River delta.

Changsha is culturally a backwater, which frees it from the pressures of Peking. I met He Liwei, a thin man and regional story writer in the tradition of Shen Congwen, and Can Xue ('Wretched Snow'), a dressmaker turned author and feminist whose *Dialogues from Paradise*, blurring autobiography and nightmare, is at the forefront of China's literary avant-garde. She wore a tartan skirt that she made herself. Later in the year she battled the Ministry of Culture's refusal to allow her to visit Japan, where she has a considerable readership, and won the case. 'I'm a funny lady,' she told me.

I met the brilliant old publisher and scholar Zhong Shuhe, who has devoted his life to needling out the complexities of literature and history concealed by propaganda in China. He has republished authors whose writing is superb, though their politics may be questionable, and he has edited a series called *Towards the World*, documenting Ching dynasty intellectuals and reformers who went abroad to seek new ideas. The work challenges the received notion that Chinese culture has been autonomous and hermetically sealed. He would like to edit a volume on late Ching intellectuals who visited Australia, but lacks primary sources.

Leaving Changsha, the train went west through the mountains to the Miao and Tujia Autonomous Region of West Hunan, another country. Bandits roam those hills, and we were warned to chain our possessions to the luggage racks. When the train stopped at remote sidings in the middle of the night, bandits could climb in the window and clean the place out. A security guard hovered by us for most of the trip. When he strolled out of earshot, the talk immediately turned to Peking. They had all heard stories of the student demonstrations in Tiananmen Square, the events of 3–4 June 1989, and other atrocities, and wanted to hear our first-hand reports. Our fellow travellers were small business people who had dropped out of the official system, honeymoon couples, elderly relations being relocated, scientists on inspection tours of West Hunan's huge reserves of manganese, antimony and tungsten.

Our first stop was Huaihua, an army town near the Guizhou border, where we were escorted to the salubrious compound that houses the People's Government. The rest of Huaihua was like a shanty town around the compound's walls. A conference on folk drama was in progress, devoted to an ancient quasi-religious kind of pantomime, the *Mulian*, akin to Tibetan drama, which had come to China through Burma and Nepal, and continued to be performed in a bastardised version in West Hunan. Among the organisers was a friend of mine from the Shanghai Drama Institute who told me that, because the political atmosphere was so volatile, performances in the surrounding villages had been cancelled for fear of being seen to encourage superstition and local chauvinism. The *Mulian* play was performed in the People's Government compound for conference delegates only. We watched as the lama king fought off life-size tigers and crocodiles.

Our journey took us on to Fenghuang, the town that Shen Congwen has immortalised. It is a walled town divided by the curving River Tuo. The beautiful three-arched stone bridge dates from 1554. Fenghuang, nestled in terraced hills and autumnal woods, is a well-preserved Ming dynasty town. The grand gatehouses indicate its history as a garrison for troops of one laird or another. The elaborate courtyard theatre with the three Taoist gods painted on the wall of the ornate little stage suggests the harmony of entertainment and belief in these parts. The old shops and houses of grey stone and mortar, weathered timber and black tiles are built along narrow alleys, or drop down to the river's edge as to a Venetian canal. They grow together into a single charming environment or work of art. I stopped at a bookstall and bought the Fenghuang Almanac. The town is closed to foreigners and the book was for internal distribution only. The bookseller got into a bit of trouble when a busybody official told him he shouldn't sell me the book. I didn't want to give the book back. The bookseller just laughed.

The local worthies welcomed us to lunch in the upper storey of a Ching dynasty pagoda that was open to the air and a view of the running stream. Our dining room was painted with a mural of flying cranes, the trademark of Huang Yongyu, Shen Congwen's nephew. We ate Miao food; wild mushrooms with wild duck, vegetable curd (as opposed to bean), pink-dyed sticky rice, and fierce young rice wine from an elegant vessel that had been designed by Huang Yongyu too. A cunning, cocky jester of a man, he had been in and out of favour for most of his life. At the time of the Peking massacre, he'd been in Hong Kong, where he had done some biting cartoons of the communist leadership, and some mournful paintings of lotuses in a field of blood and ashes. He was particularly out of favour at the time of our visit, so it was interesting to hear his efforts to preserve the town and manage the inevitable tourism development praised by local officials. Would Huang Yongyu design the Fenghuang Holiday Inn? He was ultimately under the protection of his liegelord Wang Zhen, the revolutionary veteran (then a cranky, incontinent octogenarian; now deceased) who pulled the strings of China's cultural policy in the 1980s. Hunan was numbered among Wang Zhen's fiefdoms – which was good for Huang Yongyu.

But Peking had never seemed further away. One of the sights of the town was Shen Congwen's old house and its museum of memorabilia. There was a photograph taken in 1982 when he returned home for the last time, accompanied by his translators Gladys Yang and Yang Xianyi. The black-and-white photograph shows them boating together, Shen with his wife, still afloat after all those years. Fenghuang was proud of Shen Congwen, even though it had not been correct to speak in his praise for most of living memory. It's something for a man from a small town in West Hunan, whose mother was an illiterate Miao, to become a master of world literature.

One of the deputies was a Miao nationalist. He had researched the Miao for a lifetime and did not conceal the fact that he considered their culture to be irreconcilable with that of the Han Chinese, and superior to it. I don't know how this sorted with his official position. He ate and drank heartily, reminding me, with his stories, pronouncements and passionate local loyalty, of a highland chieftain. He was involved with an international Miao federation that extended to the suburbs of Peking and the cities of South-East Asia (where the Miao are called Hmong), to the United States, to Hobart in Australia where they sell their embroideries at Salamanca market on Saturday mornings. The people in the federation were working to achieve solidarity through awareness of common Miao identity. The program was presented in a jolly, innocuous light, conforming with the Party's policies towards minorities, but it also bespoke a recalcitrant, unassimilable quality in the Miao. They could sustain themselves on legends of brave deeds, fantasies and dreams, even if there were nothing else. The last 'Miao King' killed the communists' messenger and, after a seventeen-day battle in November 1950, killed himself. His son held out in the hills until the next year when he was captured, with the help of Soviet advisors, and executed.

We sat above the town in the garden of Huang Yongyu's family home, drinking yellow tea and eating pithy pomelos from their tree. As the chilly evening wind began to blow down from the peaks, I thought of Sir Walter Scott and the border ballads.

> *Oh lang will his lady*
> *Look o'er the castle Down,*
>   *Eer she see the Earl of Murray*
> *Come sounding thro' the town!*

We were guests at a bonfire party in the small Miao village of Dehang and watched the improvised love duets that are their mode of courting. Then we travelled further to a place of weird sheer rocky outcrops, hundreds of metres high, with clumps of hairy vegetation and phallic names like Golden Whip and Turtle Head. As we climbed the steep winding paths, beside streams and waterfalls, through dense groves and drizzling rain, we passed peasant kids wearing Mao Zedong badges. Mao was Hunanese too, and has the force of a fertility spirit in this place.

I am shy about revealing the secrets of West Hunan, especially Fenghuang. It is the best place in all of China. But then again, it may not be real. Words first captured the place for me, as if the spirit of the place was a genie in a bottle of evocative language. Far away, when the stopper is taken out for a moment, one whiff transports you. When you go to the place and tread the earth, its smell mingles inseparably with the odour of those words. How can I explain it?

China, especially Confucian China, is a civilisation of the written sign. The strokes made with brush and ink embody entities that, unlike everything else in the creation, have realities of duration and meaning. People, like buildings, cities and dynasties, come and go. The written word remains, describing, defining and ordering. It names the universe.

But the universe named in Shen Congwen's writing is a world of earth, energy, fury and superstition such as words cannot normally contain or control; an irrational, profoundly anti-Confucian world. His world is there in West Hunan to be seen and experienced. Only by an act of magic, or an immense spanning of consciousness, has the author succeeded in using the means of the Confucian scholar – marks of earth and water on woodpulp – to let his people live. My homage to Shen Congwen in the journey to Fenghuang was an affirmation of the mystery that writing sometimes can quite literally take you to another world and make it indelibly part of your own.

One of my favourites among Shen Congwen's stories deals with just this phenomenon. It is called 'The Lamp', written in 1929. The young narrator is in Shanghai, at a time of great turmoil – and frequent power failures. He has an old soldier servant from his hometown, an ex-army cook who had originally followed the narrator's father. Because the young man's reading and writing are always interrupted by the blackouts, the servant gets him an old-fashioned oil lamp. The servant is a wonderful character. In a way, the old soldier is China – various, battle-weary, full of stories, but mute:

Imagine him – a man of about fifty, who had travelled nearly always on foot over the greater part of China; had witnessed the turmoil following the Boxer Rebellion and the overthrow of the Ching Dynasty; had fought many battles in the civil wars; had tasted a great variety of foods and had entrusted himself to many strange beds; had climbed over mountains and swum torrential rivers. He was a classic, a masterpiece that one could never finish reading.

It requires someone like the narrator, who can first read the servant as a person, and then find words for what he is, before his story can be told.

In the foreground of the narrative is a mistaken love story. A girl visits. The servant does all he can to encourage a marriage between his master and the girl. But the girl comes only to bid farewell to her friend before going north with another man, her lover. She is perhaps Ding Ling.

Later the narrator hears that she and her partner have been arrested as revolutionaries. The civil war breaks out. The old servant moves on, to follow the army once again. Only the lamp remains, and in its light, 'plunged in meditation – I see the old soldier as in a vision, his red face, crumpled army uniform, this steward of an ancient household. And the soundless tears torrentially flowing from his small brown eyes'.

I thought of writing about him, but how could I transform his beautiful, pure soul into sedentary prose: both his complexion and his voice had led me to see life under a different aspect, and I had to own that what I knew and wrote about was altogether too shallow and prosaic ... I seemed to be groping in the dark corners of my brain for words which possessed meaning, but all words seemed powerless now ... There were times indeed when it seemed that the peaceful soul of this most ancient and oriental people was being driven by the tides of the present into an incongruous world of struggle and turmoil. With melancholy and restraint they lived out their lives of compromise in a new world, while their dreams were still centred upon a world of light ...

The light of the old lamp comes to symbolise the zone of memory and dream that must be caught, and cherished, in the suspension of words, words which the small circle of illumination allows the writer at his work to trace.

Facing the transparent crystal lampshade and the faint yellowish glimmer that issued through it, often I would be immediately translated in company of the soldier into the dream-laden, fantastic atmosphere of a dilapidated temple of a small village inn – an inn situated in the neighbourhood of a whole battalion of soldiers and horses. I had loved these things, but they were now remote and out of my reach –

The lamp brings them back.

Shen Congwen's story has become a kind of lamp, illuminating the old soldier, the author, and the world of those songs that are sung by the young who live in the mountains under a blue sky. That glow illuminates an otherwise dark China.

I had kept putting off my journey to Fenghuang. When I was able to go at last, a circle was completed. I expected to be disappointed, but what I discovered there reassured me. I could connect what I found with the stories that had inspired my interest years before.

For weeks before the trip to West Hunan I had shared my room with Hou Dejian, the Chinese rock star who, after days of hunger-striking, had tried to negotiate with the troops, on the night the tanks entered Tiananmen Square, for extra time to enable the protesters to withdraw peacefully. In the days after the massacre Hou Dejian had sought refuge from the Chinese authorities in the Australian embassy. Every day he wrote pages of notes, and we talked for hours about his ideas for transforming China into a strong, free nation.

It turned out that his father's hometown was not so far from Fenghuang, in an impoverished border region to which the family had been driven when fleeing the Manchu invasion centuries before. Hou Dejian tackled the problems of China, which were his own problems too, with the same passionate, reckless conviction that I found in Shen Congwen, and that I recognised as a kind of obstinate poetry of the soul from the mountain periphery.

Shen Congwen, and the trip to West Hunan, left me with the same sensation as when a full meal wears off and the first hunger stirs again.

1991

My search for a shaman

Contemporary Chinese art

At a seminar at the Australian National University in 1985, Geremie Barmé discussed the poetry of Yang Lian, one of the younger members of the *Today* magazine group, in the context not only of modernisation and modernism, but also primitivism, root-seeking, myth-making, and even shamanism, the capacity to communicate with the world beyond the living, which recurs in Chinese folk religion. *Today* magazine, and Yang Lian, had emerged in association with the Democracy Wall movement of 1979–80 in Peking, when, following the death of Mao Zedong and the smashing of the Gang of Four in 1976, and the ascent of Deng Xiaoping, educated youth returned to the cities demanding change. The Democracy Wall movement was accompanied by unprecedented expressions of dissent in art and literature, but ended in suppression and the draconian sentencing of democracy activist Wei Jingsheng and others.

By the mid-1980s, such dissident artistic activities were resurfacing. They were also partially condoned. Barmé argued that the dissident culture was a continuation of older forms of Chinese discontent with orthodoxy. He drew attention to an alternative Chinese culture that had roots in the mysteries of the *I Ching* (*Book of Changes*) and the earthy energies of popular Taoism. In its cosmopolitan Peking form this culture found its Western affinities in Freud and Dada, T.S. Eliot and the Beats, rather than Marx and science. I believed that what was emerging, in pockets and spurts, of a new, or newly configured, Chinese culture offered important insights into what was going on in the society as a whole.

The kind of Taoism that Barmé had introduced me to as an intellectual concept showed in the passionate, committed, frenzied, hard-living, protean creative spirits of the Peking scene; qualities that came to the fore when the quest for creative expression was once more connected with direct political dissent, ten years on from the Democracy Wall, in Tiananmen Square in 1989. *Today* was founded by poets Bei Dao and Mang Ke. They and their friends – writers, poets, artists, performers, theorists and social activists – formed a dissenting group that had its origins in the Cultural Revolution, when the children of urban intelligentsia were sent to the countryside. Some, including Bei Dao, had since left China. Others were repositioning themselves in the 1980s, like Mang Ke, also known as Monkey, who became a kind of godfather to other writers and artists. 'After You're Dead, You Can Still Grow Old' is the title of a poem he wrote around this time.

In retrospect the period of the late 1980s is most noteworthy for the formation of a contemporary Chinese art. Visual art, working beneath or around the written language that can be so oppressive in Chinese culture, offered sensitive seismic readings of what was going on underground. I was privileged to watch, and learn, as exciting new kinds of Chinese art were fired into being by the energies of rebellion.

This phase of contemporary Chinese art began in 1985 with critic Li Xiaoshan's remark that traditional painting was dead. I saw Lin Chunyan's bold paintings from the existential *States* series at the Old Observatory in 1986, in an exhibition that was allowed to happen, although without approval, in the precarious leniency of that year. To be an artist at that time was to show oneself in a new way, rejecting tawdriness and dehumanisation by devotion to creative pursuits, however useless, in the manner of old-style literati. Works may have ended up gathering dust in a corner – that didn't matter. As an unexpected offshoot of utilitarian ideology, art subverted the society that bred it.

Ah Xian first showed me his work in private at his home and I could see at once its powerful, metaphorical political eloquence – a judgement shared by many people who have seen it since in exhibitions around the world. The way Ah Xian visualises, and even conceives of, human beings is mediated by crude, mass-produced models. Re-working Cultural Revolution models in his *Heavy Wounds* series, for example, the artist shows the sources of human creativity – brain, the sense organs, genitalia – bound and gagged. The dumb emptiness of people's faces is a travesty of the spiritual emptiness suggested by the stylised Taoist waves in the background. In other works pain and puzzlement are expressed in cross-overs of medium and form, in multiple layers and broken ill-fitting elements. Working without institutional support, Ah Xian, like most of the artists, lived and worked in modest, cramped conditions. Sometimes huge canvases were propped in the narrow hallway, with not always enough space or light to see the work properly. How moving – and reassuring – it was to see real work, with flair, originality and conviction, emerging from under the nearly fifty years of rigid Communist Party cultural regulation and the 3000 years' tradition as numbingly constructed in China's museums.

In 1986 at the China Art Gallery I singled out an oil painting by Wang Youshen, *Yugong and his Sons*, from a show of work by graduating art school students. I tracked down the artist and we became friends. He has gone on to produce work that in more conceptually sophisticated ways returns to the theme of that early work, the multiplying conformity of individuality in China. He works as art editor at the influential *Peking Youth News* and produced an installation work for the 1992 Venice Biennale: curtains of newsprint blocking the view from the window to a different, more open reality. In 1988 I also met Guan Wei, another student of the *I Ching*, whose then predominantly grey canvases of figures marked with acupoints instantly appealed to me for their cool, sharp playfulness – a rare quality in the academy art of the time, whether in traditional Chinese manner or the solemn adaptation of social realism or other newer imports. Guan Wei had stacks of paintings in his studio that had been seen by only a few friends. Standing to one side of the system, Guan Wei showed a startling inventiveness, a capacity for radical play, which gave a rare quality of humour to his work.

For young artists pursuing their own path there was virtually no access to the kind of interpretative context that exhibitions, reviews, art criticism or an art market can provide. Feedback was mostly a matter of comment from like-minded members of the artist's group. A foreigner like myself introduced another kind of response, however subjective or uninformed it might be. I saw hundreds of exhibitions in those years, and held some informal shows at my home. The scene was vigorous, and occasionally something striking would emerge. Artists came in contact with many foreign visitors, and the meetings sometimes resulted in sale of work or, in the cases of Ah Xian and his brother, photographer Xiao Xian, Guan Wei and Lin Chunyan, invitations to visit and show overseas. These salon-style showings in the apartments of foreign diplomats, journalists and teachers blurred the line between exhibition opening and cocktail party as a way of getting round red tape. Hence the phenomenon of 'dip' art. Artists whose work demonstrated the characteristics by which foreigners wished to remember China were preferred, especially if they were personally engaging too. Pre-1989 this free-and-easy art scene seemed to reflect the informality of the wider Chinese society. The tide was flowing almost too fast, however; by being part of a larger movement of change, the salons took on a degree of intellectual significance, presenting audiences with images of a China in which desire and imagination were surfacing in ways that would prove dangerous. Official venues were soon pushed to catch up.

The artists' work and the unauthorised channels they used to show it challenged the Chinese authorities and the more intransigent parts of the art establishment. A China-wide network of communication and support had developed among unofficial or unorthodox artists and other dissenting intellectuals. Such people, constituting a threat to Communist Party rule, could be harassed by the security system or otherwise obstructed in their personal and professional lives. Questions of desiring to speak or act, or simply exist in a certain way, but of being able to do so only in repressed or codified forms, haunt much contemporary Chinese art. Facelessness, and the emergence from facelessness to individuality, are predominant themes. Many artists have opted for exile outside China.

Each political movement in China brings a tightening of tension. During the Anti-Spiritual Pollution Campaign in 1983–84, for instance, Ah Xian was drawn directly into the surveillance net on the pretext of his having painted nudes, politically unacceptable at the time. During the student demonstrations and subsequent ideological suppression in 1986–87 artists were again targeted. In late-1989, during the purges following the Tiananmen Square massacre, the 'Survivors' group, which included many artists and writers who had survived from the Democracy Wall days, was condemned as 'counter-revolutionary' and an instigating cause of the 'turmoil' that followed. Art critic Li Xianting, who curated the exhibition *Mao Goes Pop* for the Museum of Contemporary Art in Sydney in 1993, was singled out for attack, not least for his part in the astonishing *China/Avant-Garde* exhibition which took over the China Art Gallery in February 1989, just weeks before the demonstrations of that year began. Because of the sensitive nexus of cultural activity and politics, independent artists have played their role in pushing political liberalisation in China, even unwittingly, and while some can be protected by high-level connections or international fame, few are completely immune from restriction and potential harassments.

The capacity to struggle, organise and tactically engage with officialdom is perhaps born out of circumstances. As I travelled around China in those years, I was able, through the network, to meet many people – printmakers in the far north-east, supportive instructors in Wuhan, outspoken critics in Peking and Shanghai, young editors from the south-west. They were individuals whose creative energies had survived, often to remould their original training, artists whose work was able to renew the arguments between tradition and modernity, inside and outside, fecundity and control, meaning and absurdity in intriguing ways, as you can see in the woodblock prints of Xu Bing and Chen Haiyan, or in Fang Lijun's drawings or Wei Guangqing's *Yellow-covered Book* pieces.

I was wary of what was happening in the art schools, despite the esteem in which they were universally held in China, because they seemed parasitic on, and finally wasteful of, their student bodies in ways that had analogies in the Chinese system as a whole. I learned not to equate avant-gardist postures uncritically with artistic achievement. Some of the most suavely, painfully sceptical art I saw came from the heart of academic realism. *Tolerance* (1988), from Shen Jiawei's series *Gallery of Modern Chinese Historical Figures*, is a collective portrait of scholars well-known during the May Fourth Movement, symbolic of the artist's democratic-humanist aspirations. It was entered in the National Art Exhibition for 1989, yet with subtle irony subverts both Chinese history and its falsification through art.

All that I have said shows that I find it hard to separate the qualities of the art from the historical moment and the circumstances of the artists as individuals and members of their particular groups. The question then asks itself: what happens to these artists when their circumstances change, especially when, in the case of those who have left China, their relationship with the struggles of their culture and society is radically altered? The striking work produced by artists after 1989 – accentuated in the exhibitions *New Art from China* (curated by Claire Roberts in Australia in 1992) and *Mao Goes Pop* – indicated tendencies towards cynicism, satire, Pop and the entry into taboo zones of privacy, fantasy and the erotic, as if even artists who continue to work in China are seeking to de-commit themselves from socio-political engagement. But how?

For artists outside China the challenge is the give-and-take with a many-faceted international art world. At a time when Asia is being enthusiastically welcomed as a new player in contemporary art, it remains difficult for Asian artists to be understood on their own terms, especially if they wish to repudiate the role of national stereotype.

There is first a need for understanding of what is culturally specific in order to allow the cultural specifics to become legible, and even transparent, as part of a more comprehensive appreciation of the artist's work. Too often the gleeful identification of something culturally specific – 'other' – brings on an awkwardness that, in the name of cultural sensitivity, declines to comment further. Usually brash critics and reviewers, wary of seeming gauche, fall politely silent, leaving commentary to the 'experts'. Artists can feel this as but another form of obstruction and finally rejection.

Ah Xian, Xiao Xian, Guan Wei, Hou Leong, Huangpu Binghui, Kathy Huang, Jia Yong, Li Liang, Lin Chunyan, Ren Hua, Shen Jiawei, Shen Shaomin, Song Ling, Tang Song, Wang Zhiyuan, Wu Di and Xiao Lu are among the artists from China now working in Australia. They remark positively on the warm reception they have had, but often go on to note the lack of any real engagement with their work from the public. People seem reluctant to explore or interpret, as if afraid of making a mistake. This timidity – if it is not indifference – forms a barrier the artists strive to overcome by reworking those aspects of their culture that travel most successfully. They risk becoming complicit in re-inscribing a cultural stereotype, or orientalising themselves for foreign consumption. Yet to expect them to forget their own artistic and social traditions in order to be absorbed into a foreign art market is also cruel, even if it were possible, because to do so would mean cutting out too large a part of themselves. Their own travel is, after all, a cultural crossing of some moment.

Guan Wei is one artist who can take on transcultural ironies and misprisions in a cool and relaxed fashion. In his painting sequences the *Sausage* series (seen in *Localities of Desire* at the Museum of Contemporary Art in 1994) and *The Great War of the Eggplant*, (seen in *Perspecta 1995* at the Art Gallery of New South Wales), he shows himself heir to the painting traditions of his native Chinese culture, where freedom is achieved within restraint. The tight discipline he imposes on himself, in terms of form, media, colour and compositional elements, creates a zone of play where postures and impostures can be acted out, and questions asked. He performs a balancing act between an idiosyncratic private vision and the mythology he has fabricated from layers of cultural dislocation. His ordered enigmas simulate narratives that are open-ended in the ways they can be read, providing trick meanings only. They are coded, but the cultural keys are elusive, and their whimsical immediacy, with blithely populist references to cartoons, cookbooks, movies and advertising, proves deceptive alongside darker references to more destructive processes of history and politics.

The Great War of the Eggplant tells a humorous and original story of how the Chinese brought the poisonous eggplant to pre-invasion Australia. Only later, when a European went looking for Chinese knowledge in turn, was a way found to remove the poison to make the vegetable fit for human consumption. It is a bizarre allegory that turns postcolonialist pieties to absurdist play. The eggplant appeals to the artist as a form in its own right, with an amazing life of its own – erotic, procreational and cross-cultural – as the artist discovered when he researched eggplant recipes through history. Yet the vegetable, like the sausage, is not without its pathos too, as a symbol or proxy for human beings who must negotiate war and reconciliation, existence and transformation, survival and consumption. It is a fantastic story – with parallels to the artist's own story of moving from China to Australia – of moments achieved, only to have them lost in the necessary move on to something else, a process of imbalances resolved at stages along the way in stunning acts of resonant equilibrium.

At the point of maximum desire for communication from one being to another, or from one culture and history to another, however, Guan Wei remains quizzical – and this quality gives his work its captivating mixture of urgency and detachment. In an anecdote the artist tells, 'Wonderful!' was the third word of English he learned when he arrived in this country, after 'Yes' and 'No'. Levels of mutual incomprehension were such that he soon found it better to reply 'Wonderful!' in response to anything he didn't understand – until he nearly ruined a friendship by responding to someone else's personal tragedy with an exclamation of 'Wonderful!' In this complex sense, Guan Wei's 'Wonderful!' is a hybrid, and makes the perfect comment on his art.

Artists seek new ways of codifying. In language one speaker must learn the language of the other. In art perhaps something different is possible – the invention of a crossover language that works for particular encounters, while needing no grammar outside itself. For me, anyway, the best new Chinese art offers the viewer the adventure of interpreting a hybrid visual language for which there is no textbook beyond the complex encounter of history and contemporaneity that has brought it into existence. In communicating between two worlds, that is shamanistic enough for me.

1994

Eunuch culture

My first warning that China was heading for a crisis came from a poet friend: towards the end of 1988 he told me not to think of leaving for another twelve months because in that time the country would blow apart.

As an agricultural journalist, he travelled the length and breadth of China and, like Cinna in Shakespeare's *Julius Caesar*, also a poet, had 'seen strange sights' – high inflation, rampant profiteering, millions of itinerant workers drifting towards the cities. The uncertain grain supply had created a gut fear in people who had known famine a generation earlier; an apocalyptic, end-of-dynasty mentality was taking hold. True to his status as scholar-gentleman, my friend feared chaos almost more than he desired change. His name was Duo Duo, another of the Democracy Wall and *Today* group of poets, who had been renamed the 'Misty Poets' as their work became more fashionably obscure.

In February 1989, when the 'Survivors' converged on Peking, Wei Jingsheng, the democracy advocate whom Deng Xiaoping made a scapegoat, was still in prison, economic reform was out of control, and demands for political reform were close on its heels. Some 'Survivors' returned from exile abroad, to celebrate the tenth anniversary of the Democracy Wall with the founding of a society, a publication and a prize. Middle-aged social responsibility mixed with their desire to keep the avant-garde torch burning. A cultural happening was planned for 8 April, narrowly skirting 5 April, the day on which Chinese remember their dead – which in 1976 occasioned the original Tiananmen Incident, a protest against Mao Zedong and the Gang of Four, in the form of mass mourning for Premier Zhou Enlai, Mao's deputy, who was perceived as a good counsellor. Tickets were hot, and the Central Drama Institute was staked with police. It was hard to say whether it was the most open underground activity for a decade, or the new establishment's takeover of the state's customary role in organising anniversaries. In the old Eastern Europe it would have turned out to be the latter. Distinguished free-thinking elders, such as astrophysicist Fang Lizhi, his wife Li Shuxian, and playwright Wu Zuguang, victims of earlier anti-liberal campaigns, graced the occasion, which consisted of poetry recitation staged with lights and electronic music, performance pieces, and rock music. A woman wrapped in plastic was painted all over, to symbolise the smothering of individuality – or was it libido? Mang Ke's friend Guo Lusheng, a middle-aged poet who had been an underground inspiration during the Cultural Revolution and had since suffered electric shock therapy for so-called 'nervous disorders', movingly read his poem of twenty years earlier:

> *Friend, trust firmly in the future,*
> *Trust in unyielding effort,*
> *Trust in the victory of youth over death,*
> *Trust the future, trust life.*

Openly anti-Party, individualistic, western – 'culturally nihilistic' in the jargon – it was also passionately idealistic and patriotic. Rumour was that it would be closed down, but it wasn't, signifying that artists could get away with almost anything. It could have been a new way of drawing the teeth of opposition. There was a fund-raising sale of avant-garde artworks in a rehearsal room, to which access was restricted, because the beer was free. The only riot of the evening occurred when those excluded stormed the door of the art space to get at the grog.

A week later the first people took to the streets in mourning, this time for Hu Yaobang, who had died – of anger, it was said, at being dumped as Party Secretary for opposing extremist policies. He was now a posthumous good guy. The demonstrations that culminated in the 4 June massacre had begun. When the authorities reckoned up the causes of the 'turmoil' some months later, the evening of performance art on 8 April was labelled an unauthorised meeting that incited counter-revolution.

At the time it had been merely an event at which to be seen. But the writers and artists involved were locked into a political culture that saw art as necessarily progressive. Their art could only find itself in attacking or subverting a reactionary status quo. 'Trust the future' presupposes a transformation of the present. If there is no chance of such a transformation, the only option is despair.

Part of the performance evening was a candlelit recitation in memory of a young poet, Haizi, a law graduate from Peking University, who had thrown himself in front of a train ten days earlier. He wrote the lyric 'Four Sisters' on 23 February 1989, just before his death:

> *Atop a desolate ridge stand four sisters*
> *for whom alone all the winds blow*
> *for whom alone all the days are shattered.*
> *A stalk of grain high as my head waves in the air.*
> *Standing atop this desolate ridge*
> *I remember my empty room, covered in dust.*
>
> *Four sisters embracing a stalk of grain*
> *that waves in the air*
> *embrace yesterday's snow, today's rain*
> *tomorrow's flour, tomorrow's ashes:*
> *it is the grain of despair.*
> *Please tell those sisters, it is the grain of despair*

it will always be this way.
Behind the wind there is wind
beyond the sky there is sky
beyond this road continues the road.

Just as the 8 April meeting retrospectively became a counter-revolutionary event, so Haizi's suicide has been fused with the Peking massacre. The hundreds of poems discovered among his papers have become one expression of the moment and the movement.

Before the protests had started in earnest on 15 April, artistic expressions of dissent were in search of a focus. In poetry, fiction and drama, visual art, film and pop music, keeping up-to-date quickly became a matter of running on the spot to stay in step with the latest imported fashion, of daring to do what had already been done elsewhere. Chinese culture had encountered one of the legacies of modernisation – the problem of lateness.

Duo Duo's *Selected Poems*, published underground, was launched at a lugubrious cocktail party in early 1989 in Peking. It was run like a Party meeting by fellow poet Bei Dao, who was asserting his leadership of the younger poets' community after his recent return from abroad. Each guest had to make a speech in praise of Duo Duo, who became all things to all speakers. Pop singer Hou Dejian, who had defected from Taiwan to the mainland in 1983, noted that performers had to endure heckling from the audience – unlike poets. He unveiled a new song called 'Get Off the Stage'. Once the protest movement started, the song was taken up as a chant to sing at China's leaders. Hou Dejian became a hunger striker in Tiananmen Square when the momentum of protest was waning after the declaration of martial law. He was carried out of the Square on a stretcher, hidden under a blanket. He made it to the diplomatic compound. Many weeks later he was allowed to return to his home in safety. But he couldn't keep quiet about his political views, so the Chinese authorities threw him back to Taiwan.

I last saw Duo Duo in Tiananmen Square in the early hours of the morning a few days before the massacre. Like Cinna, he was moved 'to wander forth of doors'. He was filling time before his flight to London to participate in a poetry festival. He had a ticket for 4 June. I next heard his voice on the BBC, speaking from London on 6 June. Cinna was accused of being a conspirator, and torn apart. Duo Duo had escaped Cinna's fate and became a hero. His poems were rapidly published by Bloomsbury as *Looking Out from Death*. The death to which he referred was actually that of his baby daughter some years before, but it had become a metaphor. He had ridden a wave on to the international circuit – for a time.

The movement and the crackdown re-established conditions of creativity that were familiar and venerated in China. Artists and audiences alike understood the context of struggle, repression, sacrifice and patriotism.

The festivals and commemorations that dot the Chinese calendar express a preoccupation with numbers and cycles. The dynasty legitimates itself through celebrating its high days and holy places, and the Communist Party has been no exception. May Fourth, Yanan, Tiananmen Square: such moments and places are sacred, open to claim and counterclaim, interpretation and re-interpretation. They exist in time and space, but also in a realm of myth. Analogies can be found elsewhere, for example in the history and historiography of seventeenth-century England, where absolutist monarchy contended with a parliament that became revolutionary. The scaffold that Charles I mounted to lose his head and crown also became a disputed site.

In China the struggles of the present are understood and aggrandised through relationships with events of the past that are ordained and reinforced by the powerful traditionalism of Chinese society. In seventeenth-century England, the debate about Charles I's head was couched in terms of the Norman yoke and the rights of free Britons, and of the pros and cons of an earlier historical precedent, Brutus's assassination of Julius Caesar. For the Chinese, tradition is embodied in the written language rather than in notions of the common weal and common law. It is the inscribing of a name that brings an event into the domain of proper discourse and into alignment with sanctioned historical fact and wisdom. The name must be the right one. Inscribing the appropriate name is the key rite of the Confucian scholar-minister, since it involves bringing what is happening in human life into line with what is written in the classics. Fixing the right name is the statesman's solemn act of setting human affairs to rights. The protest movement was set on its tragic course when the official government newspaper, under instructions from Deng Xiaoping, defined the demonstrations in mourning for Hu Yaobang as 'activities designed to instigate counter-revolution'. That was the name given. In defiant response, the demonstrations grew, with the demand that the movement should be redefined as 'patriotic'.

The problem of naming continues unresolved, with Peking's disgruntled intellectuals recognising that until the 4 June 'peaceful suppression of counter-revolutionary rebellion' is re-classified as a fascist crime against the people – which can happen after Deng's death – Tiananmen 1989 is still unfinished business.

The students' appeal for their movement to be labelled 'patriotic' was partly a claim that the 1989 movement represented the rightful continuation of the patriotic May Fourth democratic movement in which students and intellectuals demanded that China strengthen itself against foreign incursions into its territory. There are photographs of students demonstrating at Tiananmen in the summer of 1919: photographs taken in May 1989 show that, seventy years later, the location, the style and even the slogans have not changed. May Fourth provided a glorious precedent, and gave the 1989 students a place in history, making them at the same time part of a re-enactment.

Political twists and turns in the People's Republic have been heralded by political campaigns and mass movements often described as 'stage-managed', 'concerted', 'orchestrated'. The language indicates a quality of performance, taking place within accepted guidelines. 'Ironically,' as Geremie Barmé has written, 'movements have become the most natural form of popular political expression for the people themselves ... Although the style of participation in a movement is rigidly limited and the process itself quite routinised, it is a charade with a deadly significance, a form of mass theatre that can have devastating consequences.'

The tents and banners that covered Tiananmen Square in 1989 were the props of street theatre. The huge posters on the monument proclaiming 'Hunger Strike' were also announcing a new oppositional rite to be performed in this sacramental place. A portrait of Hu Yaobang, painted by students from the Central Academy of Fine Arts, was erected in the Square opposite the portrait of Chairman Mao Zedong: a subversive icon in a political play. Later Mao's portrait was splashed with paint, in an act of defilement that was also the creation of a new agitprop image. Dancing, snack-vending, speechmaking, love-making and display laps by the Flying Tigers motorbike squad were other carnivalesque activities, while those with more important roles – the ambulance escorts, the hygiene monitors, the persuaders and the power-brokers – comported themselves with the rhetorical gestures of high political drama: sirens, loudhailers, spotlights, cameras, manifestos, press releases, sallies and withdrawals. A group of drama students formed a ring of bodies around a makeshift altar where a hunger-striking comrade lay in the sacral space, beneath a lurid banner that quoted May Fourth author Lu Hsun's heart-felt 'CRY!' The colours of headbands and other costume details, together with slogans and caricatures carried aloft on banners, contributed to the iconography of the huge festive pageant. One example was the cartoon of an overturned stool or *dengzi*, homophonous with the surname of the paramount leader. The smashed 'little bottles' (*xiao ping*), homophonous with Deng Xiaoping's given names, became a recurrent symbol of the movement.

The inversion of iconography confirmed that this was a 'world turned upside-down', to use the phrase taken from seventeenth-century English radicals by historian Christopher Hill to describe his English 'century of revolution'. It was an initially festal re-enactment of anarchy designed to admonish corruption and reinstate decency, order and good government. Behind it lay perhaps a Rousseauean ideal commonwealth, a version of pastoral. When the police had been forced off the streets and the students took over the tasks of law and order, the citizenry became more polite, decent and harmonious than I ever knew them in Peking before or after. Literary critic Ian Donaldson comments on the role of carnivalesque festivity: 'A society with an acute sense of the necessity of everyday social distinctions allowed itself briefly to re-enact an apparently "ideal" state of anarchy which it had no wish to bring permanently into being.' He is writing, in *The World Upside Down* (a title echoed by historian Christopher Hill), about early modern England.

The supreme symbol of the anarchic – or democratic – ideal in China's case was presented when student leader Wu'er Kaixi, at that stage a virtually unknown member of the student body, pushed forward by the throng, was received at the Great Hall of the People in his pyjamas and carrying his intravenous drip, weak from the hunger strike. Premier Li Peng was tense and twitchy as he heard out the young student's demands for reform. Nationally telecast, it was a classic tableau of the role reversal that can be implied in the cry of liberty: the leader is reduced to the level of the student dorm, while the student enters the palace.

The authorities later said that the 1989 movement had developed because of slackened control over education and ideology, including culture. The parameters of artistic activity subsequently altered and narrowed. A firm line of opposition to 'bourgeois liberalisation' was pushed, and a temporarily heightened political consciousness only made artists and their audiences keener to find subversive meanings. The revolutionary model operas, revived in the theatres, were greeted with nostalgia for a time against which the cynical present regime could be found wanting. A television series celebrating the triumphal history of communism was popular for documentary footage that could be decoded to tell another story. With a restricted diet of news and information through the media, rumour and gossip flourished – what Peking playwright Liu Shugang calls 'folk literature' – extraordinarily inventive, scurrilous, hilarious, often deadly accurate, running like a communally produced soap opera. It can be manipulated, but never entirely; it can be contradicted, but never suppressed. It bounces back and forth between palace and people, creating a charged ground for disbelief, mockery, inversion and exposure.

Film production froze after the events of 4 June 1989. Folk literature had associated Deng Xiaoping with the Empress Dowager, who is a popular topic for film and television drama. Searching for a permissible topic, some film-makers lighted on Li Lienying, the powerful eunuch adviser to the Empress Dowager. The film *Li Lienying* turned out to be a subtle study of what happens when an individual surrenders to a subservient relationship with a hierarchical power, what the film-makers Tian Zhuangzhuang and Jiang Wen called 'eunuch culture'. There is a scene in which Li Lienying orders that a group of reformers within the palace be beaten to death. The cruelty and callousness are dwelt upon: the reformers are bent over, locked into stocks, while their spines are slowly beaten to bloody pulp. The audience needed no more specific allusion to the Tiananmen massacre. The film's final image, in which Li Lienying as an old man flips over onto his back, like a turtle, and dies because he cannot right himself, speaks eloquently of the enfeeblement of the once-mighty.

On stage too, only tried-and-true socialist classics could be performed. Lao She's 1957 play *Teahouse*, a panorama of Peking life over some fifty years from the Manchus to the dawning of New China, had been performed hundreds of times in its original production, defining the achievement, and limitations, of drama in the People's Republic. It had become a sacred cow. When it was revived for the Asian Games celebrations in 1990, as virtually the only play deemed safe enough, it became a rallying point. There is a moment in Act III when police agents beat up intellectuals who are protesting against Kuomintang spinelessness. A poster on the teahouse wall says 'Please Don't Discuss State Affairs'. But the owner accuses the police agents: If you beat up lawful protesters, does that make their protest *unlawful*? The line was greeted with cheers and applause from the audience. The show became a sell-out, the houses full of young students. The Peking authorities, considerably embarrassed, had to meet to discuss taking the play off. Once again, the tightened political environment had breathed new life into art. Even George Bernard Shaw's *Major Barbara*, staged in 1991, proved susceptible to a similar, subversive re-invigoration.

Given its hothouse nature as the capital of a society that stresses cultural continuity to the point of claustrophobia, Peking provides fertile ground to observe the energies, creative and destructive, that immersion in the processes of history and politics can give to art. The excitement of an artist's struggle to reclaim part of the historical or cultural heritage for a particular contemporary moment can be a difficult quality for the critic to gauge. It requires attention to the interaction between public and private meanings, between orthodoxy and subversion in the contemporary reshaping of received stories and images.

Certain periods and environments are more likely than others to generate double-edged political art. Nat Lee's play *Lucius Junius Brutus* was received 'with great applause' on the London stage in 1680, but taken off after six performances because of 'very scandalous expressions and reflections upon the government'. Lee's Brutus gives his blueprint for national reconstruction:

> . . . *a Balanc'd Trade,*
> *Patriots incourag'd, Manufactors cherish'd,*
> *Vagabonds, Walkers, Drones, and Swarming Braves,*
> *The Froth of States, scum'd from the Common-wealth:*
> *Idleness banish'd, all excess repress'd,*
> *And Riots check'd by Sumptuary Laws.*
> *O, Conscript Fathers, 'tis on these Foundations*
> *That Rome shall build her Empire to the Stars.*

The language here is stimulated by the cunning excitement of veiled debates. In being a poet, Nat Lee, like the poets of Peking, has become political actor, a conspirator too.

1991

The beat goes on

'You are at the centre of the world,' said a friend who called me from London during the Tiananmen Square demonstrations. It was as if the Middle Kingdom had once again earned its name. In Tiananmen Square a drama of protest was being enacted that would change the course of China's history. The world watched avidly. Never before had China's political life been available for so close a scrutiny week after week, proving more compulsive than soap opera and as elemental as Greek tragedy. The full weight of the world's reporting and analytical powers was brought to bear. How ironical, after the excitement died down, that people started to wonder if they really knew what had happened.

I was warned by a wise old woman before I first came to China that it was a very different country. Many of the foreign observers who arrived cold in China in 1989 to cover Soviet President Mikhail Gorbachev's May visit were unprepared for the demonstrations that had been growing since late April, and didn't know what to make of them. For some it was People Power from day one, with the triumph of democracy inevitable. The estimates they made of the number of participants often had a nought too many. Swept up on the all-but-spontaneous student activism, reporters failed to consider what might be going on in the black hole that passes for China's top leadership, where it must have been clear all along that the demonstration would end in suppression. China's difference is indeed considerable. The Philippines and Poland, for example, offered only distant points of comparison. There have been atrocities in Tibet, and earlier in the history of the People's Republic, of which we have only the vaguest idea. The brutal suppression of the pro-democracy movement in the heart of the capital, where all could see, conveniently for us and inconveniently for the Chinese leadership, provided an opportunity to put the record somewhat straight.

A diplomat was quoted in the September 1989 issue of the *Independent Monthly* as saying: 'There are no facts.' How diplomatic can you get? If there are no facts about what happened in Peking, there are no facts anywhere. Eyewitness accounts, photographs, footage, bullet holes, tank treads, scars, missing people. Are these not facts? There are difficulties, of course, in assembling the information into a coherent, verifiable picture of what happened. Caution must be exercised in extrapolating from individual versions to an overview. What happened in Peking was not a television drama series in which no threads were left hanging. But to acknowledge that new information might lead to revision of original accounts, in the interests of greater accuracy, is quite different from saying as in the *Independent Monthly*'s headline, 'We Got It Wrong'.

It is unedifying for journalists to quibble over the figures of how many people were killed, where and at what time, with the sneering implication that the whole thing could have been a beat-up. The terms can be defined so narrowly that it can be truthfully stated that between 4 and 5 am on 4 June in a certain central area of Tiananmen Square very few people were killed. But that is a schoolboy debating tactic. Richard Nations of London's *Spectator* has movingly described how the Tolstoyan pop singer Hou Dejian joined forces with the Dostoevskyan literary critic Liu Xiaobo to persuade the last group of students to forsake empty self-sacrifice and peacefully leave the Square. Liu Xiaobo was imprisoned and interrogated, probably under torture; his account has not been made fully available. Hou Dejian's account, published in Hong Kong in August

1989 after he came out of hiding, confirms Nations's story. Hou adds that at that time and place, with his own eyes, he saw no one killed. It impugns neither report to add, however, that not all the people whom Nations and Hou Dejian saw move off safely actually made it home. Nor does either report conflict with Amnesty International's conservative conclusion of 1300 dead and many thousands injured. There was a massacre. It happened all over the city, but was concentrated in the area that the locals refer to as Tiananmen.

I suspect that journalists, like all of us, have a certain amount of bad faith towards their profession. A journalist's aim is to be there on the spot when the big story breaks. That is the *raison d'être* of 'our correspondent in Peking'. But it is not surprising that a journalist, whose code of ethics is to guard against distortion, is the one who knows best how easy it is to con the public with sensational sets of words, images and figures. And the Australian public, whose perception of a place like China might be little more than a weird and wonderful congeries of images, will run with the sensation. In a postmodern culture, where everything is believed and disbelieved with equal halfheartedness, the time will come when the sensation dies down, the words and images will be replaced by others, and people will start asking: 'Did it really happen?'

Such modish scepticism, which prefers hypothetical interpretations to fact, suits the betrayed lover. Australia, with other Western countries, was hurt by the break-up of its love affair with China. When the outrage wears off, the pain is soothed by confessing that you don't really know what happened, that you never understood and that you don't care if you never see her again. The attitude approaches that of the Chinese government, which insists that foreigners should not meddle in China's internal affairs because they do not know the whole story and cannot understand. Many ordinary Chinese take a quite different attitude, placing on the West, especially Western media, the responsibility of broadcasting a truthful record of their plight.

The current regime in China has put its hopes in its capacity to make people doubt the facts. By suggesting that uncertainty about some of the details could lead to a major revision of what happened, the *Independent Monthly*'s correspondents play into the hands of those orchestrating 'the big lie'. In Peking, propaganda is a form of hermeneutics in which as much depends on eroding reality as on fabricating falsehoods. In an interview with a French journalist, Premier Li Peng showed his skill as a master of the art of interpretation. He said:

Doubtless you saw the sequence in which a man remained unmoving as a tank approached him, finally persuading the tank driver to stop. These images convinced President George Bush that the man was an extraordinary man, single-handedly able to stop a column of tanks. But there is another explanation. If one looks at the sequence objectively, doesn't it display the humanitarian aspect of the Chinese army and the orders of non-violence that had been given? As if a man could stop a tank all by himself.

According to an account widely circulated in the West, army tanks rolled over people in Tiananmen Square, with blood flowing in streams, bodies reduced to minced meat. But I am sure you have not seen pictures actually showing someone being crushed by a tank.

If you've seen it, says Li Peng, it doesn't mean what you think it means. If you haven't seen it, it didn't happen.

The propaganda campaign continued on a massive scale, working its way into all areas of society. From senior officials and teachers to hotel employees and taxi drivers, people spent days watching videos of the 'peaceful quelling of the counter-revolutionary rebellion', studying texts, hearing speeches, and being asked to explain their behaviour around 3–4 June. Fortunately, if they could stay awake, they too could exploit the art of ambiguous interpretation. 'I am clear now, I understand, I know what really happened,' they say and, if they're lucky, they pass. Meanwhile, every night the television news lists half a dozen bumper harvests. The mood of the people of Peking is another kind of fact: not quite as palpable as the stone with which Dr Johnson refuted Bishop Berkeley, but almost. A city is not easily filled with a sense of moral anger and righteous hatred – not to mention shock, anguish and despondency so profound as that which existed in the weeks afterwards.

Autumn is the favoured season in Peking, a time of brilliant blue skies and golden days, of festivals and abundance. The market stalls groan with grapes as big as plums, crisp Chinese pears, mountains of melons, and the mutton carcasses brought in for the Mongolian hotpot that is eaten as the weather gets colder. The quality of produce is better than it used to be, thanks to the reforms, including the increased use of chemicals in farming, but inflation has driven prices dramatically higher. People are still buying, but this year there is a sense of garnering in. The price offered by the money-changers has dropped. There is a move away from imported goods. The demand for colour television sets has eased, perhaps in revulsion at the propaganda campaign waged on TV: short-wave radios are a hot item for listening to the Voice of America and BBC.

The government has ordered an austerity campaign, and the people have responded in their own way by battening down the hatches. Families are making long-term plans. There is a widespread but unspoken feeling that things could get worse before they get better. Economic collapse, famine, even civil war, are not impossible, and the spectre of the latter has made many people determined to get out of China. The government distributes largesse – eggs and fish – to mark the festival period, and then orders employees to buy government bonds to the value of a month's pay. He that giveth also taketh away.

The real festival this autumn is the 100 days anniversary of the Peking massacre, and the regime is reaping what it has sown in a harvest of popular alienation.

The students at Peking University, subject to intensive re-education and threatened with assignment to the countryside on graduation, bang their chopsticks on the canteen tables and hoot when the newly-appointed hard-line president speaks. They slow-march around campus, lugubriously singing, 'Without the Communist Party there'd be no New China'. A solitary old woman burns paper in a residential courtyard to mourn the death of her son on 4 June, and the neighbours gather silently. A young man jumps to his death in front of the martial law troops, from the bridge where the tanks were stationed. On a streetside stall, the bookseller draws browsers' attention to an essay by Yan Jiaqi, one of the dissidents now organising abroad. All night long, people are losing themselves in a purposeless frenzy of gambling, clicking the 144 mahjong pieces, which they satirically call 'Reading the 144th Directive of Deng Xiaoping'. Others respond in a more upbeat way, wearing smarter clothes, more make-up, wilder hairstyles – as if, in the sophistication born of the new-found clarity with which they regard their rulers, they are determined to indulge their 'bourgeois liberalisation' to the utmost.

The regime seems to be nervous, paying paranoid and counter-productive attention to detail in the measures taken to stop further unrest. How crass to erect the styrofoam sculpture of united workers, peasants, intellectuals and soldiers where the Goddess of Democracy had stood in Tiananmen Square! For Peking is a city which has not been permitted to grieve for its dead, and the festering grief and shock have produced a lasting defiance, which is the most threatening possible force in a society based on deference. The empty, cordoned-off square at the heart of the state remains haunted ground, an unavoidable reminder. And while this mood continues people are waiting, edgily, for the next explosion.

The determination of a people is not something that can be seen in an organised resistance or spelled out in manifestos, and for that reason it is impossible for the regime to dispel it. Whatever restrictions are imposed, the spirit of 1989 will find its way.

At Liubukou, outside the forbidden quarters where China's leaders live, and where one of the bloodiest encounters took place on 4 June – like doubting Thomas I have seen the bullet hole in a friend's leg – a new nightclub opened, valiantly continuing the entrepreneurial spirit. A newly formed Chinese band is playing. They call themselves '1989 Love You'. The place is packed, jumping to versions of 'Hey Joe', 'Get Back' and 'Let It Bleed' only metres from where hundreds of people were bleeding only weeks before, in one of the grimmest nights of recent Chinese history. The point is lost on no one. When the band concludes its gig with one of the obligatory patriotic songs, they turn 'Without the Communist Party there'd be no New China' into a weird, cacophonous twenty-minute improvisation that can be interpreted as a musical re-enactment of events still imprinted on everyone's mind. It is electrifying. Nothing is said, and nothing needs to be said.

There are those who claim that the situation in Peking has returned to normal. There are photographs of tourists going to the Great Wall, of old men exercising their birds, of children singing charming songs for the leaders, and merchants signing deals. As the poet W.H. Auden observed, the farmers in the field don't even look up as Icarus falls from the sky, and 'the torturer's horse scratches its innocent behind on a tree' even as the torturer goes about his work.

But look again. The dangerous liaisons and secret meetings go on, and people disappear in the middle of the night. Perhaps the civil war has already begun, in a clash of cultures and values, regions and generations. Let us hope that moderation and pragmatism prevail, and that a way forward is found, before the armies line up to fight again.

1989

Screen dreams

'The old man is fond of dragons,' she said. 'It's one of our sayings. This old guy was a dragon fanatic. He studied them, painted them, filled his house with toy dragons. One day a real dragon popped its head in the window. The old guy died of fright. It means you like the idea of a thing, but you can't cope with the reality.'

Writers having their novels turned into film or television drama are rather like the old man in the Chinese saying, quoted here in a passage of dialogue transferred verbatim from my novel *Avenue of Eternal Peace* to its television adaptation, the mini-series *Children of the Dragon*, shown on ABC television in 1992. Dreams can turn into nightmares when they come true. Stories abound in the film industry of writers of original works storming off the set, cursing and suing. As complaints are almost mandatory when the final product turns out to be based on the book more 'loosely' than expected, let me say at the outset that I have found the experience fascinating and instructive. I am happy about the way I have been treated personally, and relieved that the end result works so well on its own terms.

But the process of transformation was as complex as they all seem to be. *Avenue of Eternal Peace* weaves together a web of stories set mostly in Peking in 1986. The main strand concerns an Australian cancer specialist who, having failed to prevent his wife's death from cancer, goes to China in search of insight into non-Western approaches to the disease. Discovering an old Chinese professor who may have known his grandfather, who worked as a doctor in China at the turn of the century, Wally Frith also discovers that East and West are one, at least in the human struggle with mortality. The Chinese woman he has fallen in love with is revealed as the professor's granddaughter, but she stays behind at the end when the Australian returns home to continue his work. Running alongside Wally Frith's story are the stories of other Pekingers, local and expatriate, which culminate in the eruption of protest demonstrations, swiftly suppressed, in Tiananmen Square in December 1986.

The novel evolved from ideas with which I went to China, to teach Australian Studies, in early 1986. The draft was completed by the end of 1987. My agent Rosemary Creswell showed it to independent Sydney-based producer John Edwards, who excitedly took up an option – eighteen months before the more famous Tiananmen Square demonstrations of April–June 1989. A year later Sandra Levy, then head of ABC TV Drama, had joined forces with Edwards to form the production company, Xanadu, and Robert Caswell (*Scales of Justice*, *Evil Angels*) was signed to work on the screenplay. I had accepted an appointment as cultural counsellor at the Australian embassy in Peking, where my time was taken up with a bonanza of bicentenary cultural exchanges. Revision and editing were delayed, and the novel was finally scheduled for publication in mid-1989. As the 1989 protest movement unfolded on television screens around the world, Xanadu and its British partner Zenith, with encouragement from the ABC and the BBC, renewed their commitment to the project and sent associate producer Wayne Barry, designer Murray Picknett, and China consultant Linda Jaivin on a research trip to China. They were there when the massacre happened on 3–4 June. By the time I was evacuated to Canberra, the publishers already saw that my book could be associated with the momentous events that have come to be known in shorthand as Tiananmen Square.

Wanting to distinguish the novel from the quickies that would soon appear, and to acknowledge that the events and personages in my black comedy, originally entitled 'Searching for the Shaman', and later 'Crackers', were to be perceived through a new, tragic frame, I added an afterword connecting the conclusion of my fiction in 1986 with the historical developments to 1989. The title was changed to the more sombrely ironic *Avenue of Eternal Peace*. Xanadu, by now merged with Southern Star, liked the title and commissioned Caswell to rework the script in the direction of a political thriller culminating in Tiananmen Square. I was called in to have a look at that script early in 1990.

Names and characters had been altered as the scriptwriter put his mark on the material. Blundering Australian Wally became angry Englishman Will Flint, the flinty male will at the heart of a new age parable about learning to own your pain under the higher spiritual/erotic influence of the mystic East. Caswell and his partner visited China for three days during one of the epochal moments of modern Chinese history and laid their mineral water at the feet of the million or so demonstrators filling Tiananmen Square, before the pollution, Chinese food, heavy smoking and spiritual bankruptcy of the place compelled them to leave. Back in Los Angeles after the massacre, Caswell's commitment to the struggle of the Chinese people surfaced in his readiness to continue with the project, and his inspired idea to re-focus the story on youth. It was the foreign doctor's son, not his wife, who had died, and his Chinese lover was given a daughter, one of the idealistic student leaders whose safety is threatened after the military crackdown Those young Chinese are the 'children of the dragon' (referring to the pop song by activist Hou Dejian sung in the Square) who dare to challenge the dragon: a title arrived at after months of debate between the British and Australian production partners. As a brilliant technician, Caswell did a construction job on the script that imposed a drama of self-channelling, self-realisation and democratic determination onto the quite different structure of the novel, which leads through an apparent maze to the open-ended awareness that East and West form a false opposition.

In the mini-series Will and the girl student manage to escape on a

Qantas jumbo, in a gripping rework of the Casablanca ending, while the Chinese are left behind to fend for themselves. Changes to the script meant that, to avoid human and financial risk, the arrangements made through Jaivin with a television production group in Peking had to be abandoned for a shoot done predominantly in Australia, offering employment as extras to thousands of the Chinese students who flocked here round that time. One extra appeared on set at the reconstruction of Tiananmen Square on a airfield outside Sydney wearing the same clothes he had worn to demonstrate in Tiananmen Square in Peking – and was told by wardrobe to go and change into something less colourful.

The visual recreation of China, however, and the look of the production as a whole, are a remarkable achievement. Locations identified by Picknett on his visits to Peking were recreated with great attention to detail, with help from Chinese production staff who had film and television experience in Peking.

Casting proved to be more problematic. The vagaries of co-production meant that alongside Bob Peck as an Englishman working in Australia was Australian actor Linda Cropper as the American feminist/bimbo Monica, a character invented for the adaptation (replacing the novel's more idiosyncratic Dulcia) to lure American interest. Local Chinese communities were searched high and low for a leading lady who could act in both Mandarin and English, and who had the right mix of sharpness and austerity to play a middle-aged Northern Chinese intellectual, beautiful without being glitzy. Lily Chen, a Chinese costume-drama star, was eventually brought from Texas. Stilted though her performance and delivery are at times, reflecting in part different conventions of acting and body language, she seems to me right in the part.

The production gave opportunities to a great many local Chinese performers, some of whom were found through casting agents, others through restaurant searches and other grassroots activity. There are some real finds, such as Linda Hsia (from Radio Australia, Melbourne) and Mimi Phu, daughter of a great Chinese stage star, who should put paid once and for all to the excuse that Asian parts cannot be written in Australian drama because they cannot be cast. There are also some regrettable cases of 'all-Asians-look-the-same' casting. The Chinese opera in Peking is sung by a Sydney-based *Cantonese* troupe. Filipinos and Indonesians masquerade as citizens of Peking – rather like some of the boat people, who apparently come from Guangxi near the China–Vietnam border area, but claim to be political refugees from Peking.

The gay relationship loses impact through casting against type in the case of Gary Sweet and his Chinese boyfriend, who is presented in a studious Hong Kong image rather than the haughty, histrionic style favoured in Peking – and perhaps also because the screenplay and direction have a general residual awkwardness about Chinese sexuality, falling for oriental clichés despite strenuous efforts to avoid doing so. The hardest part to cast, interestingly, was the old Chinese professor. Actors in China were traditionally regarded as little better than courtesans. An elderly actor was more likely to be suited to playing the scheming eunuch or the old queen than the dignified Western-educated professional. The old are also cautious in China, having learned too much about the pendulum swings of policy. For this reason the senior actors in China and senior scholars and professionals from the Chinese community in Australia who were approached for the part invariably turned it down. It is a worldwide shortage, which has created a niche for one Chinese actor based in the United States who specialises in playing Chinese sages. He is much in demand at a price well beyond the budget of this production. Shooting had already started when Wan Thye Liew, an amateur Cantonese opera enthusiast from Adelaide, was brought forward from among the extras. He gives a charming performance.

Questions of authenticity can be academic. Neither novel nor television drama claim strict factual accuracy. But the changes and transformations that are made in the interests of creating a story, tightening a scene, attracting investors, coming in under budget or, most fundamentally, making the product compatible with expectations of the makers and the hoped-for audiences, reveal social and cultural attitudes at work. Historical drama stylises and concentrates material, and in the process distorts. In *Children of the Dragon* the corruption the Chinese students protest against is dramatised as the passing of a cash bribe to a shady go-between, a simple and blatant act that can be shown clearly in a television scene. The all-pervasive, invisible, decorous and far more insidious institutionalised corruption of the society is beyond our television's capacities. The student protester is shot in front of his foreign lover's eyes in Tiananmen Square. With legal exactitude the Chinese authorities could claim that no such thing happened and that to show it as happening is to fall victim to the designs of propagandists intent on subverting the Chinese state. If it happened, it would have been just *outside* Tiananmen Square. But the economies of representation dispense with such niceties.

Much of the adaptation has a cartoon-like logic and directness, reflecting an American style of television. It was a tendency resisted in production by director Peter Smith (*A Perfect Spy*) in favour of a slower, more intricate, more ironically literate unfolding – in the BBC mould with which Smith and Peck are more comfortable. The British style of leisurely bemusement was in turn resisted by the Chinese involved in the production, led by director's assistant Wang Ziyin, who wanted a tough, raw, passionate quality, even if at the expense of polish. Interpersonal and intercultural frictions have bequeathed to the finished product a powerful kind of tension, warts and all, that meshes with the narrative-focused direction and Peck's highly strung performance. At times the expressions on Peck's face, on the umpteenth take, suggest he is doing the acting for all the participants in the scene at once

The strength of tradition and the weight of history, the invasion of personal lives by social control, the desperation for change, the supportive yet burdensome webs of relationships, the ineptness of Westerners in the encounter: such central issues of China are pursued down a winding path until we are brought to the blood-stained centre. *Children of the Dragon* deals with the drama of China with a maturity and range that, given the constraints, may not be easily matched by other international screen versions of the events surrounding Tiananmen Square 1989.

Cultural materialists use sophisticated methodologies to analyse television drama, and television drama responds to such interest in its procedures. From *Twin Peaks* to *GP*, the product offered is highly sensitised to the ways in which its structures will be decodified, its messages read.

Television drama is engaged in what the Propaganda Department in the People's Republic of China would call 'thought work', with big rewards if it is got right. The changes made in adapting literary works carry the hidden meanings a Chinese writer would recognise when warned by television authorities that some changes to the script will be required. It is a process of bringing into line, for a greater good. The often eccentric and private world of a novel must be changed if it is to be communicated to the potentially larger screen audience. The story must be made to work. It must have no stray elements, no redundant characters. It must, ultimately, suit the taste of the makers, whose job is to second-guess the taste of the consumers.

Taste, a neat eighteenth-century invention, is designed to harmonise the potentially conflicting areas of enduring truths and passing fashion, personal choice and social desiderata. It looms ever larger in a society where everyone is watching everyone else to find out what is 'correct' and hence what will take off. The marketing manager and the contemporary moralist occupy the same space.

1992

Green oil

Media images of Australia/Asia

My guide to the island of Rodrigues, a little-known adjunct of Mauritius, where part of my novel *The Rose Crossing* (1994) is set, was François Leguat, a Huguenot who was part of a short-lived settlement there in 1691–93, the place's first human habitation, of any kind, apparently. His detailed account of the island, *Voyages et avantures de François Leguat, et de ses Compagnons, en deux Isles désertes des Indes Orientales*, published in London in 1708, was widely read in its day as the chief authority on Rodrigues. Closer to our time, the book became the subject of critical study by a young American academic keen to make his name. Geoffroy Atkinson's work on extraordinary voyages in French literature was published in 1920 and 1922. The scholarly world seemingly concurred with Atkinson's conclusion that the account 'which had hitherto been believed to have been founded on a real voyage ... is purely an imaginary novel', allegedly written in a London armchair, not even by Leguat but by one Maximilien Misson. Leguat and his information about Rodrigues were discredited for half a century. It is only since the publication in 1979 of *The Vindication of François Leguat* by Mauritian historian Alfred North-Coombes that Leguat's account of the island of Rodrigues has again been reclassified as fact not fiction.

Going and seeing a place with your own eyes, as Leguat had so arduously done, doesn't necessarily convince people that what you say is true. If there is no disposition to believe you, or inadequate corroborating evidence, fact can readily be discounted as fiction. By the same token, the convincing lie, the one that works carefully on what people expect or like to hear, can be accepted as truth.

When Mauritians heard that I was including their island in a book on the basis of a brief visit, they were alarmed. They insisted I supplement my own random impressions with information obtained from meetings with government ministers. I didn't have time. At last they simply asked that I 'write something positive' – something to attract visitors, investment and international friends to the island. 'Write something positive': you are conscious everywhere of the same wish. Something that serves the interests of those you are talking to, as representatives of their group, community or state. It is a natural wish – no one likes to be bad-mouthed – even as it identifies writing with propaganda or advertising copy. You are seldom encouraged to 'write something truthful', unless by the disenfranchised who want a voice for their cause, and almost never to 'write something *un*truthful'. Yet how often really can readers tell the difference?

Write fantasy. Fiction as a kind of licensed lie, pretending less, may reveal more. It seems to have a capacity to cause greater offence than error or misrepresentation in factual reporting. We should remember that the television series *Embassy* and the film *Turtle Beach*, about which there has been so much fuss from Malaysia, are blatantly screen dramas. As with Australia's libel laws when applied to works of the imagination, the voodoo fear of images exceeds concern about fact.

If you write for television, you are told that there are only ten plots. In order to fit the conventions of the form, the mass of characters, themes and narrative elements must be boiled down to one of the known structures. Reading Western newspaper reports from Asian countries, you could be forgiven for thinking there were far less than ten stories. In the case of China, there are three. There is the free-wheeling capitalist road story, prevailing in stories of the Shenzhen stock exchange and Shanghai real estate. There is the oriental communist despotism story, which covers restriction of human rights, arbitrary detentions, forced abortions, as well as lighter matters such as Peking's No Flies Bid for the 2000 Olympic Games. Thirdly, there is the freak story – the record-breaking athletes, or the report of green prawn shell use as human skin substitute in cosmetic surgery.

An experienced correspondent will know which of the categories a possible story falls into, and which of the current categories is the go. If a story mixes the categories, the desk editor will generally sort it out, to achieve a result which clearly reads China as up, down or sideways. There's not much room for complication and confusion. Editors know how the China card plays among others in the deck. They know the larger stories the community is telling itself about China, which are not easily challenged.

The media in China, and in other countries where the media are less than free, are just as responsive to the preconceptions and wishes of their audiences as in Australia. Media that work explicitly in the service of the state also depend for their effectiveness on interacting with the larger stories that people are telling about their place in the world. Nor are the contrasting systems of information management as independent of each other as talk of free or controlled media cultures might suggest. The Western journalist in China, for instance, will supplement personal impressions and sources with official press reports (appropriately reinterpreted), the official/unofficial Hong Kong press, and the swirl of palace gossip – leaks, rumours, straws in the wind – that is part of a more subtly orchestrated process of opinion-forming. The journalist's story, like the diplomat's cable, is then dropped into a moving current back home.

The domestic political agenda is a variable that mediates the reception of foreign stories. In the case of stories from Asian countries, the Scylla and Charybdis of fear of immigration and anxiety about relative trade competitiveness regularly exert their influence. For China, the good/bad switch is flicked off and on in ways that can link with the Immigration Department's headaches in dealing with refugees and boatpeople.

The Chinese who wish to come here are in turn lured by conceptions of Australia prompted by information in the Chinese media, including our own press releases, as part of our cultural diplomacy, that promote Australia as a peaceful, prosperous, democratic, free and multicultural land that is developing rapidly. Such positive views are, of course, set against a good deal of negative propaganda, including pieces from the Chinese press in Australia that document hardship, homesickness and discrimination. The moral according to the Chinese press is that, in the end, you'll return gratefully to the bosom of the motherland. That's the moral – which those reading it apply to everyone but themselves.

The understanding of Australia in varying Asian communities is built up through a mixed application of logic, fantasy and extrapolation from what is already known. One small example nicely illustrates the vagaries of the process. An article in the Japanese English-language press headlined, 'Passion for equality keeps Australia's global profile low,' adds the subtitle: '"Tall puppy" syndrome makes heroes of underdogs.' The author has heard of hot dogs and top dogs, and, by extension, the Australian sympathy for the underdog. A typo or mishearing takes the analogy, with impeccable plausibility, a stage further to invent the 'tall puppy'. It could just catch on.

In constructing an image of Australia, whatever is available will be used. We, as Australians, have little control over the process, and not much idea of the ingredients to hand in any particular Asian community, but we must live with the consequences. The need to 'improve' Australia's image in Asia by providing more and better information is regularly indentified in government reports and other documents, yet implementation is fuzzy, partly for want of understanding of the mental environments in which the changing images are to grow.

By contrast with mainland China, Taiwan has been a minimal target for Australian government cultural diplomacy over recent decades. But there are longstanding unofficial links between Australia and Taiwan, and substantial trade. I was fascinated, therefore, on a recent visit to Taiwan to see what kind of image of Australia exists, where there has been almost no official effort to shape one, except for the purposes of tourism. (The Gold Coast rings bells.) Then I discovered Green Oil. It is an extremely popular Taiwanese product that, in the tradition of tiger balm, goanna salve and snake oil, claims to cure 'headaches, nose complaints, cuts, burns, bites, abrasions, muscular pain, stomach ache, and seasickness'. It is advertised widely, on billboards, on radio and television. People associate it with Australia, which I understood when I heard its advertising jingle (in English):

> *Kookaburra sits in an old gum tree,*
> *Merry merry king of the bush is he,*
> *Laugh, kookaburra! Laugh, kookaburra!*
> *Gay your life must be!*

The healing properties of Green Oil symbolise an unspoken identification of Australia as a healing place, a clean zone of purity and nature. White beaches and fresh food imports are aspects of this image. A Taipei taxi driver assured me there is so little dirt in Australia that you need wash only every third day. Green Oil, the packet tells us, contains 15 mg of eucalyptus oil – probably from Thailand, since eucalyptus oil plants are virtually a thing of the past in Australia.

Green Oil. It is a wonderful image for Australia to have in Taiwan. I have no idea how it has come about. We couldn't have manufactured it if we'd tried. It provides a fine foundation to work with, and suggests a lesson. In nurturing its image in Asia, Australia must be aware of what already exists over there, which will differ significantly from place to place, yet must be worked with, because it won't be quickly changed. Every society has its Green Oil, in the sense of a ground of awareness – film and lubricant – which leaves its mark, sometimes its stain, on stories and images coming from elsewhere. It is an environment, or medium, a *bricolage* of economics, politics, history, personal and imaginary associations, into which any new conception of a foreign country will be immersed. In considering how information from an Asian country is mediated for Australia, or how our own images will be seen by a neighbouring community, it is worth stopping to ask: what is the Green Oil this time?

1993

Taiwan: treasure island

Beautiful island. Lost paradise. Strongroom of Chinese treasure. Sentinel against Gargantua across the water. Mountain of gold. Dragon economy. Diplomatic orphan.

Contemporary culture in Taiwan arises from a time-and-place intersected by contending historical narratives, geopolitical mappings and cultural affiliations, where nation-building strategies have succeeded only in producing noisy dissent about what might constitute culture or nation. The society's storytellers – artists, filmmakers, writers and critics – project cacophonous tales about themselves to a double audience of insiders and outsiders. While no individual artist's work can be categorised solely according to the place and time of its production, the art of contemporary Taiwan can nevertheless be grouped under the banner of a twisting, fantastic and polemical set of stories, mutually dependent, mutually antagonistic, in which creative making is tied inextricably to specific, yet always disputed circumstances.

Indigenous Taiwan, named Formosa, the Beautiful Island, by colonising Europeans, became the offshore refuge of Ming loyalists from southern China when the Manchus invaded the Chinese heartland from the north in the seventeenth century. Two centuries later the Manchu collapse, hastened by the depredations of Western powers, led to Japanese occupation of Taiwan. Japanese defeat in the second world war brought Chiang Kai-shek's Nationalists to take over the island as a base for their claim to govern China. When the United States and other countries recognised the People's Republic of China in 1976, diplomatic isolation followed for the rival Republic of China and the quest for 'local soil' Taiwanese identity intensified. By the 1980s Taiwan had become an economic powerhouse, following Japan to 'developed-nation' status, yet without Japan's strong national form. From 1987 Taiwan has pursued a rough-and-tumble democracy in which Nationalist rule has become less secure and the movement for 'independence' from mainland China has grown. The mainland Chinese Communist Party reserves the right to use force to 'recover' the renegade province of Taiwan, while the Nationalists on Taiwan sit prepared to wait for the collapse of the 'bandit' communist regime across the straits before ultimately 'retaking' the motherland. Much of this must seem like dream or nightmare to the majority in Taiwan who identify their long-term future as simply Taiwanese, and who realise that, if they are to have a future at all, the stories they tell must contain arguments for political, social, environmental and cultural transformation.

From early times, creative spirits in Taiwan have grouped together to make alternative blueprints to occupation, authoritarian assimilation or marginality, working obliquely in art and literature when to be explicit was impossible. 'What the artist felt, what the philosopher thought, and what the patriot dreamed of, were all put into song by the poet,' writes one historian in reference to the dynamic role of literary gatherings in the evolution of civil society from late-seventeenth-century Taiwan onwards. In the late-twentieth century, Taiwanese artists, while jealous of their individual trademarks in the vigorously competitive critical and commercial marketplace, continue to position themselves in groups according to lineage, locality, training (including overseas experience) and ideology.

The stories that artist Huang Chin-ho tells about himself and in his work, for example, are as pointed as they are entertaining. Born in 1956,

Huang Chin-ho describes himself as thirteenth-generation Taiwanese, from a family that migrated from Fujian in southern China three hundred years ago – and perhaps with some hypothetical Dutch blood. He speaks Taiwanese or *minnanyu*, the dialect of Fujian. He shares the distinctive, popular Taoist/Buddhist spirituality of Taiwan. In paintings such as *Journey to Paradise* and *Garden of Earthly Delights*, he draws on Taoist symbols and colours against a philosophical background of Buddhistic detachment from material desires and physical passions. In Chiayi in west-central Taiwan, where Huang Chin-ho was born, the incoming mainland Chinese Nationalists were especially severe in their attempts to annihilate local opposition. The memory of the 28 February 1947 'incident' and the subsequent White Terror, in which an estimated 50,000 people were killed throughout the island, was a catalyst for the development of Taiwan consciousness among the population of the area.

Huang Chin-ho was initially self-taught as an artist. Failing to get into art school, he studied philosophy and history, developing a special interest in Taiwan's history. Painting came later. In the early 1980s he was an abstract expressionist and in the later 1980s moved on to neo-expressionism; by 1989 he had achieved his ambition to work in New York. It was in New York, far from Taiwan, that he realised that the art he most passionately wanted to produce was inseparably bound with Taiwan itself. In 1990 he left New York and returned to Taiwan to embark on his quest for a new, locally generated style. In a series of remarkable paintings from 1990 on, Huang Chin-ho has used local elements and materials to articulate a Taiwanese aesthetic that is different from China's and different from prevailing modes in the West. Part horrifying, part celebratory, these works show the newly prosperous denizens of Taiwan in a world of exuberant grossness and garish transformation. Traditional symbols, such as peaches (for longevity), sugarcane (for good luck) and lotus leaves, jostle with the imitation-classical façades of karaoke bars and strip clubs in exquisitely painted garden settings where humble cabbage grows in the foreground and overweening power lines soar behind. The artist talks of Taiwan's 'migrant' and 'colonised' culture as having produced a flamboyant, ostentatious aesthetic, a brash ersatz rococo which, for all its intense physicality, expresses the pathos of untrammelled or unachievable psychological and spiritual desires and states.

Huang Chin-ho is engaged in a kind of striptease himself, peeling the clothes off his fleshy figures to show them empty of soul underneath, or lacking head and heart. In *Journey to Paradise*, he seems almost to peel the skin itself off the famous singer who has ended up working the meat markets. Elsewhere he exposes the hybrids of a crossover society, pumped-up beasts in bikinis, robots with dictator faces, transsexual, hermaphrodite, party animals all crossdressed-up with no place to go. In these wild, warning scenes, the artist is concerned with the meaning of Taiwan's history, the consequences – especially for the environment – of Taiwan society's materialism and pragmatism, and, fundamentally, with a contemplation of human existence in which the world of spirits hovers, perhaps trapped, within the fiery, brightly coloured world of passion and mortality.

Narrative elements are no less present in the work of other contemporary Taiwan artists, whether it is the retelling of political histories, conversation pieces, fantasy illustrations, esoteric story-fragments or Zen diary entries. Hong Kong gallery director Johnson Chang Tsong-zung, one of the first observers to mediate Taiwan's new art for an outside audience, identifies the inscriptive impulse in a number of Taiwan artists as 'a continuous, often unconscious exploration of the self in relation to environment or family, as though the artists are unsure of their own "shapes" and need to define themselves through a re-constitution of a familial or environmental world'. Looking 'at Asian countries newly liberated economically', Chang sees 'a growing self-awareness. With this will inevitably come an art which attempts to re-align one's orientation in the world from an individual perspective. Speaking generally, the need for constant re-affirmation of one's local identity will also grow with an increasingly shifting, fast-moving world.'

In this sense, localism is also a global phenomenon, and Australians can readily find points of contact between Taiwan's cultural situation and our own. The comparison was not lost on the early historian of the island, an Australian himself, whose rhetoric transfers with prophetic quaintness to 1995. In *Formosa: A Study in Chinese History* (1966) W.G. Goddard writes of

a striking similarity between the making of this Formosan character and that of the Australian . . . In both cases the toll of life and labour's enterprise was terrific . . . In both cases another element, this time human, entered into the struggle to intensify it and add to the casualties . . . Historians have recorded the lawlessness that resulted, but out of the struggle . . . developed that spirit of independence and that love of freedom, so characteristic . . . [and] also, perhaps, that resentment against authority.

This, of course, is merely another story. It remains to tell how later generations are revising it. Now, at any rate, Taiwan's contemporary culture can speak to us with surprising, if partially deceptive, directness. Its quite particular energies and exuberance are unexpected, fascinating, and even, perhaps, like the gilded temples that are sprouting like mushrooms all over the Beautiful Island, inspirational.

1995

Cultural trading

What have we got to show?

One of the things that appeals to me about Chinese culture is the notion of the 'scholar-official', in exile from the court, who goes on chastising the emperor even when the emperor is not listening.

The brows of Australian officials furrow over Australia's image abroad, particularly in Asia. Australia already had an image problem in 1688, when William Dampier arrived at the north-west coast of what was then New Holland and recorded in his journal that the natives were unfriendly and the place unfit for civilised life. But that apparently negative image has never stopped Australia from attracting people, whether they have come here as invaders or investors, dreamers, migrants or tourists.

A rough way to understand this paradox is to split Australia into 'land' and 'people', as the word 'Australia' refers both to a physical place and a nationality. It doesn't matter that, in fact, the land, Aboriginal Australians and everyone else are inextricably linked, for better or worse, sharing histories, the present, and putative futures. The split between land and people exists as a construction in many minds. When Australians overseas are homesick, for example, they often speak of missing 'the light', 'the sky', 'the smell of gumleaves', in order to express what is perhaps a more complex, and more *cultural*, feeling of absence.

Discussion of Australian culture for consumption overseas often, in my experience, works with narrow or wishful notions that, in a similar way, split culture from its connections with the other parts of Australian life, whether physical, economic or political. In this way the possibilities of cultural relationship are diminished. Culture becomes something of a vanity exercise, the packaging and not the package. A broader conception is needed, one that might see culture as the expression of all a community's values and that might encompass all kinds of imaginative interactions between people, both individually and collectively. The discussion has opened up in the 1990s, and there is a new awareness – or sense of urgency – about Australia's cultural relations with other societies. Perhaps that also means an opportunity to do things differently.

The realisation that Australia is able to relate more closely to other countries in the Asia-Pacific region has brought the question of culture to the foreground in a new definition, referring not to painters and pianists, but – as in the now-common phrase, 'cultural sensitivities' – to a broad range of values, customs, etiquette, lifestyle, including core cultural concepts, such as human rights, environmental issues, religion and so forth. Australia's preparations to become a republic, along with Australian-style multiculturalism, as part of a determination to re-make our history, are altering the domestic consensus about what Australia is. Mabo, symbolising 'reconciliation' between Aboriginal and other Australians, incorporates a process of cultural relationship that cannot be separated from political, economic and broadly human means and consequences. It is part of what Australia wants to show the world in the 1990s. Indeed, showing the world is an integral part of achieving the domestic vision: Asia, the Republic, Mabo – all have a dimension that engages with perceptions from outside. What have we got to show, culturally speaking, that other people might be interested in? The creations of our society include the major intellectual processes in the life of our society, which should not be cordoned off because they have also become items on the government's agenda. These value-laden mappings of an emergent society are shapes which it will take a whole host of more specific activities to fill out. Australian Studies, presence in print and electronic media networks, long-term interaction between arts communities, arts export, tourism, shared environmental and heritage practice, and people-to-people exchanges of all kinds are only some of the means at our disposal. There is much at stake, then, in cultural relations.

Prime Minister Paul Keating has referred to the overseas dimensions of culture, noting that the arts industry is an export earner 'in Asia and elsewhere' and that Australia 'needs to be a country which releases self-expression and which can sell to the world an unmistakeable identity'. These two strands combine in initiatives foreshadowed in *Creative Nation: Commonwealth Cultural Policy* (1994) 'to develop an international cultural marketing structure that encourages cultural exchange' and 'to develop an international marketing strategy to increase export potential'. One aim is to support Australia's independent standing as an originator of culture; another aim looks outward 'to improve understanding and recognition of Australia as a natural and long-term partner in regional development'. Just how these ideas will translate into practice remains to be seen.

In addressing itself to issues of Australian culture overseas, *Creative Nation* has tried to take into account the different Australian government agencies (quite apart from the array of market forces) with rival interests in this area. The Australia Council is aiming at a more export-orientated international strategy. The Department of Employment, Education and Training is a player, through its support for Australian Studies abroad and through the International Development Program of Australian Universities and Colleges. The Department of Communications and the Arts has plans for its own off-shore activities to assist cultural export. Obliquely, the Department of Immigration too plays a significant role in projecting Australia's image to the wider world.

Crucially, the Department of Foreign Affairs and Trade (DFAT), through the Cultural Relations and Overseas Information Branches, and through bilateral councils such as the Australia–China Council, has had a longstanding interest in Australia's cultural presence in Asia. In my experience, however, there is a public expectation of the role of Foreign Affairs that differs markedly from the department's own definition of its role; an outside perception, in arts communities and even their administrative organisations, such as the Australia Council and the Australian Film Commission, that DFAT should or could play a larger role than it does. The reality is that DFAT's allocation of staff and resources to cultural relations is under siege. The Australia–China Council's budget, for example, has dropped by about half in real terms since its founding in 1978–79, while the council has broadened its area of activity to include Hong Kong and Taiwan as well as the People's Republic of China, where things are much costlier than they were fifteen years ago.

Perhaps out of desire to delimit his department's cultural objectives, in contradistinction to those of contending agencies, the Minister for Foreign Affairs and Trade, Senator Gareth Evans, has sought to describe quite specifically the domain of what he calls 'public diplomacy'. Senator Evans emphasises that 'public diplomacy' is 'no longer . . . an optional extra in our foreign and trade policies'. A major task of 'public diplomacy' is to build 'a more accurate and rounded image of Australia than currently exists', especially in Asia.

This can seem like a very general undertaking, encouraging Australians and Asians 'to devote more attention to Australia and Asia "in each others' minds"' – to quote Ross Garnaut – but there are exclusions, according to Senator Evans. 'It is important to stress that our cultural relations are not designed to assist the Australian cultural community, or to directly involve the government in establishing links between cultural disciplines in Australia and overseas.' '"Public diplomacy" is not about tethering community groups to the government's foreign policy agenda. It is not even about co-ordinating government and non-government activity.' The sentiments are echoed in *Creative Nation*: 'the principal reason for sending arts overseas under DFAT's auspices is to enhance our national image at critical times or to support particular goals'. Notice too that 'dialogue' and 'exchange' have been overtaken by a one-way process of projecting outward.

These demarcation lines must puzzle an outsider. There is an emphasis on 'image' rather than 'substance', that perhaps risks hiving off too much. The then head of DFAT's Cultural Relations Branch, David Ambrose, clarified this point in a speech in 1993, when he said that 'Australia's successful long-term economic engagement in Asia has to be underwritten by a widespread appreciation among our neighbours of the socio-cultural *realities* [my emphasis] of contemporary, multicultural Australia, not frustrated by incomplete, partial, or inaccurate stereotypes not representative of us at all.' Ambrose gives to 'image' such a generous interpretation that it almost becomes 'substance'. So perhaps Cultural Relations can look beyond massaged images after all.

I would start any discussion of Australia's cultural relations in the region with two empirical observations. First, wherever you go, you find almost no Australian-published books – in libraries in Taiwan, in bookshops in Hong Kong, even in Australian Studies Centres in China. (The observation is confirmed by the Australia Council Literature Board's 1994 report on International Publishing and Promotions.) Second, wherever you go, you must eventually expect the White Australia policy to be raised. (It was current until very recently, for example, in the entries on Australia in Taiwanese school texts.) I sympathise with Senator Evans who must have had White Australia trotted out to him often, and tendentiously.

I suspect there is a connection between these two empirical observations. The absence of books and other publications is an absence of substance. It is the absence in other societies of access to our society's information about itself, our ideas and imagination, which not only stimulate the purchase of more books, and translation rights and film rights and all those industry benefits, but are also the basis for study and research, and travel, and understanding. The absence of books is a prime instance of the absence of 'presence', from which many of the image and other problems arise. Fortunately the situation is improving, slowly.

There is an opportunity at present, as well as a necessity, to re-conceive Australia's overseas cultural relations in the national interest. Although Senator Evans describes his department's 'public diplomacy' as not about co-ordinating government and non-government activity, it is hard to see where, other than Foreign Affairs, with its international perspectives and infrastructure network, such guidance could be offered. Or should other agencies re-invent the wheel, because there is no way to quantify what Foreign Affairs might, or might not, have achieved in the past? For a relatively small country such as Australia to achieve an identity in the world, co-ordination of and communication between all parties that share the same broad interests is surely desirable, if limited resources are to be managed to achieve maximum results. Co-ordination and communication only follow where there is real commitment and political will. That will only come when cultural relations are understood as not a matter of image enhancement but an integral part of articulating what Australia is. Culture is substance: the total package. That will be evident as cultural relations activities draw on the energies of their constituent communities – sponsors, target audiences, host societies, artists and writers – enabling the interconnected workings of the medium, the message and the market to be better understood and appreciated.

Hong Kong, as the exchange hub of the Chinas and of East Asia, is as good a place as any to start. From Hong Kong, dynamic, ever-changing, endlessly responsive, it might be possible to look back and out at Australia's presence, at what we have to show for our efforts in cultural trading so far, as a basis from which to suggest strategies that, using all possible resources, will make us as present in the regional networks as anyone else.

1994

Out of Hong Kong

Timothy Mo

Almost everyone has passed through the transit lounge of Hong Kong. For tourists and business people the gateway to China, for mainland Chinese the door to the West, for local residents a springboard to Canada or Australia; Hong Kong has been created by the vagaries of history as one of the world's most remarkable interfaces, a determinedly international, offshore island where anything can be bought or sold. Yet Hong Kong is sad.

In the shadow of the negotiation of the Sino–British Joint Declaration by which it returns to Chinese sovereignty in 1997, if not sooner in practice, Hong Kong has matured. With high living standards and education, economic hypersensitivity, community self-consciousness – and widespread corruption – has come a sharp political sense. Yet remarks such as Deng Xiaoping's opinion that the people of Hong Kong are not ready for democracy must be passively heard out with the realisation that Hong Kong's political will has very little means of expression.

Mainland visitors defend themselves against the colony's success story by commenting that Hong Kong has no culture. Europeans make a similar complaint, that Hong Kong has sold its soul to business. Both China-lovers and Chinese tend to dislike Hong Kong's deviation from venerable tradition in the money-making name of 'total Westernisation'. Cultural product is as smoothly international as the city itself; in literature, for instance, historical epics like the Taipan novels of Australian-born James Clavell, or spy stories like very British John Le Carré's *The Honourable Schoolboy*. Yet of all marginal, not-quite-postcolonial cultures perhaps Hong Kong's has been the most marginalised; the split between the resilient cultures of coloniser and colonised sharpest.

What is the voice of Hong Kong? What is the language of the territory Le Carré calls 'a smug, rich British rock run by a bunch of plum-throated traders whose horizons go no farther than their belly-lines'? Cantonese speakers in Hong Kong need to study both English and Mandarin to have their futures covered. A Hong Kong memoir in which the narrator considers the problem of finding a language to do justice to the range and depth of her experience is called *Borrowed Tongue*. The book is written jointly by a Hong Kong couple, he British, she Chinese, under the pseudonym Tao Yang. Here it takes two to encompass the necessary range of expression and acculturation, to reckon up the penumbra of Chinese culture in the bright light of the West. The writers work the border.

What passport Timothy Mo carries doesn't matter. He is described as the Hong Kong-born son of an English mother and a Cantonese father. Educated in Hong Kong and England, he now lives in London. His theme is the co-existence of opposing peoples who have been brought together by history, fate or accident, dynamically interacting or linking arms against each other; a condition of which Hong Kong is a rich exemplar.

His novels are each pinpointed in time and place. *The Monkey King* (1978) is a dry domestic comedy set in 1950s Hong Kong in the peace following the Japanese occupation, when the place was a relatively complacent colonial outpost, despite the fear and loathing of the 'Reds' running high as a result of the Korean war. It is the story of an outsider, a shrewd, wacky young man from Macao who through an arranged marriage penetrates the household and at last takes over the business empire of a Chinese patriarch. As in a game of *Go*, a comic battle of will takes place. Through risk, calculation and sheer good luck, the enterprising new man out-manoeuvres the old master, but with the master tacitly approving because the tradition (the family business) survives. Monkey is a character from the Chinese classics who, under magic protection, succeeds by wildly unconventional methods. So the Portuguese-Chinese hero delicately outwits the nepotistic British bureaucracy, the opportunistic Chinese trading network, the peasant chiefs who deal illegally with the Reds, and the local communist sympathisers. Through scenes of low-key farce filled out with brilliant social observation and droll dialogue, a youthful tale unfolds, under a patina of irony. Over the shoulder are glimpsed social and historical forces held in shifting equilibrium. In the foreground lightness and deftness balance a precocious worldliness – all with a poker-faced humour just slightly removed from callousness:

'At least we Chinese was the cleanest people of the world.' It was a habit of Mabel's to preface her odder pronouncements with the phrase 'We Chinese'. It enabled her to get away with many things.

At the same time the local Chinese are forever reminded of another world whose unfathomable ways must be fathomed if they are to get on. The education they prize seems to buy only absurd irrelevance:

History essay. Number one: 'Was Alfred's Navy the major factor in his success against the Danes?' (Who the hell this Alfred was anyway? We maybe had a Alfred here for a governor one time . . .?) Number two: 'Did the Conquest alter the character of English life?' Number three . . . He broke off incredulously, with stagey amazement. The boys looked at him with hurt, reproachful expressions. The youngest spoke: 'Father, why were you laughing?'

In this world the hero's success lies in working the crazy seams of disjunction. His signal victory is to drain the floodwaters that threaten to ruin the rice crops of an entire village. To do so, he draws on a knowledge of hydro-engineering that the farmers think is geomancy. He manages the slippery element of water no less skilfully than he manipulates the flow of human credulity and suspicion. In *The Monkey King* it's the traditional Monkey hero who triumphs by un-Confucian means.

In *Sour Sweet* (1982) it's the Chinese family writ large and small. A tiny emigrant Hong Kong nucleus of husband, wife, baby son and wife's sister survives London in the 1960s by bonding together. Yet the tightness of Chinese family bonds also obliges the husband to remit a large sum of money to Hong Kong to cover his aged father's hospitalisation. He is assisted by an organisation that exists to lend a hand to Chinese brothers in need: thus the Triad claims him. By framing his attentive and heart-warming account of a migrant family's struggles in a new land within a chilling thriller of drug-smuggling and gang warfare, Mo charts both the benign and malignant effects of bonds that begin in natural human feelings but are elaborated into rigid, arbitrary and inhuman rites. In the motives of the Triad it is impossible to distinguish greed and power lust from the maintenance of an ancient quasi-masonic order; just as in the family the strict control, slavery and penny-pinching (not to mention the many infringements of the host country's alien law) are administered in the name of love.

Mo's tone is one of dark detached humour, where sympathy for foibles and fiascos alike is muted by the exposure of meagrely self-interested motives and larger impersonal processes. There is no scope for tragedy here, rather a steady reckoning of the constant, fluid interchange of material goods and personal powers. Here what could be called a Taoist dynamism comes to subvert Confucian stasis.

No man is an island, we are reminded in Mo's third novel, *An Insular Possession* (1986). No island is an island either, especially if it is Hong Kong: geographically and historically part of the mainland and the main routes of international trade. Mo's novel covers the circumstances by which Hong Kong came into being as a Crown possession, telling of the foreign traders who operated in Canton in the 1830s and the British insistence on opening up the Chinese Empire, by fair means or foul, diplomacy, opium, and at last gunfire, until they were forced back to what proved after all a most convenient bastion off the coast: the first opium war which ceded Hong Kong to Britain in 1841, where the novel ends. But, though no direct reference is made, it is impossible not to read the book against the background of Hong Kong's return to China. Where does the extraordinary sequence of events initiated over a century ago come to a close? Where does the story end? This prodigally open-ended novel is much concerned with the problem of endings, knowing that there is one 'category . . . which does love an end' while 'the world is not like that – it is untidy, there are no reasons, the final sum never balances'. The novel carries a debate between the completeness of art and the fractious truths of history – yet what Mo offers is a version of Hong Kong's pre-history that has since been suppressed by the glorious victors. It is noted, for instance, that the name of Captain Charles Elliott, one of the good guys, 'is uncommemorated in the colony he founded'. Mo's defeated heroes are those who tried to stop the opium trade, who tried to achieve a degree of understanding, fairness and decency in relations between Chinese and Europeans, those who were routed in the end by British pride, militarism and sheer determination to maintain intact an economic and power machine that stretched from India, enslaved Africans and came home to ghastly factories in the midlands: what Mo calls the two 'unholy trinities', triangles of trade 'Cartesian almost in their ruthlessness and clarity'. It was the opium traders, not the humanitarians who prevailed.

The author bends over backwards to be fair and just in his account of the ways and motives of both Chinese and foreigner, and if the balance tips in favour of the Chinese, that is because they suffered more. He understands that the outcome by which the two sides came to live in enmity developed inexorably from countless misapprehensions and pettinesses, the obverse of edgily accommodating co-existence:

Remote Emperor, wily Mandarin, ruthless British Free Trader, hard-headed Yankee interloper, pompous Company official, swaggering secret-society smuggler, and opium-growing Bengal ryot are linked by a devious web of dependence and repulsion, necessary co-operation and mutual hostility and, curiously enough, without the tension inherent in the confrontation of opposites, the system would probably not have held together so long.

Mo eschews the tragic quality which is surely inherent in his source material. There is an unending assessment of rights and wrongs, goods and bads, actualities and alternatives, conclusions and non-conclusions.

The novel for him is God, who sees all, understands all, redeems all. Its divine perspicuity not only sees the skin, close-up, warts and all, but also gets under the skin to register the shadings of right and wrong by which human character and moral action must be judged.

When a man writes . . . you get his soul. That is, you are presented with his essence, but essence is clear stuff. Race, culture, quirks, physical appearance, they've all been boiled away . . . When the souls go to the Day of Judgement will God differentiate between us as Americans, Africans, Indians or Chinese? As tall, short, thin, fat?

So writes the narrator of The Redundancy of Courage (1991), Mo's novel set on East Timor. Only the novel can deal so fair-handedly, with a conception of universal humanity and the uniqueness and equality of individual souls, even while, ironically, the stuff it deals with, especially in Timothy Mo's hands, is precisely 'race, culture, quirks, physical appearance'.

The creative decisions behind The Redundancy of Courage are impressive, despite the title. A lesser novelist, even Graham Greene, would have simulated a factual account of the Indonesian invasion of East Timor and the Fretilin resistance. Mo takes the step into fiction; which both generalises and also focuses. The story of the failure of the resistance movement is the story of Adolph Ng's survival. As a Chinese, he belongs neither to the native race nor to the invaders. He breathes in the interstices between vanquisher and vanquished.

Ng is a citizen of the world who makes his accommodation with power in order to clear a space in which he can be left alone. In that sense, he is on the side of freedom. He realises that while power enforces its own hierarchy, there are bonds of personal loyalty, love and respect that form a durable human reality not easily brought into the service of power. Ng is also homosexual, which opens up for him another invisible network of human bonding. He is clever, well-educated, dirty-minded, discriminating, and does what he has to do. Ultimately it is little more than his sense of himself – which Mo gives us richly, comically and compassionately – that brings him through. In the first part of the novel, he sets himself apart from the passionate revolutionaries who are his friends, priding himself rather on the foreign-style toilet bowls he has refurbished in his hotel. In the central section, he finds himself fighting in the hills with the guerillas, and, from being a humiliated outsider, proves his courage and commitment when circumstances require. In the final part he survives as wily courtier to the household of the invaders (an 'Indonesian' colonel) who have captured him. At the conclusion he is one of a handful of survivors of the resistance movement. He changes his name to Kawasaki and leaves for Brazil.

Although he is splendidly individuated, Ng is, in the context of the clash between coloniser and indigenous people, the definitive Chinaman. As he feels it and as others see him, his race and the unexpected legacies of his culture enable him to stand at one remove, judge more shrewdly, act more quickly – and survive. But he cannot survive alone. His skill depends on attaching itself to the needs and commitments of others. Therein lies Ng's bond of nature.

W.B. Yeats once suggested that the East has no tragic sense: 'The East has its solutions always and therefore knows nothing of tragedy'. Yeats's intimation is that tragedy itself is limited – 'it cannot grow by an inch or an ounce' – and that beyond the tragic there is gaiety and wisdom. Perhaps Hong Kong today is an example, politicised, ironical, 'enisled', one of Mo's favourite words, in shifting and shifted loyalties, with no direction home. Only faith in solutions, in pragmatism, in new lamps for old. Its glassy optimism and glittering frenzy allow no glimpse of tragedy.

At midnight when the streets are cleared, stylish teenagers gather on the road through Hong Kong's Statue Square, by the Courts of Justice, to dance a formation cha-cha. The ghetto-blaster sings: *I want to be ha-ha-ha-ppy/But I can't be ha-ha-ha-ppy/Till I make you happy too!* Such is the extent of self-determination.

1987/1991

Ice city

How to make friends in China

When I took the job, I expected the usual gibes. 'What culture?' the Europeans would say. 'Ah, the cultural spy!' would whisper the Chinese. 'The Les Patterson of the Orient,' the Australians would throw in. I suppose I lived up to expectations. At any rate, most of my neckties are stained.

For New Year 1988 I went to Harbin, once the 'Paris of the East', in China's frozen far north. With a few remaining onion-domed churches, it is reminiscent of Middle Europe. Or Dickens. After dark, on foggy, cobbled streets, vendors sell roast chestnuts and blackened frozen persimmons. Harbin used to be famous for bread before the cold war and the Sino–Soviet split brought on a double isolation. It still produces export-quality vodka and passable caviar. But the echoes of Paris have faded. Harbin is now Ice City. In winter, with temperatures below twenty degrees Celsius, the city fills with fantastic ice-sculptures, an art form that, however ephemeral, is taken seriously by the locals. But the ice festival was not my reason for visiting.

The Anti-Bourgeois Liberalisation Campaign of 1987 had made it difficult for unofficial art to be exhibited in Peking, but in the China of the economic reforms the Heilongjiang Provincial Museum was willing to take the risk. The only active part of the museum was a display about human reproduction and the one-child policy. Foetuses in ascending sizes lined up in jars alongside anatomical cross-sections of genitalia. Siamese twins and specimens of elephantiasis provided a freak show that people would pay to see. Otherwise the museum's enviable collections of porcelain and bronzes, fossils and stuffed animals, were deteriorating quietly in unvisited halls. As an entrepreneurial gesture, the museum had decided to experiment with hiring out space to any self-styled artist with the cash and the nod. From an earlier period of rustication an artist friend in Peking had mates in the local Artists' Association who had talked the bankrupt museum into holding an unprecedented, officially sanctioned display of bold contemporary oil paintings. The warps in China's reform process made such unlikely things possible.

The visit of an Australian cultural counsellor was a rare event in Harbin, so meetings were arranged with the local artists, who hang off official structures like barnacles off a pier, maintaining their factions and their pseudo-independence. But first I wanted to sightsee. Before my breakfast meeting, we set off from the colossal Soviet-built Friendship Palace along the frozen Songhua River. As we trudged along, the safe markers disappeared under the falling snow, and suddenly the ice broke. My two companions, an Australian woman and a Chinese man who couldn't swim, yelped as they sank into the freezing water. Both were dressed in great-coats, walking boots, caps and gloves. The cold was so intense it virtually catapulted them out. I grabbed at them, hauling them on to slabs of ice cracking beneath us as we pulled backwards, the river flowing fast under the frozen surface. Then we ran, ice still splitting, towards the bank. My companions' clothes were hard as boards by the time we reached the hut where a local committee was in session around the pot-bellied stove. We burst in. The Australian woman ripped off her clothes by the stove, down to her thermal underwear, while the committee members took notes.

We were late for our meeting. Drink is an important habit of solidarity in northern China. Our host, Liu Zhi, a benign painter of Van Gogh-inspired landscapes, was a veteran. He was a man who had lived his life within iron limits, but who inwardly had gone to extremes. To accompany the breakfast dumplings, he provided champagne glasses of ferociously strong spirits for the self-congratulatory toasts. In thanks for our deliverance from the Songhua River, we began downing the stems, proclaiming friendship and co-operation between the artists of Harbin and Australia.

My head seemed to float from my body. I could hear people around me putting questions that I did not respond to. I could hear them asking, 'Is he all right?' I sat there with my eyes open, but as if unconscious. In the two-room flat, tables had been set up, laden with food, around which twenty artists were crammed. Somehow I stumbled to the door and down three flights of stairs to the street and the snow. A search party came after me to fetch back the foreigner, the diplomat in flight. Back in the flat I was laid in a tiny room filled by a double bed and a television set that was showing Donald Duck quacking in Chinese. I lay on the quilt, the room turning, and heard them say, 'He's thrown up.'

The next day I went back to apologise. The tables and chairs had been folded up out of sight, the cement floor washed down. The artist's wife was wringing out sheets in a tub. The down quilt was strung on a line across the room where it would take forever to dry. Liu Zhi shook my hand and offered me a drink. I turned green at the thought. He told me I was one of them.

Acheng means Old City. It is south-west of, and even colder than, Harbin, reached by the kind of long, straight road, lined with bare poplars, through mile after snow-covered mile of country that you associate with Tolstoy. The Acheng Print Creation Workshop, my reason for coming, was in a barracks clad with padded tarpaulin. A brunch of dog ribs, sparrow skewers and stewed frogs awaited us. The founder of the workshop was Shen Shaomin, a solid, long-haired woodblock artist whose fame had reached Peking. The Great Northern Wilderness was home to a native tradition of printmaking that had been harnessed to the Communists' requirement for art to serve the revolution. Local woodblock printing assimilated styles of socialist realism and revolutionary romanticism. Nearby were the miraculous oilfields of Daqing, which workers had dug with their bare hands. Woodblock printmaking also had roots in the lively folk customs of the district. After the Cultural Revolution, younger artists, including many people demobilised or otherwise stranded in the Great Northern Wilderness, became restless for a more contemporary direction. In setting up the Acheng Print Creation Workshop, Shen Shaomin and friends had drawn the threads together, creating an informal support group for young artists. Workers who by day designed prints for the local cotton mills would by night turn their skills to self-expression.

Asked to sing, we sang that old standby, 'The House Of The Rising Sun' as, more warily this time, I toasted artistic co-operation. The visit subsequently opened the way for Australian woodblock printmakers Ruth Burgess and David Marsden to attend the fortieth anniversary celebrations of the Great Northern Wilderness Printmaking Movement, and a continuing series of exchanges between Australia and artists linked to the Acheng Print Creation Workshop. The Art Gallery of New South Wales has acquired two of Shen Shaomin's best works from that time: *Red Wind*, depicting the red gales of socialism, the desert or the prairie fire sweeping through a field of sunflowers, and *Autumn Sunflower*, the flower withering as it releases seed into a sickly green environment.

Since the collapse of the Soviet Union, there have been troop reductions along the banks of the Amur River that marks the northern border. It is an open border now, crossed in both directions by streams of people looking for business opportunities. The risk-taking Chinese have the better of the situation at the moment. Russian is being studied once more in Harbin's schools, blond Russian women are employed in Harbin's night spots. Not far away, since the death of Kim Il-sung, the scar dividing North and South Korea moves towards healing – perhaps. Harbin is on the map again, if not the Paris of the East, then a plausible *entrepot* town.

I keep in touch with the Harbin gang. When I left China a few years later, they told me that I had only shown my true self to them twice in the time they had known me. The first was when I didn't save my Australian friend from the frozen water at the expense of the Chinese who couldn't swim. The second was when they drank me under the table. Maybe that's why they continue to deal with me.

1990

Selected Bibliography

List of works cited, and suggested further reading by authors mentioned in the text.

Barmé, Geremie and Jaivin, Linda (editors), *New Ghosts, Old Dreams: Chinese Rebel Voices* (New York, 1992)

Barme, Geremié and Minford, John (editors), *Seeds of Fire: Chinese Voices of Conscience* (New York, 1988)

Barnstone, Tony (editor), *Out of the Howling Storm: The New Chinese Poetry* (Hanover and London, 1993)

Berry, Chris, *A Bit on the Side: East-West Topographies of Desire* (Sydney, 1994)

Blofeld, John, *City of Lingering Splendour* (London, 1961)

Broinowski, Alison, *The Yellow Lady: Australian Impressions of Asia* (Melbourne, 1992)

Castro, Brian, *Birds of Passage* (Sydney, 1983)

Castro, Brian, *After China* (Sydney, 1992)

Chang Tsong-zung, Johnson (curator), *Man and Earth: Contemporary Paintings from Taiwan* (Centre for the Visual Arts, Metropolitan State College of Denver, Colorado, 1994)

Chang Tsong-zung, Johnson, Li Xianting and Doran, Valerie, *China's New Art, Post-1989, with a Retrospective from 1979-1989* (Hong Kong, 1993)

Dobson, Rosemary, *The Three Fates and Other Poems* (Sydney, 1984)

Donaldson, Ian, *The World Turned Upside-Down* (Oxford, 1970)

Duo Duo, *Looking Out From Death* (London, 1989)

Dutton, Michael and Williams, Peter, 'Translating theories: Edward Said on Orientalism, Imperialism and Alterity', *Southern Review* 26 (1993), pp. 314-357

Fitzgerald, C.P., *Why China? Recollections of China 1923-1950* (Melbourne, 1985)

Goddard, W.G., *Formosa: A Study in Chinese History* (London, 1966)

Hart, Deborah (curator), *Identities: Art from Australia* (Taipei Fine Arts Museum, Taipei, 1993)

Heyward, Michael, *The Ern Malley Affair* (St Lucia, Queensland, 1993)

Jose, Nicholas and Yang Wen-i (editors), *Art Taiwan* (Sydney, 1995)

Jung Chang, *Wild Swans* (London, 1991)

Kaptchuk, Ted J., *The Web that has No Weaver: Understanding Chinese Medicine* (New York, 1983)

Kates, George N., *The Years that Were Fat: Peking, 1933-40* (1952, reprinted Hong Kong, 1988)

Leys, Simon, *The Burning Forest: Essays on Chinese Culture and Politics* (New York, 1986)

Lu Peng and Yi Dan, *Zhongguo xiandai yishu shi, 1979-1989 [A History of Chinese Modern Art]* (Changsha, 1992)

Miller, Alex, *The Ancestor Game* (Ringwood, Victoria, 1992)

Morrison, G.E., *An Australian in China* (1895, reprinted Hong Kong, 1985)

Morrison, Hedda, *A Photographer in Old Peking* (Hong Kong, 1985)

Oodgeroo, *Kath Walker in China* (Brisbane, 1988)

Pearl, Cyril, *Morrison of Peking* (Sydney, 1967)

Roberts, Claire (editor), *In Her View: The Photographs of Hedda Morrison in China and Sarawak 1933-67* (Sydney, 1993)

Rolls, Eric, *Sojourners* (St Lucia, Queensland, 1992)

Said, Edward, *Orientalism* (London, 1979)

Sang Ye (with Nicholas Jose and Sue Trevaskes), *The Finish Line: A Long March by Bicycle through China and Australia* (St Lucia, Queensland, 1994)

Shen Congwen, *The Border Town and Other Stories*, translated by Gladys Yang (Peking, 1981)

Shen Congwen, *The Chinese Earth: Stories by Shen Tseng-wen*, translated by Robert Payne (London, 1947)

Shen Congwen, *Recollections of West Hunan*, translated by Gladys Yang (Peking, 1982)

Stewart, Harold, *Phoenix Wings: Poems 1940-6* (Sydney, 1948)

Storey, Robert, *Taiwan: A Travel Survival Kit* (Hawthorn, Victoria, 1990)

Stow, Randolph, *A Counterfeit Silence: Selected Poems* (Sydney, 1969)

Taam Sz Puy, *My Life and Work* (Hong Kong, 1925)

Yahp, Beth, *The Crocodile Fury* (Sydney, 1992)

Yang Lian, *Masks and Crocodile*, translated by Mabel Lee (Sydney, 1990)

Zhang Xinxin and Sang Ye, *Chinese Lives: An Oral History of Contemporary China*, edited by W.J.F. Jenner and Delia Davin (London, 1987)

Zwicky, Fay, *Ask Me* (St Lucia, Queensland, 1990)

Index

Aboriginal culture - 22, 54, 63, 103, 112, 113, 117, 118, 120, 121, 176, 177
Acton, Harold - 38
Adelaide - 66, 95, 163
Ah Xian - 135-7, 139
Amnesty International - 33, 154
Anti-Spiritual Pollution Campaign - 94, 110, 111, 118, 137
Asian thrust - 50, 65
Auden, W.H. - 88, 158
Australia-China Council - 95, 96, 104-7, 109, 178, 179
Australia Council - 22, 95, 109, 110, 178, 179, 180
Australian Studies - 108, 111, 118, 160, 178, 180
Backhouse, Edmund - 37
Barmé, Geremie - 39, 119, 133, 134, 147
Beaton, Cecil - 88
Bei Dao - 134, 145
Berry, Chris - 69, 70
Blainey, Geoffrey - 105, 109, 111
Blofeld, John - 86, 87, 90
'bourgeois liberalisation' - 78, 95, 149, 157
Bredon, Juliet - 90
Brisbane - 96, 99, 119, 120
Broinowski, Alison - 60, 61, 63, 65
Buck, Pearl S. - 38, 97, 124
Buddhism - 14, 24, 45, 86, 173
Burchett, Wilfred - 37

Campbell, David - 41, 56
Can Xue - 126
Canberra - ix, 86, 96, 99, 122, 160
Canton - 64, 111, 112, 184
Castro, Brian - 51, 52
Chang, Victor - 45, 105
Chen Haiyan - 137
Chen Kaige - 83
Chen, Lily - 162
Chey, Jocelyn - 105, 107, 109
Chiang Kai-shek - 23, 113, 115, 172
'China/Avant-Garde' - 137
Chinese Communist Party - 42, 47, 83, 95, 98, 110, 112, 123, 135, 136, 146, 156, 162, 172
Christianity - 52, 79, 87, 98, 100-2, 105
Chuang-tzu - 68
Ci Xi - 74 (see also 'Empress Dowager')
Clark, Manning - 109, 111-14, 119, 120
Clarke, Marcus - 46
Clavell, James - 183
Confucianism - 37, 46, 52, 69, 123, 129, 130, 147, 185
Conrad, Joseph - 38, 42
contemporary Chinese art - 108, 134, 137, 190
Coward, Noel - 38
'Creative Nation' - 178, 179

Cropper, Linda - 162
cultural diplomacy - 107, 108, 169
cultural relations - 110, 177, 178, 180, 181
Cultural Revolution - 68, 74, 78, 92-6, 98, 102, 110, 134, 135, 143, 192
cultural sensitivity - 25, 71, 138, 177
Cusack, Dymphna - 38
Darwin - 95
Democracy Wall - 133, 134, 137, 142, 143
Deng Xiaoping - 75, 78, 93, 94, 133, 142, 147-9, 157, 182
Ding Ling - 122, 123, 130
Dobson, Rosemary - 41, 51, 56
Du Fu - 56
Du Yuesheng - 88
Duo Duo - 142, 145, 146
East Timor - 187
Empress Dowager - 37, 74, 78, 84, 89, 149, 150
Empson, William - 40, 88
Evans, Gareth - 62, 179, 180
Fairweather, Ian - 61
Fang Lijun - 137
Fang Lizhi - 143
Fitzgerald, C.P. - 51, 87-90
Fitzgerald, Stephen - 26-7
Fleming, Peter - 38
Foley, Gary - 117
Formosa - 21, 37, 171, 175 (see also 'Taiwan')
Fujian province - 103, 173
Gantner, Carrillo - 108
Garnaut, Ross - 108, 179
Gaunt, Mary - 51

George, Lloyd - 77
Gleeson, James - 72
Goddard, W.G. - 175
Goldsworthy, Peter - 63
Gorbachev, Mikhail - 152
Guan Wei - 135-6, 139-40
Guangdong province - 103, 125
Guangxi Zhuang Autonomous Region - 119, 125, 163
Guizhou province - 125, 126
Guo Lusheng - 143
Haizi - 144-5
Hall, Richard - 45
Han Suyin - 37
Harbin - 189-93
Harris, David - 38
Hart, Sir Robert - 89, 90
Hawke, Bob - 103, 104
heritage - 27, 53, 82, 113, 151, 178
Hewett, Dorothy - 38
Hobart - 128
Hong Kong - 23, 44, 46, 47, 58, 59, 64-6, 79, 94, 107, 112, 125, 127, 153, 163, 168, 174, 179-83, 185-6, 188
Hou Dejian - 132, 145, 153, 154, 161
Hou Leong - 139
Hsia, Linda - 162
Hu Wenzhong - 108
Hu Yaobang - 104, 144, 147, 148
Huang Chin-ho - 172-4
Huang Yongyu - 122, 127-9
Hubei province - 125
Hughes, Billy - 76, 77
human rights - 26, 39, 70, 76, 78, 80, 168, 177

Humphries, Barry – 24
Hunan province – 123, 125-30, 132
I Ching – 133, 135
'Identities: Art from Australia' – 21
immigration – 58, 59, 64, 79, 80, 99, 111, 168
Isherwood, Christopher – 38, 88
Jaivin, Linda – 160, 162
Jiang Wen – 150
Jiangxi province – 125
Johnson Chang Tsong-zung – 174
Johnston, George – 40-1
Jung Chang – 62, 96
Kang Sheng – 91
Kates, George N. – 85, 90
Keating, Paul – 50, 178
Kiriloff, Con – 86, 90
Kristeva, Julia – 40
Lao She – 83, 150
Lao-tzu – 53, 54
Le Carré, John – 183
Leys, Simon – 35, 38, 41, 75
Li Peng – 149, 155
Li Po – 56
Li Shuxian – 143
Li Xiannian – 104
Li Xianting – 108, 137
Lin Biao – 97
Lin Chunyan – 134, 136, 139
Liu Guoguang – 108
Liu Xiaobo – 153
Lu Hsun – 41, 97, 148
Mabo – 177
Macao – 183
Malley, Ern – 72

Malraux, André – 38
Mang Ke – 134, 143
Mao Zedong – 42, 68, 75, 78, 79, 91, 93, 96-8, 106, 117, 129, 133, 143, 148
'Mao Goes Pop' – 137, 138
Marshall, Alan – 38
Maugham, Somerset – 38, 88
Mauritius – 166
Meale, Richard – 60
media – 60, 81, 104, 149, 154, 168, 178
Melbourne – 45, 80, 108
Miao people – 123, 126-9
Miller, Alex – 51, 52
Mitrophanow, Igor – 90
Mo, Timothy – 183, 185-8
Mongolia – 23, 46, 64
Morrison, George Ernest – 37, 74-82
Morrison, Hedda – 82, 85
multiculturalism – 47, 69, 79, 169, 177, 180
Murdoch, Keith – 77
Murdoch, Rupert – 77
Nanking – 24
Nicolson, Harold – 77
Nolan, Cynthia – 51
Oodgeroo – 109, 112, 113, 116-21
(see also 'Walker, Kath')
Orientalism – 49, 50, 61, 70-2, 80, 139
O'Rourke, Dennis – 69
Patterson, Les – 189
Payne, Robert – 41
Peacock, Andrew – 104
Pearl, Cyril – 74, 77, 79-81
Peck, Bob – 162, 164

Peking – x, xi, 14, 16, 19, 23,
  28-34, 39, 41, 42, 64, 69,
  74, 75, 78, 82-99, 107,
  108, 110, 111, 113, 118,
  125-8, 133, 134, 137, 142,
  145, 147, 148, 150, 151,
  153-8, 160, 162, 163, 168,
  189-91
PEN International – 33
Polo, Marco – 36
Preston, Margaret – 61
Psalmanazar, George – 37
Qantas – 25, 34, 111, 162
Qu Yuan – 40, 41
racism – 61, 63, 78, 79, 117
Radio Australia – 104, 162
refugees – 61, 69, 79, 163, 168
republicanism – 78, 81
Richards, I.A. – 40
Richardson, Henry Handel – 49
Roberts, Claire – 138
Rodrigues – 166
Rolls, Eric – 45
Ru Gu Lake – 16-19
Russell, Bertrand – 88
Said, Edward – 49, 50, 70
Sang Ye – 45, 92-102
sea slug – 103, 117
Shanghai – xi, 23, 38, 58, 59,
  64, 80, 88, 90, 96, 103,
  109-12, 118-19, 127, 130,
  137, 167
Shaw, George Bernard – 38, 150
Shen Congwen – 122-32
Shen Jiawei – 138, 139
Shen Shaomin – 139, 191, 192
Shenzhen – 167
Sichuan province – 15, 16, 125
Sima Qian – 97

Singapore – 5, 44, 46, 64, 66
Sitwell, Osbert – 36, 88
Stewart, Harold – 51, 72, 73
Stow, Randolph – 51, 53, 54
Sun Yat Sen – 75, 94
'Survivors' group – 137, 142
Sweet, Gary – 163
Taam Sz Pui – 47, 48
Taiwan – 20-5, 44, 46, 64, 78,
  99, 145, 169-75, 179, 180
Tang Song – 139
Tao Yang – 183
Taoism – 52, 68, 72, 127, 134,
  135, 173, 185
Terrill, Ross – 37, 38
Terzani, Tiziano – 38
Thubron, Colin – 38
Tian Zhuangzhuang – 83, 150
Tiananmen Square – x, 29, 33,
  41, 59, 64, 75, 84, 94, 103,
  112, 120, 126, 132, 134,
  137, 143-50, 152-8, 160,
  161, 162, 164.
Tibet – 14, 23, 46, 64, 117, 153
tourism – 28, 67, 128, 169, 178
Tranter, John – 41
Trevaskes, Sue – 45
Trevor-Roper, Hugh – 37
Tujia people – 126
Turner, Caroline – 109, 111,
  113, 117
Walker, Kath – 109, 111-13,
  117, 121,
  (see also 'Oodgeroo')
Wang Gungwu – 45, 106
Wang Shuo – 39
Wang Wei – 56
Wang Youshen – 135
Wang Zhen – 128

Wang Zhiyuan - 139
Wang Ziyin - 108, 164
Wei Guangqing - 137
Wei Jingsheng - 133, 142
Wen Yiduo - 40-1
White Australia - 46, 61, 76, 79, 180
Whitlam, Gough - 96, 106
Wilde, Oscar - 71, 72
Williams, John - 102, 103
Wollongong - 22, 24
Wright, Judith - 121
Wu Di - 139
Wu Zuguang - 143
Wu'er Kaixi - 149
Xiao Lu - 139
Xiao Xian - 136, 139

Xu Bing - 137
Yahp, Beth - 51, 53
Yan Jiaqi - 157
Yang, Gladys - 99, 128
Yang Lian - 133
Yang Shangkun - 101
Yang, William - 48
Yang Xianyi - 34, 88, 99, 128
Ye Qun - 97
Yeats, W.B. - 188
Yi people - 16-18, 101, 102
Yuan Shikai - 74, 75, 78
Yunnan province - 16, 18, 40
Zhao Ziyang - 104
Zhou Enlai - 143
Zhuang people - 119
Zwicky, Fay - 41, 51, 54-6

Wakefield Press

Beautiful Lies

AUSTRALIA FROM KOKODA TO KEATING

Tony Griffiths

Beautiful Lies is an original account of the people, events and trends that have shaped Australia since Menzies declared war on Germany in 1939. It is racy, maverick and impartial – a tour de force.

ISBN 1 86254 284 8   RRP $14.95

Scandinavia

A MODERN HISTORY

Tony Griffiths

Tony Griffiths tells the story of two centuries of change in the Nordic nations, focusing on the exchanges between Scandinavian artists and their politicians that have produced many of the western world's archetypal cultural and political motifs.

ISBN 1 86254 263 5   RRP $19.95

Wakefield Press

Black Horse Odyssey
SEARCH FOR THE LOST CITY OF ROME IN CHINA

David Harris

This intriguing book tells the story of David Harris's search for archaeological evidence of a city built 1200 kilometres south-west of Beijing thirteen centuries before Marco Polo 'discovered' China for the western world.

'Utterly absorbing and unique ... The most extraordinary and moving non-fiction book I have encountered since the late Bruce Chatwin's sublime masterpieces.' Giles Hugo, Mercury

ISBN 1 86254 270 8   RRP $12.95

Wakefield Press

A Case to Answer

THE STORY OF AUSTRALIA'S FIRST EUROPEAN WAR CRIMES PROSECUTION

David Bevan

On Australia Day 1990, a seventy-three-year-old man was plucked from the Adelaide suburbs and accused of helping massacre nearly nine hundred men, women and children in Nazi-occupied Ukraine. David Bevan describes the legal manoeuvrings that followed in a compelling work of courtroom drama.

'David Bevan has produced a fascinating book describing a unique and dramatic event in Australian legal history. His approach is thoroughly objective and impartial. Readers are left to assess for themselves the trial judge's decisions.' Australian Law Journal

ISBN 1 86254 323 2   RRP $16.95

Wakefield Press

Sentence: Siberia
A STORY OF SURVIVAL

Ann Lehtmets and Douglas Hoile

Ann Lehtmets is one of few people alive in the western world to have lived through Stalin's holocaust. This is her tale of survival in a world where existence was difficult for all and deadly for most.

> 'A marvellous and calmly told account of endurance and undefeated spirit.' Sir Arvi Parbo

ISBN 1 86254 313 5   RRP $18.95

Wakefield Press

The Shark Arm Murders
A TIGER SHARK AND A TATTOOED ARM

Alex Castles

This true story of one of the world's great unsolved murder cases begins one quiet Anzac day when a giant tiger shark, on display in the Coogee public baths, coughs up a tattooed arm. What follows is a spell-binding tale of detection in the 1930s Sydney underworld, concluding with Alex Castles' solution to a riddle that has baffled police and scientists for decades.

ISBN 1 86254 335 6   RRP $16.95

Wakefield Press

Nature Strip

A NOVEL

Leonie Stevens

'What would you suggest, weather like this?'

She didn't have to think at all. 'Procure a good-looking man and some drugs, then draw the curtains. I tell you, this is not a good day.'

Life on the dole was easy that summer, and the dealers in Melbourne made housecalls. Doomsday had passed for Caitlin, or so it seemed, until her friends in the backstreets started dropping like flies.

'This book is good ... beyond the movie *Dogs in Space*, beyond *Monkey Grip*, beyond other novels by extremely fabulous local writers ... this book has warmth and humour.' Melbourne Times

'A magnificent first novel.' Stuart Coupe

'An incisive account of urban drift.' Juice

'Gritty and corrosive ... witty and ironic.' Helen Daniel, Age

ISBN 1 86254 308 9   RRP $14.95

Wakefield Press

The Devil You Know
A THRILLER-ROMANCE FOR THE NINETIES

Frederick Guilhaus

Corruption in the boardroom,
murder in the wilderness,
a woman's fight for all she believes in ...

Brady Martin, unemployed and fed up, ignites rebellion among Tasmanian farmers who are being forced off their land by the banks. Meanwhile in Sydney, the directors of a new investment corporation play a dicey game with the nation's superannuation funds ...

The Devil You Know is a thriller-romance for the nineties.

ISBN 1 96254 341 0   RRP $18.95

Wakefield Press

The Original Mediterranean Cuisine

MEDIEVAL RECIPES FOR TODAY

Barbara Santich

Here is a book that brings authentic medieval food to today's table, with seventy recipes translated and adapted from fourteenth and fifteenth century Italian and Catalan manuscripts.

'*The Original Mediterranean Cuisine* is a fascinating and intelligent book on a riveting subject. It is packed with gems of information and also provides delicious eating.' Claudia Roden

'A book to be placed both on the history shelves and on the kitchen table.' Maggie Beer

'One of the most uncommon cookbooks to reach shelves groaning under the weight of cookbooks.' Tony Baker

ISBN 1 86254 331 3   RRP $24.95

Wakefield Press

This is My Friend's Chair

A NOVEL

Geraldine Halls

This beautifully paced saga, told through the eyes of Sophie Conway, spans forty years from the early twenties to the sixties. Set between Adelaide and London, it is a story of family life, betrayals and reconciliations, conveyed by a series of vignettes, finely crafted dialogues, and subtly manipulated variations in time and mood. Sophie's love–hate relationship with Lizzie Grey, the 'intruder in the Conway family' forms a constant thread in this epic drama of a family's decline and disintegration.

'In a world of relentless hype and fifteen-minute fame, I am wary of lavishing the superlatives on this book; they would only diminish it.'
Tony Baker, Advertiser

ISBN 1 86254 342 9   RRP $19.95

Wakefield Press

Wakefield Press has been publishing good Australian books for over fifty years. For a catalogue of current and forthcoming titles, or to add your name to our mailing list, send your name and address to Wakefield Press, Box 2266, Kent Town, South Australia 5071.

TELEPHONE (08) 362 8800   FAX (08) 362 7592

Wakefield Press thanks Wirra Wirra Vineyards for its support.